WHEN I SEE
BLUE

WHEN I SEE

BLUE

LILY BAILEY

Orion

ORION CHILDREN'S BOOKS

First published in Great Britain in 2022 by Hodder & Stoughton

1 3 5 7 9 10 8 6 4 2

A CIP catalogue record for this book
is available from the British Library.

ISBN 978 1 510 10980 3

Typeset in Trebuchet by Avon DataSet Ltd, Alcester, Warwickshire

Printed and bound in Great Britain by Clays Ltd, Elcograf S.p.A

The paper and board used in this book
are made from wood from responsible sources.

Orion Children's Books
An imprint of Hachette Children's Group
Part of Hodder & Stoughton Limited
Carmelite House
50 Victoria Embankment
London EC4Y 0DZ

An Hachette UK Company
www.hachette.co.uk

www.hachettechildrens.co.uk

To everyone who has ever lived inside a noisy head

In memory of David Jones, who told me
my first stories

1

1.1

Hilltown Secondary School looks so unlike a school that I don't even realise it *is* a school until Mum says, 'Here we are, it's just through those red doors, I think.'

My old school was built in Victorian times, so it was all bricks, points and long arched windows. It even had separate entrance doors that said *Boys* and *Girls*, from a time when it wasn't OK for us all to use the same door. This school looks like it could be a block of flats.

A big group of kids walk by, heading for the red doors. They are all talking over each other, loud and fast.

'Hey!' says Mum. 'Those might be your new friends. Why don't you go and talk to them?' I look at her like she has just suggested I paint my body with blood and go and swim with some sharks, and wonder if it's true what my older brother Kyle says – Mum *is* completely nuts.

2

Every single one of these kids has a backpack glinting with keyrings. My backpack doesn't have any. It is a TARDIS blue backpack (the only OK type of blue). TARDIS stands for 'time and relative dimensions in space', and it is the spaceship that the Doctor travels in through time and space. The Doctor is the main character in my most favourite ever, *ever* TV show, *Doctor Who*. The Doctor looks like a regular human, but *really* he is a Time Lord, which means he is from another planet, has two hearts and can live for hundreds and hundreds of years. The Doctor travels around in his TARDIS solving problems all over the galaxy. He's always fighting monsters and stopping wars and saving the world *just* in time.

The Doctor would be seriously peeved if you tried to decorate his TARDIS, so I keep my TARDIS backpack neat and keyring-free.

'You'll be fine,' says Mum, interrupting my thoughts. 'Go on – off you go.'

I tap my feet on the floor four times, because four is my special number, and it keeps me safe. There are four people in my family, and I am born in August. The bad thing about being born in August is that you are nearly always the youngest in your year, and everyone treats you like a baby. But the

3

excellent thing about it is that August is the eighth month, and I was born on the 2nd. If you divide eight (for the month) by two (for the date), you get four *again* – which *must* be a sign it's a special number for me.

When I see the number four in my head, I see myself sitting in the triangle that the left side of the four makes, with my knees bunched up to my chest, the line above my head making a nice slanty roof. I can't remember exactly when I knew four was my number. It feels like maybe I always knew. I do remember that when I used to walk in fours, Mum and Dad would pick me up and carry me, because it was easier than waiting for me to get somewhere. Then I used to scream and scream, because they didn't understand that I had to do it to keep us all safe.

They stopped picking me up eventually. Maybe it was because of the screaming. Or maybe I just got too big. One of the most difficult things about doing things in fours is walking. I count my steps in fours, and I like each step to feel the same size. Sometimes I'm not sure if the steps are the same size, or something about them just *feels* wrong, and then I have to go back and do the steps again. When I'm walking down the road, I like the fact that cars have four wheels, but if I see a bicycle, motorbike or one of those long lorries with six wheels, then I have to count four cars to make things feel OK. If that doesn't make it feel OK then I times that by four and count sixteen cars, and if that doesn't work then I times sixteen by four and count sixty-four cars, and if that *still* doesn't work then I times sixty-four by four and count two hundred and fifty-six cars.

Sometimes it can be pretty hard to find two hundred and fifty-six cars in Essex. So I guess that's a good thing about moving to London, even if there are lots of scary things too, like going to a new school, and not knowing where anything is.

I feel Mum's arms reaching out to hug me goodbye, but I don't want her to hug me in case the other kids see and think I'm a baby, so, still facing away from her and towards the door, I say under my breath, 'Can you just say the magic words, please?'

'The quick brown fox jumps over the lazy dog,' Mum whispers, which is a pangram – that's a sentence that contains every single letter of the alphabet, which means it sort of contains every good thing in the world that you could possibly need to say to bring you luck. I ask her to do it three more times to make four, and she does.

And then she squeezes my shoulders and says, 'Off you go, Benny. I love you, you'll be fine.'

I head through the red doors, knowing that red is the colour of anger, and that every day when I walk into school I will now wonder whether I am causing Mum and Dad to have another argument with each other.

Because it's the first day, there are paper signs on the walls with arrows telling you which way to go. Mum told me that I am in class 8A, so I follow the signs to the fourth floor (good sign), and head into a room that is not square, and has six corners (bad sign). A man at the front of the room with a paper register tells me that his name is Mr Montague, and he is teaching this class. 'Find a desk, any desk you like!' He grins as if the fact there is no assigned seating is a good thing.

If you are an unpopular person, this is basically the apocalypse.

There's an unoccupied twin desk by the front window, and I scoot over there. The other kids are sitting on each other's desks and swinging their legs, talking about what they did during the summer holidays, and messing around. I stare down at my desk and count its four corners with my eyes. I have decided at this school that I will be invisible. I stuck

6

out a lot at the Essex school, so being invisible basically requires me to reinvent myself, a bit like the Doctor. When the Doctor dies, he doesn't die like us. He regenerates into a different body, and the new Doctor likes different foods and might be a bit sillier or grumpier than the last one.

I am not a Time Lord, so I can't regenerate, but I can try and do something similar. This is The Rule that I have made for myself: I will only do things in my head or with my eyes, no matter how much I want to physically tap, step or repeat. I will not talk to anyone, or say anything in lessons, and maybe, if I'm *really lucky*, no one will notice I'm here at all.

Mr Montague claps his hands and calls for quiet. He takes a register, and I count the names, so that I will know how many people are in this class. I count thirty-four, which is not divisible by four (extremely bad sign). Then Mr Montague welcomes us all, and tells us that there is a lot to look forward to this term, including that there are some new after-school clubs, *and* a Halloween disco.

Then Mr Montague says, 'We have three new pupils in this Year Eight class, who've transferred from other schools. Now, guys. Think about when you first started here last year, or when you've been somewhere before that you didn't know, and

7

remember that saying hello and being friendly only takes a second. So – so that we can get to know our newest pupils – would all the new kids like to stand up and tell us their names?'

Around the room, a couple of girls shuffle out of their seats, stand up briefly and tell us their names are Jia and Rachel. I can feel eyes looking around the room for the third new student, but I stare hard at my desk, feeling grateful that at least Mr Montague said the new students only had to stand up if they would like to.

Mr Montague tells us that he is our form teacher this year. He'll be taking us for maths, English and science, and we'll have other teachers for geography, French, religious studies, history, PE and drama. 'Our first lesson of the day is going to be maths,' he says, 'and I know how excited you'll all be to hear that today we'll be starting algebra!'

The class groans, and a girl a few seats away from me wearing leather lace-up boots, which really do not look school-uniform compliant, mutters the rudest swear word I know. I like algebra, but obviously I do not announce this, because I do not have a death wish. At the Essex school, my maths teacher used to give me extra algebra worksheets to do because I had finished all the other stuff in the

textbook. At the time I just did them, b
back, I don't think it helped my 'I am not ﾋ
case very much.

Mr Montague does an example using real appﾋ
and oranges that he has brought in, and no one
seems too confused, but then he moves over to the
whiteboard and replaces apples with X and oranges
with Y, and now people are, as Kyle would say,
'losing their freaking minds'. Mr Montague explains
the equation and asks us to find X, and a red-haired
boy with freckles in the second row points to the X
on the board and says, 'It's there, sir,' which makes
everyone snicker.

After a few more examples, Mr Montague hands
round some worksheets for us to try. He tells us
there are two sections, but we won't be able to do
the second one yet because he hasn't taught us that
bit. I could very easily do the second section, but
then I remember that I am being invisible, which
means not standing out in any way at all. So after I
finish the first section, I just do the second section
in my head. Mr Montague walks round the desks
to take a look at what everyone has written, and
asks the red-haired boy why he isn't filling in the
worksheet. 'Cos you don't need algebra in the
real world,' the boy says, and Mr Montague tells

9

.im that while they'll have to agree to disagree on that one, you might need some GCSEs if you want to get a job 'in the real world'. Which makes everyone go 'oooooooh' and someone shouts, 'Burrrrrn, Bradleeeey!'

Bradley looks like he is going to punch Mr Montague in the face.

I've finished answering section two in my head, so I start counting corners. I feel safe when I am in square or rectangular rooms with exactly four corners, and I can move my eyes round and round counting them, but unfortunately this room is not square or rectangular. However, if I count the six corners of the room twice it's twelve, and plus the four corners of my desk it's sixteen, which is the square of four, so that feels kind of workable.

I'm darting my eyes round and round, and have done this 107 times, when Mr Montague arrives at my desk to check my work.

'Wow, you've finished the whole first section,' he beams. 'You're the only one who's even got close.' He checks through my answers. 'And they're all right!' He looks like he could dance. 'Have you done this before?'

I am annoyed for making myself stand out. But I glance round the class and no one is looking our way – in fact, everyone is talking so loudly that Mr Montague could probably give me a badge for mathematical excellence and no one would notice.

'A bit,' I say quietly. Mr Montague says I should try the next section, and sits at the desk next to me to explain what I need to do. I nod and say, 'Thanks,' while wondering if it is a bad kind of lying to pretend you don't know something when you do.

*

We break for lunch at 12.30 p.m. The canteen is on the ground floor. It's a massive room with three white walls and one red wall, and a plasticky blue floor that has sparkly purple flecks in it like the inside of a geode. There are eighty-six long plywood tables, and the room is heaving with people. At one of the tables towards the back I spot Kyle, crammed in with a load of guys and girls who you only have to look at for a couple of seconds to know are the popular kids. Kyle is showing a girl with a high swishy ponytail something on his phone, and she is looking at whatever it is and laughing.

For a moment it's sort of . . . shocking: seeing Kyle already surrounded by brand-new friends after only one morning of school. But really, there's no reason for me to find this surprising. Kyle is extremely good at 'fitting in'. Mum says Kyle could make friends in a vacuum. I couldn't make friends at a Friendship Convention.

Kyle is also extremely good at pretending he doesn't know me. He insisted on walking to school by himself, ten minutes after Mum and I had left. He has given me instructions not to approach him at school ever, under *any circumstances whatsoever*. So I look away and pretend I haven't seen him. It's so loud that the people in the queue have to shout to the dinner ladies to tell them what they would like to eat. I join the back of the queue.

The trays are red, so I don't want one. As well as meaning anger, red can also mean harm, because red is the colour of blood. So if I use something red, it could cause someone I love to have an awful accident and even die. I figure I'll just take the plate that the dinner lady gives me. But when I get to the counter the dinner lady says I have to have a tray; it's a health and safety thing. I remember The Rule about fitting in, so I just nod my head and leave the counter to grab a tray, and join the back of the queue again. At least the room is rectangular. I say the word *rectangular* over and over in my head, but I know I'm blushing, and I can hear my heartbeat in my ears. My hands are clammy, and I'm worried that they'll be making a damp mark on the red plastic and someone will notice. I sneak a glance down. The tray is covered in wet smudges from my fingers and palm. *Rectangular, rectangular, rectangular, RECTANGULAR*, I repeat in my head, but—

'What would you like to eat today?' someone is asking me. I refocus my eyes and realise that I have made it to the front of the queue and am standing in front of the same dinner lady again.

'One sausage, mash, peas and a Yorkshire pudding, please,' I say.

'Speak up, dear.'

'ONE SAUSAGE, MASH, PEAS AND A YORKSHIRE PUDDING!'

'It's mash or a Yorkshire, not both.'

Oh, flip. I do not want to have three things on my plate. But I remember The Rule. Ideally, I need four different foods, but I think of a quick way to make things work.

'OK, TWO SAUSAGES, PEAS AND MASH, PLEASE.'

The lady nods and starts spooning things on to my plate. The tips of one sausage are touching the mash, and some of the peas are actually ON TOP of the mash, but – absolutely worst of all – she has given me three sausages, so now there are five things on my plate. At the Essex school, the dinner ladies knew to always give me four things, and not to let anything touch. Mum had written a letter when I first started, explaining that there were things I needed done in certain ways.

And then the lady takes the ladle from inside a vat of gravy and lifts it above my plate, about to pour it over everything—

'NO!' I shout. She raises an eyebrow, stops, and hands me the plate. I take it from her and place it on my tray. In the back right corner of the room I can see a long table with four unoccupied places at the end. To get there I will have to pass Kyle at a distance of approximately ten metres. Kyle can be a total jerk, but right now I want more than anything for him to notice me panicking and help me decide what to do about my food. I feel like if I stare at him and he happens to notice me needing help and come over, then that won't count as me approaching him. I stare hard at him, willing him to notice me. At the last second he does, but he just stares back at me, and shakes his head – *no* – so subtly I wonder if he really did move his head at all, all the while continuing to say something to the girl that is still making her laugh.

So I grip my tray hard and keep walking until I get to the table with the four spaces. I sit in the seat closest to the wall. I look at the plate. As well as my blood-coloured tray having a plate with five things on it, there are two blobs of gravy solidifying on the side of the plate, from where the ladle dripped.

I wonder if I could count the peas as individual items. If I count them all up, and add the mashed potato as one item, the sausages as three items and the gravy splodges as two items, there is a one in four chance that the food on my plate will add up to a multiple of four. It's worth a shot.

First of all, I separate the food so none of it is touching any more. Then I start counting.

It turns out peas are pretty difficult to count. I keep losing track of which ones have been counted and which ones haven't. I try separating them but they end up rolling into the mash. Everything feels wrong, and I know that if I eat this food Bumble will get hit by a car when Mum takes him for his walk. I see him lying and bleeding in the road, totally still. Then I have the terrible thought that maybe I *want* something awful to happen to Bumble.

I picture his big furry happy face hurtling towards the door, like it always does when one of us arrives home from being somewhere.

I don't want to kill Bumble! I don't want to kill Bumble!

I realise I am saying this out loud, because the older kids a few seats away have turned to look at me. I also realise that my eyes are filling with tears. This is very much not ideal, and in clear violation of The Rule.

'Sorry,' I mumble. I pick up my tray and take it to the trolley at the other end of the room. I leave the canteen, but I have no idea where I'm going. I was hungry before lunch, now I feel like throwing up. I walk through two doors and down a long corridor; I take some stairs four flights up and walk down another corridor – this school is *huge* – and reach a green door that has a peeling laminated sign on it with a ClipArt picture of a swirly treble clef and the words: *Music Department*. I walk through it and into a new corridor that is approximately twenty metres long with lots of small rooms on each side. The doors all have a small meshed window. I peek through and see pianos and silver stands holding pieces of paper with music language on them, and instruments in grey and dark-green fabric cases. In total, I count twelve small rooms, and eleven of them are empty. One of them has a kid who looks a bit younger than me in it. He's standing by the window, droning out the same notes on a clarinet over and over. I head straight for the one on the right, which says *Music Room 4* on the door. It smells musty, like charity shops and my grandma's house. This one has a piano, but the music stands don't have music paper on them, and there aren't any cases for instruments.

I sit on my bum in the third corner from the door. This room is a near-perfect square, and I let my eyes move round and round from corner to corner.

Why didn't Mum write a letter to school telling them about me needing four things on my plate and nothing touching? Mum and Dad are always squabbling over whether to 'give in to Benny', which means letting me do things my way. Dad says that I should learn to fit in with the normal world and not do everything in fours or scream if things aren't the right colour, otherwise how will I ever grow up and be a normal adult? Mum says that it is easier for everyone if things are done my way, and what is wrong with 'giving in to Benny' if it makes me feel better?

Maybe Dad has finally convinced Mum that 'giving in to Benny' has to stop.

Or maybe she just forgot. Dad keeps telling her to stop being such a space cadet, and when I asked Kyle what that meant he said a space cadet is a person who is an astronaut but without the brains. I said everyone has a brain. Kyle said, 'OK, well, not a very good brain.' So I said that astronauts actually have exceptional brains, otherwise they wouldn't be astronauts in the first place, and also they wouldn't pass their training. Then Kyle got a bit annoyed and said, 'OK, smart arse, but the way Dad means it is someone who stares at nothing at all for a long time, is not very good at replying to you and generally doesn't really understand anything at all.'

So maybe Mum was being a space cadet.

I decide to stay in Music Room 4 until lunch break is over. I suck at playgrounds because boys are supposed to charge around and play football, and I tend to trip over my legs. Pokémon cards were popular in Year Three and there was a brief five-week period in Essex where I was actually quite good at the playground because I knew the name of every single one. I had been collecting Pokémon cards before anyone else so I had the best cards and everyone wanted to see them. Tarek and Jamie even started calling me Spoink. Spoink is a cross between a metal spring and a pig, and everyone knows he is pretty much the most rubbish Pokémon ever (he has to bounce just to keep his heart beating). Kyle was horrified when I told him, and said being called Spoink was extremely offensive and I needed to put a stop to it right away.

It didn't matter, even though I would much rather have been called Charizard, because people were actually talking to me.

I'm glad I brought my backpack with me to lunch now, because that means I can read my comic. But as I unzip it, I can see a small crumpled piece of paper that I don't remember putting in there. I reach in and unfold it.

It's lined paper that's been torn out of an exercise book, and written in capitals it says:

NEVER RUN WHEN YOU'RE SCARED.

1.2

The Doctor's rules are a set of guidelines for his companions to follow if they want to hang out with him, although they do change pretty regularly. The exact rules depend on which incarnation of the Doctor is telling you about them, but *NEVER RUN WHEN YOU'RE SCARED* is number seven on the eleventh Doctor's (played by the actor Matt Smith, 2010–2013) list of rules.

I have absolutely no idea how it got into my backpack.

I look out of the window. I can see some construction workers in fluorescent orange jackets and yellow hard hats drilling at a tower block opposite, and people walking down the street with their pushchairs and shopping bags. I open the door and peek into the silent corridor, and I check that all the other music rooms are empty, apart from the one with Clarinet Boy in it.

I don't know who or what I'm expecting to see,

but I feel like someone is watching me.

I look back down at the jagged thin black letters:

NEVER RUN WHEN YOU'RE SCARED.

This is extremely weird. Who on earth sent me this? Should I be concerned about my safety?

I sit trying to work out who the mysterious note sender might be for the rest of my lunch break, but I can't come up with a single person who seems at all likely. I don't think anyone even knows my name. I can't work out whether receiving this note makes me very frightened . . . or very excited.

I wait until 1.25 p.m. and then open the door to go back to the classroom for afternoon lessons. I don't know what the rules are here, but in Essex we all had to be outside for the whole of break once lunch had finished. I do not want to get caught, because I plan on spending every lunch break here, so I sneak down the three corridors back to the classroom, looking over my shoulder every few seconds – I still feel like someone is watching me.

This afternoon we have English, history and religious studies – which is bad news. I always think of them as 'story' subjects. I know this is not exactly right because history is not just stories but actual real things happening to real people a long time ago, and different religions are always telling you that things did *really* happen, even if you know that they can't all be true at once, otherwise there would be way too many gods all fighting for sky space. But anyway, what I mean is, I do like the bit where the teacher tells you the stories. I just don't like what comes next.

We have English first, and Mr Montague reads us the first four chapters of a book called *Kensuke's Kingdom* by a man named Michael Morpurgo. I'm not sure who the Kensuke guy is yet, but Mr Montague says it is an adventure story and what has happened so far is that a boy on a boat with his mum and dad has lost his dog overboard in a storm and has jumped in to rescue him and they have both ended up stranded on an island. Bradley says that this was a really stupid thing to do, but I like it because I would definitely do that if Bumble fell into the ocean, even though I am not very brave.

Mr Montague says the task for the rest of the lesson is to write our own adventure stories where *we* are the main character who has to rescue an animal or person from a life-or-death situation. This is the bad bit. I find it very difficult to get words on paper. I don't like writing down words that don't have four letters, or don't have a number of letters that is in the four times table, which makes it difficult to write much at all. Also, instead of thinking about what I'm writing down in front of me, I can't stop looking around the room and wondering if the mysterious note sender is in here or not.

So far I have written:

Woof said mutt name Champion

Mutt is another word for dog, and I tend to just miss out in-between words if they don't make the right number. Kyle says this means I write like a five-year-old, but Mum says there are lots of famous authors who write in unusual ways that were considered wrong at first, but now people see them as creative pioneers, which means that they discovered a new way of doing things that people ended up thinking was cool.

My teachers tend to agree with Kyle.

A shadow comes over my exercise book. Mr Montague has been walking round the classroom checking people's work, like he did earlier in maths.

'Huh,' he says, looking over my shoulder. He sounds a bit disappointed. Maybe he thought I was going to be his star pupil because of maths.

'Can I help?' he asks.

I nod, and he takes a pen out of his pocket and changes my sentence to:

'Woof!' said ~~a mutt~~ *a dog* ~~named~~ *called Champion.*

Mr Montague starts explaining the corrections: did I know that you need an 'a' or 'the' before 'dog' in a sentence, and mutt is too informal a way to talk about dogs in English lessons – but all I can think is what kind of teacher marks work with glittery purple gel pen?

Maybe he is an alien rather than a proper teacher, and actually that would make a very good story . . .

*

I told Mum that I don't want her to come and get me from school because I am old enough to walk home by myself. This is what adults call a white lie, meaning that while it is not the truth, it's not a *bad* lie because you do it for a *good* reason.

The truth is that being invisible definitely means no more Mum at home time. Because 'Mum At Home Time' was one of the major reasons why we had to move from Essex to London in the first place. The first time it happened, I was in Reception. Mum turned up a bit late, and she wasn't very steady on her feet. When she spoke to my teacher, the words came out of her mouth funny – like a long word slug rather than individual words and sentences with spaces between them. It was hard to be sure exactly what she was saying.

And then I started to find bottles of clear liquid in our cupboards at home. It looked like water, except I noticed that when Mum drank from them she would change into this person who knocked things over and didn't speak normally, so I soon realised it wasn't water, because that never happened to me when I drank water.

One time I unscrewed one of the caps and took a sniff to see if I could work out what it was. I remember thinking that it smelled funny. It had the same chemical sting as Mum's nail varnish remover. I knew that Mum had been drinking from the tall clear bottles before she came to pick me up. Obviously *now* I know that it's alcohol, but back then I didn't have a clue.

The second thing that happened was that sometimes Mum would forget to pick me up at all. School ended at 3.30 p.m., but 3.40 p.m. would come and go, and soon the only kids left would be me, Jamie and Nathalie, and we'd get sent to the school office. It was kind of OK for Jamie's mum to be late, because she was a foster mum with five other kids all at different schools, and she would always apologise and say that the traffic had been terrible. Nathalie's mum was a police officer, and sometimes her shifts would overrun because you can't stop chasing a criminal down the road because your daughter needs to be picked up. But I wasn't quite sure why *my* mum wasn't there. School would call our home phone, and one time I heard the receptionist tell my teacher that it sounded like Mum was 'sloshed'. I didn't know what this word meant then, but I sure do now.

The final and worst thing that happened was one day last year when Mum arrived with her hair even messier than usual and her face so white she looked like one of those paintings of Queen Elizabeth I in my history textbook. The green vein that runs down the centre of her forehead was throbbing out like an angry snake. She was tripping over nothing and got into a row with Christie's mum because she 'looked at her funny'. She called her some things that I'm not going to repeat here.

Mrs Hansen put her hand on Mum's lower back

and asked her to 'please calm down'. She tried to walk her away from the playground, but Mum swore at her too. Mrs Hansen could be a real pain in the bum, but still, seeing Mum talk to her like that was . . . kind of horrifying. Then Mum had to meet Mr Jones, our head teacher, the next Monday morning before school started. I would have given anything to be the one who messed up – to have been sitting opposite Mr Jones with Dad in her place, looking down at the ground and twisting my fingers, saying sorry over and over. I wasn't there, but I knew that that's what she'd be doing.

Mr Jones said that Mum, Dad and I had to meet with the school counsellor to talk about what had happened.

Mum told the counsellor that 'she had no idea' what had happened, that she must just have had too much to drink at lunch with a friend, and, yes, she truly regretted it, and, no, it wouldn't happen again.

I looked at Dad, waiting for him to ask her which 'friend' she was talking about, since Mum doesn't have that many friends apart from her sister Kate, and best friend from school, Tina, and neither of them live in Essex.

But he didn't say *anything*.

27

So then the counsellor *asked* him what he thought.

'I think that this was very unlike Leila and that she is very sorry about it,' he said tightly.

This was very unlike Leila. That's definitely what he said. Those words were so outrageous, it was like they got imprinted on my eyeballs. Because even though I suppose it *was* unlike Mum to start shouting at someone she barely knew, it was definitely like her to 'get sloshed' in the day.

And I knew Dad knew it. Even though they seem to have this weird deal where as long as Dad doesn't *see* her drinking we can all pretend it doesn't happen, and I'm pretty sure he actually *tries* to get home after Mum's in bed, but there were definitely times when he caught her. I have heard him shout at her twice to 'for god's sake, stop it' because 'I can't take it any more!' and one time he went away for three days and I honestly thought he might not come back.

I had seen enough movies to know that you are supposed to be honest when you talk to a counsellor or a doctor, and that Mum and Dad were telling lies. In fact, I knew this so well that three months ago, when we got a scary letter from the children's mental health service (??!) saying that a teacher (which one?!) had noticed I spent a lot of time engaging in 'compulsive behaviour' (also ??!) and that I needed to go to a local centre for an 'assessment', I answered the questions the doctor there asked me as honestly as I could. I then worried all the way home that my answers would mean I would be taken away somewhere to be fixed. So far, nothing has happened. I think they've probably forgotten about me.

But I suppose I went along with the lie with the counsellor at school that day too, because when she asked me what I thought, I took one look at Mum and Dad's eyes, both pairs of which were looking at me the way Bumble looks when he wants some of your dinner.

Like they were saying: 'Please, please, PLEASE.' So I said, 'I think she just made a mistake and everything will be fine.'

We left after fifty minutes and we never spoke about it again.

Christie was in with the Populars, and anyway there was no question about whose mum was in the wrong. They spent the next few weeks playing 'Benny's Mum': someone would scream, 'BENNNNYYY'S MUUUM!' and everyone else would drop whatever they were doing and pretend to go all wobbly and swear at anyone in earshot.

I hadn't been very good at fitting in before anyway, because it is hard to seem like a regular kid when you are always touching things in fours and opening and shutting the classroom door. So I guess it is true that Mum could have been a gorgeous popstar or, better still, just a normal mum who turned up on time and wore V-neck sweaters, and I still wouldn't have had an easy time at school.

But it is also true that people teased me *a lot* more after the incident with Christie's mum.

And by the end of summer term last year, I flat out refused to go to school. Then Dad had an opportunity to take a new job in London, and he sat us down and told us he thought it would be good for us all to make a 'fresh start'. This made Kyle very angry: it wasn't his fault that his mum couldn't stop drinking and his brother didn't know how to make friends, so *why* should his whole life be uprooted because of 'those freaks'? Dad sent him to his room and we didn't talk about it again. The next month, Dad announced that we were moving for definite.

Five days ago we moved into our London home, and *I* announced that I didn't want Mum picking me up from school and that I would walk home on my own.

Mum wasn't sure, but Dad said, 'You should

30

let him. It will be good for Benny to be more independent.' Mum tugged at her bun with one hand and chewed the thumbnail of the other, as Dad continued, 'Benny remembers literally everything. It's not like he's going to get lost.' And that was that. Mum and I agreed that she would walk me to school on my first day to show me the way, and at the end of the day I would walk home by myself.

*

That afternoon, RS and history were as bad as English: instead of Mr Montague we had a different teacher called Mrs Williams. Mrs Williams has a short grey bob and half-moon glasses, and she stomps round the classroom between the desks when she talks. She drones on with her eyes focused on the ceiling and her hands clasped behind her back, like a policeman in a cartoon. She gave us a 'brief' history of religion in this country across the last millennium, which *felt* like a millennium. Everyone was talking and texting, but either she didn't notice or didn't care. But much, *much* worse than Mrs Williams's lesson was having to resist doing things in fours *during* her lesson so that no one thought I was a weirdo.

So by home time, I feel utterly exhausted, and I

can't wait to get home from school, but I've only walked halfway down the high street away from the school gates when I start to get The Thoughts.

The Thoughts say: *I'm going to get home and Mum will be in bed with the lights off and the blinds shut and the fan going* vrrrrrrrrrr *on the loudest setting so that you have to shout for her to hear you over it.*

Dad is going to get back from work a few hours later and shout and shout at her to get up.

Mum will not get up.

He'll say, 'Benny, have you had any tea?'

I will say yes because I don't want her to be in trouble, but he'll know anyway, because there aren't any plates in the dishwasher, and—

. . . and I'm not sure I really am old enough to walk home from school by myself after all, because I've stepped on one pavement slab, two, three, four and then back three, two, one, and then done the whole thing over again sixteen times before I've even thought about what I'm doing—

Stop it, Benny, I say to myself, because that's what Mum or Dad would say if they were here.

There are going to be lots of kids from school on this street and you're just lucky you haven't bumped into any of them yet and ruined your entire life.

I try to keep walking, but The Thoughts say I have to step in fours if I don't want to find Mum like that. I turn off the high street past a white pebbledash house with a wooden gate that has the number sixty-four spray-painted on it in white. White is the cleanest colour: it's pure, like fresh sheets and angels. Sixty-four is four cubed, making it a power number.

Trace that number with your finger four times and when you get home Mum will be acting fine.

I do it four times and walk a little way away. It's not enough.

The Thoughts say, *Just another four times*. And then, *Just once more*. And then, *Try again, because that time wasn't quite right* – and I'm getting so angry, my body feels like the time I burned my fingers on the stove, except I'm burning all over. I want this to stop. I want to scream that I'M NOT GOING TO DO IT, but I go back every time, even when I manage to get to the end of the road, away from the stupid gate, I feel like the last trace wasn't quite right; my finger wasn't exactly in the middle of the numbers, I have to go back, and then because it seems I'm never going to get it right, I end up bending down to touch my toes sixty-four times, which sometimes makes The Thoughts stop. *Someone from school's going to see me and tell everyone! But don't I want Mum to be OK? I'm sure I do, I'm sure I do – fifty-four, fifty-five, fifty-six, fifty-seven—*

I feel hands on my shoulder shaking me and turn round to see Kyle. 'Are you OK, Benny?' I tell him yes, but I feel like I'm underwater and I can't take in enough air, and after each breath my throat starts flexing up to the sky a few times a second, and my mouth and tongue start making clicky noises that I can't stop. I've been feeling this a lot lately.

'Stop it, Benny, stop it. It's fine. Hey, bro, calm down. It's all good!'

'Let me finish!' I shout, because I was almost at sixty-four. It's ruined now; I have to start from one. Just as I bend down to start toe-touching again, Kyle scoops me over his shoulder like everyone used to when I was small. I kick his tummy and punch his back, but it's no good, he's way stronger than me.

'I knew they shouldn't have let you walk home by yourself,' he says.

Well, if that's what you think then why can't we walk home together? I want to shout. *It's not like we're coming from different places.* But when Mum had suggested it, Kyle had said, no, no *way.* He wasn't going to walk home with Benny, because firstly if anyone saw us together it would be

34

unbelievably damaging for his 'vibe', and secondly, 'It takes four times as long to get anywhere with him walking up and down the same road until it's dark . . .'

But now here Kyle is, carrying me along the road. He puts me down once we're round the corner and crouches so his face is at my level. He tells me that, 'We're going to walk home now, together, like normal people.'

Every time I try and do my backwards stepping Kyle grabs me by the wrist and yanks me along. We walk in silence towards the new house, which we have lived in for five days.

I don't want to get there. I walk slow, I try and make Kyle play Pokémon Go with me on his phone, I ask him what music he's listening to at the moment even though we both know I won't know any of the singers. But it doesn't do any good. Pretty soon I can see the house, which looks old from the outside – sturdy red-brick walls, with a chipped bottle-green and once-white-now-brown tiled path leading through a tiny overgrown front garden. It's on one of those streets where the houses all attach to each other on either side, and wiggle down the road like a giant caterpillar.

Before, when we lived in Essex, we had the

whole house, and a big garden with Mum's studio shed for her pottery. In this new house we just have the two top floors, and there's another family living in the flat downstairs. Dad says that we have 'upgraded', but I don't understand how, because this house is half the size of our old one. Dad says it is to do with the *value of property*.

There are two doors to the house: a peeling blue one with bronze numbers that say 28a, and a red (also peeling) one that says 28b. Twenty-eight can be divided by four, which I'm pleased about, *and* I'm relieved there are no sixes in the number, because six is my ultimate bad number. But I still start to feel really nervous, because, as I've said, red is the colour of blood, anger and arguments – The Thoughts tell me whether it means anger or harm (or both) every time I see it. Blue is also bad, because blue is the colour of sadness. When I see blue, I see Mum asleep on the sofa with the curtains shut even though it is the middle of the day. I see still, hot days with nothing to do but count the walls.

When we first arrived here five days ago, Dad opened the blue door before I could even decide which door was worse. Probably the red door would have been worse, because I'd rather we felt sad sometimes than that one of us had a bad accident.

Still, I wasn't exactly thrilled about having a sad-coloured door.

Kyle opens the blue door for us, and my stomach feels like it's going to fall out of my bum, the way it has done every time I've walked through our front door so far.

But when we get upstairs it turns out Mum's fine. Actually, more than fine.

The kitchen is steamy and she's stirring a massive pot of something that looks like a stew for tea and humming some song. She is wearing an apron that says THIS IS WHAT AWESOME LOOKS LIKE on it. We got it for her for Christmas two years ago and I have never ever seen her wear it even once. Weird. Did my stepping and tracing make her OK?

Kyle tells her to stop playing house and marches upstairs. I don't know what that means.

I am thinking that maybe things will be better with Mum now? And maybe Mum and Dad will even be happy together . . . The night we moved in, I made Mum and Dad laugh a lot, and they seemed pretty good. Mum had told me to look around the flat. She said, 'I think there's a bedroom overlooking the garden that's got your name on it,' and squeezed my shoulders from behind.

I walked around looking at every door, but I

couldn't find one that said 'Benny' on it. The flat was almost entirely empty, because the removal van with all our furniture wasn't here yet. Dad said it was a mess before, and that's why he had to paint it all white. But I felt like a character in a book on a giant sheet of blank paper.

I pushed open a door and saw a square room with one big (rectangular) window that looked out over the garden that belongs to the people who live below. I thought, *So this must be my room*. I was so relieved that the room had four corners that for a few seconds I couldn't do anything except stare into it happily. Then I flitted my eyes round them all – one corner, two corner, three corner, four corner – and I stood there counting them until I had counted them sixteen times.

I followed the sound of Mum's voice back down into what would be the sitting room, where she and Dad were sitting on the floor with mugs of steamy tea. Mum's legs were crossed lightly under a flowy lilac skirt, while Dad was on his knees in corduroy brown trousers looking a bit stiff and uncomfortable, but still happy. I noticed that his hand was on Mum's thigh. An open door led directly into the kitchen, and I could see that the yellow kettle (which had come with us in the car along with four mugs because Dad said they were 'priority items') was plugged into the wall by the sink of the otherwise empty kitchen.

Mum told me to 'come sit' and asked me if I liked my room.

'Yes,' I said. 'But it didn't have my name on it.'

This is the thing that they found *extremely* funny. 'You take everything so literally, Benny boy,' said Dad. 'When you say something has someone's name on it, it means that it's perfect for them. It's just an expression.'

'Oh,' I said. 'OK.'

'Taking things literally' is when someone says something that they don't actually mean, but you think that they do. So if someone says, 'It's raining cats and dogs,' you might think that there are pets falling out of the sky, but actually it just means that there is heavy rain.

It is true that I do take things literally. This is because I think it would be sensible for people to say things that they actually mean. When I was little, Mum and Dad were talking about Grandma Sarah (Dad's mum) in the car. They called her two-faced. Later on, when we got to Grandma and Grandad's house, I lifted her hair from the back of her head. She asked me what I was doing, and I told her I was looking for her second face. The room went horribly quiet. It turns out being two-faced means that you aren't very nice, and not that you are a mutant creature with four eyes.

Anyway, the point is, they were really, *really* laughing about me taking the 'it's got your name on it' thing literally. And they seemed genuinely quite happy.

Kyle thundered down the stairs past the living room, and Dad called that he should join us.

Kyle poked his head round the door.

'No, thanks – I'm off to explore – find out what's going *down*.' He smirked. I imagined cool things, events and people all over London tumbling down flights of stairs. 'You guys have fun playing happy families, though.'

The door to our flat banged shut, and then the front door too.

'Shall we watch something while we wait for all our stuff to get here?' said Dad.

'Yes!'

'What would you like to watch?'

I picked *Doctor Who*, because we'd never be able to watch it if Kyle were here. Kyle says *Doctor Who* is babyish, which is ridiculous, because while it *is* a family show, its audience are actually mainly adults. Which makes sense, because the Doctor knows about pretty much *everything*, and so is very good at solving problems, and adults seem to have lots of problems.

We had to watch it on the laptop, sitting on the carpet, because our TV and sofa were still in the van with all the other furniture. Dad hit play.

I leaned against Mum. Dad laughed in all the right places and didn't look at his iPhone once. I counted the four corners of the laptop over and over while we watched, feeling like if I did it enough times, then maybe every night could be like this.

Anyway, the point I am making is that things were going well, and I was hoping that maybe we could all watch *Doctor Who* together again tonight, since it had been my first day of school.

But 8 p.m. and 9 p.m. come and go, and Dad still isn't back from work.

At 10.14 p.m., I am sitting up in bed wearing my Dalek pyjamas that say *EXTERMINATE!* in capitals up the arms. The Daleks are the Doctor's greatest enemy: they are hostile aliens that are half living creatures, half machine. They have wheels rather than legs and they want to kill anyone who isn't a member of their race, so they are always screaming '*EXTERMINATE!*' and blowing up whoever is in front

41

of them. I'm reading a comic with my torch and I really do *not* feel like being interrupted, but that's when Kyle walks in without knocking.

I think he's going to take one look at me and call me a loser geek, but what he actually says is that if he finds me like that on the street again he will tell Dad that I can't walk home by myself.

Then he comes closer and sits on the end of my bed. He says, 'Bro, you don't want to be teased again, do you? Like in Essex?'

I say, no, of course I don't, because seriously what kind of person wants to be teased?

He says, 'Good. Then you'll walk in a straight line on your way to school and back.'

He puts his fist out for me to fist-bump him. This is something we used to do when I was younger, but we haven't done it in years. The worse my fours got as I got older, the more I seemed to annoy Kyle, and the less he wanted anything to do with me. So it's weird . . . Kyle being kind of nice to me.

Kyle leaves, and I read my comic for another sixteen minutes before clicking off my torch four times and trying to sleep.

Bedtime is a bad time for The Thoughts, because I feel like everything must feel right before I can go to sleep. The Thoughts fill the blackness like monsters crawling out from under the bed: *open and close the curtains four times or Bumble dies, switch the switch by the bed sixty-four times or Kyle really does think you're a freak and wishes you weren't his brother . . .*

So I get up and do the curtains, and the switches, because I am sure that if I listen carefully enough and follow everything The Thoughts say properly, then I can stop anything bad from happening.

The problem is, once I've sorted one thought, another one seems to pop up right away. It's kind of like Whac-A-Mole: that game where a mole comes up and you have to hit it back down with a hammer, except that as soon as you have sorted one mole, there's always a new one that immediately pops up again.

Read sixteen more pages or Mum will leave, open and close the door four times or you'll never make any friends, do the switches another sixty-four times or Dad will lose his job, touch the ceiling four times and you can make all these things not happen . . .

I like that last one. Anything that makes all The Thoughts go in one is brilliant news.

I switch my sidelight on and look up at the ceiling. I try jumping and stretching out my fingertips, but the new ceiling is too high for me to reach. My bed is low, so standing on that doesn't work either. I pull my wheelie chair out from under my desk and climb on to it so I'm standing. I can reach the ceiling easily like this, but the chair swivels and swerves out from under me. I fly off it and hit my head on the cupboard, before landing with a crash on the floor.

I lie there, breathing hard into the dark, my head throbbing where I hit it. I wonder if someone will come. I think I want someone to come. Is someone going to come?

No.

1.3

Dad is making this big thing about us all having breakfast together on the weekend. So when I open my bedroom door on Saturday morning I'm hit by a massive waft of bacon (yay) and coffee (no, thanks). Downstairs, Mum is at the table, stirring her tea excessively into little brown whirlpools. Dad is at the stove negotiating four different pans. Kyle swaggers in just after me and goes to put the TV on, but Dad says, 'Not today, Kyle.' So the two of us sit with Mum and wait for Dad to serve up.

It's weird to feel awkward with your own family, but that's how it is now, waiting for Dad. Like we've only just met and we don't know how to talk to each other properly yet. Because we *haven't* only just met, we can't even do the pointless small talk thing. Dad tries to start up some conversation about how our weeks have been, but Kyle interrupts him.

'Dad,' he sneers, and from his tone I can already tell that whatever comes next has been strategically calculated to annoy Dad as much as possible. Mum pivots towards Kyle, gripping the table edge, her mouth slightly open. She looks like a child. It's only the bags under her eyes, grey and silky, like little sardines, that give her away. 'Do you think that if you make a big effort with breakfast and play happy families for an hour, then nothing else that happens in the week matters?'

Mum drops her spoon on the floor. The kitchen tap goes *drip drip*, like a heartbeat on TV.

'Kyle,' says Dad warningly, stirring the baked beans and flipping an egg, which hisses.

'Whaaaaat?' he replies, his eyes all glittery and innocent. 'I'm just asking. Because I'd started to think we weren't a very good family, but, you know, maybe I'm wrong?'

Drip, drip! In the silence that follows, the kitchen tap makes the loudest noise in the world.

Dad's knuckles clench white on the kitchen worktop, as if he's on one of those really tall rollercoasters — the moment where you're suspended; you know you're about to fall, and all you can do is wait. He shakes his head, but he doesn't *look* angry. He looks . . . tired.

'Go to your room,' he says.

Kyle snickers and scrapes his chair out (extra

loudly), and a few seconds later the door to his room slams. I think he might actually be obeying Dad's instructions for once, but then I hear the *thunkety thunk* of his footsteps coming back down the stairs, and the front door slamming on his way out.

Sometimes I wonder why Kyle hates Mum and – especially – Dad so much. I always come back to this thing he said in Essex to me, that they wouldn't have stayed together if Mum hadn't got pregnant with Kyle – they'd only been dating for a few months at university, it wasn't supposed to be long-term. Mum was doing a ceramics degree and looks like a hippie in all the pictures – Dad was studying marketing and management and being in the economics society was his idea of fun. Their paths probably never would have crossed if they weren't studying in the same place, and then Kyle accidentally came along. Mum dropped off her course and they had a speedy wedding. Apparently Grandma Sarah went ballistic.

Things weren't working out – they argued constantly and over everything. They thought having another child might cement the family together better. That's where I came in. Kyle said the whole thing was stupid – they should have just accepted they had nothing in common and moved on with their lives. I didn't know how Kyle knew this. Did he overhear them or did he just *know*? I also wasn't sure whether it was worse to be the one who accidentally glued two unsuitable people together, or the one who couldn't fix it.

*

Today is my first day walking to school by myself. I'm not sure whether it *was* my stepping and tracing on the way home that made Mum good last week.

Either:

    a) They worked.

or:

    b) They didn't count because Kyle didn't let me complete them, so Mum was OK even though I didn't finish keeping her safe.

My rule has always been that doing things in fours can't do its special magic unless it is completed, so most likely it is b).

If so, maybe Mum doesn't need four protection? Maybe she is better now, and I can walk to school without stopping to do routines and she'll be fine. Plus, Kyle's going to ruin my life if I don't.

I make it to the third street only doing small

backwards movements with my arms in fours when The Thoughts say, *If you don't step back on the pavement, you won't be able to be invisible at school today and everyone will realise you're a freak.*

I try to tell The Thoughts that's silly — there's much more chance of ruining my invisibility if I start marching backwards and forwards down the street. It doesn't really work, though, and I still end up doing quite a bit of backwards-stepping down the final long road to school, terrified someone will see. I'm pretty sweaty by the time I get to my class and take my seat at my loner double desk.

I sit counting the corners of the room and repeating the phrase 'easy peasy lemon squeezy' in my head without really thinking about it. This is a phrase Dad always uses to convince us everything will be OK when he's about to do things like unblocking a sink or changing a lightbulb.

Mr Montague comes in, throws his green leather shoulder bag on to his chair (a proper throw; it flies approximately two metres before landing there), and says that rather than having physics as our first lesson, we are going to go round the room and say our name and one thing we like about ourselves. There's a group cheer of 'Yes!' and Farid does a fist pump. Apparently, it's so that the three of us who are new this year can get to know everyone and they can get to know us back. Not that Rachel and Jia need this – they seem to be fitting in *just fine*. Must be nice to be able to acclimatise to a whole new social habitat in one day! If you'd told me this morning that I had to guess who the new students were, I wouldn't have been able to pick them out. I'd have just said myself three times.

Maybe I should have thought a bit harder about whether to use Dad's phrase to bring luck, because actually he is pretty terrible at DIY so it always turns out not to be *easy peasy lemon squeezy* at all. This is obviously not going to be either.

Mr Montague starts with the back four desks on the left-hand side of the room. There are three girls sitting there who are all wearing pink lipgloss. Lauren says she likes her lips best because they are already big and so she won't ever need to have surgery to make them that way, Aliya chooses her waist because it's the thinnest in the class, Michelle picks her eyebrows becaue everyone says they are naturally 'on fleek' – whatever that means.

I didn't know people had surgery to make their lips bigger. It sounds painful. What do they do? Pump them up with air like a bike tyre? Do they put something else in? What if one day you accidentally pricked your new lips with a fork when you were eating tea and they exploded and everyone was sitting around the table covered in your fake lip insides?

I thought Mr Montague might tell them to pick something more interesting, and a boy nearer the front calls back, 'Why don't you try not being completely self-obsessed and vain for a change?'

'Dylan,' Mr Montague says, 'I didn't give any specifications, so if the girls want to preen and you don't like it, then you're just going to have to sit tight and when it's your turn you can tell us all something mind-blowingly deep about you to make up for it. OK?'

Jules says she likes that she is good at cooking, Sophia says her faith in God, and Ezinne is good at roller blading. When we get to Dylan he picks being good at football, and Isiah thinks he is a good mate. 'I'm really good at making stuff,' says Farid. Bradley picks his sense of humour, because even though it gets him into trouble at school, his dad says it will be the making of him. We're getting closer and closer to me and I'm freaking out about what I can say that no one will remember. The girl with the black boots, April, actually picks her shoes, because they're great for kicking anyone who gets in her way. I have no idea if she's joking.

Everyone is looking at me now because I'm next and I need to say something.

'I'm Ben,' I say. 'My favourite thing about me is my black Converse – I mean, they're at home right now. But I like wearing them at the weekends.' I could add that they're especially great because black feels like the colour of strength and power, and when I wear them I feel like I'm protected wherever I walk (even though they're getting too small for me), but I'm pretty sure no one would get it.

'He just copied April!' says Bradley. Oh, man. I probably did. I still hadn't thought about something to say and April made me think of just picking something you wear, so I picked my shoes . . . just like her.

And now I'm definitely not invisible, because my eyes are darting round the corners of the room like they're on fast-forward, and I can feel my throat doing the gulpy thing and my mouth and tongue going *click, click, click, click*, and the more I tell myself to stop gulping and clicking the faster and bigger it happens.

'I also didn't say that people can't pick the same things,' said Mr Montague. 'Do you think you're the only person in the world who likes their sense of humour most about themselves? It *happens* to be my favourite thing about me.'

He keeps going round the room.

'Everyone says I'm mature for my age,' says Rachel.

'I'm good with animals,' says Jia.

'I can run really fast,' says Daniel.

'I write good stories,' says Niesha.

'I'm kind to everyone,' says Grace, which makes Bradley snort.

I'm very glad when this activity is finally over and we can just get back to normal school stuff. We have biology after break and learn how plants make their food using carbon dioxide, sunlight and water. It is called photosynthesis.

Mr Montague has got three plants and we're going to put them in different conditions (one with light and water, one in a black box with no light, and one without water) to see how this works. I am not keen on this idea, because surely it is obvious that if they don't have the things they need then they will start to die, and do we really have to torture plants just so we can learn something we know already?

'Did you know that they did this study, and they found that saying nice things to plants can make them grow better and that the ones who had nasty things said to them didn't grow as well?' says Niesha.

People start laughing and Dylan tells Niesha she's a nutjob. But Mr Montague doesn't laugh, and he just says, 'Well, maybe we could all learn something from that.'

I'm very hungry by the time it's lunch, but I head to Music Room 4 to wait it out because I don't want the canteen drama again. I seriously wish *I* could photosynthesise. I check all the rooms – Clarinet Boy is back, otherwise it's empty. I shut the door to Music Room 4 behind me. I've brought my comic to read, and I unzip my backpack to get it out.

There's a folded piece of paper right at the top.

I am excited; I am terrified. I want it to be there; I wish it wasn't. I pull it out and trace my finger round its edges sixteen times before unfolding it. How did someone get it in there without me noticing?

The same thin black capitals ask me:

IF YOU ARE SO DESPERATE TO STAY ALIVE, WHY DON'T YOU LIVE A LITTLE?

Another *Doctor Who* quote! This one is something the tenth Doctor says to Lady Cassandra, who used to be a human but in this episode, which is millions of years in the future, she's just a sheet of skin stretched across a frame so that she can survive. Basically, Lady Cassandra is seriously boring and not very nice, and I'm *nothing* like her!

Why would someone send me this? I need to find out who they are.

I try to read my comic to take my mind off the nasty swirly feeling in my stomach, but I can't concentrate on it at all. Then I realise lunch break is almost over and I'd better hurry back to the classroom.

Mr Montague isn't there. Instead, Mrs Williams comes to teach us history. I scan the classroom again, wondering who here could possibly have sent me the note. Because it has to be someone in this class.

Mrs Williams is pacing round the classroom again, and her stepping is extremely out of sync. She'll go for a lunge when she's excited about something and then start shuffling when the drama dries up. 'So, as you can imagine –' LUNGE – 'it was utterly shocking when Henry VIII told the Pope to shove off and introduced another religion called Protestantism –' LUNGE – '*just* so he could divorce his wife.' LUNGE. 'When Henry VIII died, his young son Edward VI, awfully frail boy, succeeded him, and the European Reform that would entrench Protestantism got under way.' SHUFFLE. 'There were new prayer books; the order of service completely changed.' SHUFFLE, SHUFFLE. 'But he died and then his sister Mary, who was Catholic, came to power, and started setting people on *FIRE* if they wouldn't convert back.' LUNGE, LUNGE.

The wonky steps make my insides feel all squirmy, like I've swallowed a load of slugs and they're all having a slime convention in my tummy. I feel my throat going gulpy and I have to move my hands under the table to cancel out Mrs Williams's steps, which is super-risky because someone might notice.

I'm glad when the lesson is over and Mr Montague comes back to teach us for maths, but the problem of the note is still demanding most of my attention, and it's not until Mr Montague comes over and asks if I'm OK that I realise I haven't answered a single question on the worksheet he handed out fifteen minutes ago.

After school, I find that I have walked most of the way home without having to retrace any steps. I've been too busy thinking, *How can I find out where the notes are coming from?*

When I get back to 28a, only Mum is home. She

says Dad will be working late, and Kyle has his first evening shift at the local gaming arcade, because the first thing Kyle did when we moved here was go down the high street handing out his CV looking for a job. The arcade needed another person to sit changing people's notes for coins at the desk for the slot machines. Dad praised Kyle for being 'industrious', which means hard-working. Kyle narrowed his eyes and laughed with a snort, right into Dad's face. It's rare that I understand Kyle, but I knew what that meant. Kyle can't stand being around Mum when she's been drinking. 'I'm not industrious,' he might as well have said. 'I'd just rather be anywhere else than here. And you know what, *Dad*, I think you feel the same way too.'

When I think about Kyle now he's never around, sometimes I get a bit sad. I miss the days where we played video games together, and the times where he used to make me laugh by pulling faces behind Dad's back whenever he was talking about something serious. That feels like a very long time ago. I guess it was. Once I get sad, I start to feel worried: what if something happens to Kyle one of these days when he's out so late? What if he gets hit by a car, like Casper our old cat? Our neighbour Mrs Klein brought him home in a towel; she'd found him in the middle of the road leading out of the town. 'Dead in such a neat way, you wouldn't have known,' she'd said.

I sneaked a peek under the towel, then wished I hadn't. *I* knew.

Casper was nimble. If he could get hit by a car, Kyle definitely could, especially while crossing the road scrolling through his messages with his headphones going *thump thump thump*.

I used to go to Mum when I got worried like this, and she'd just smile and pinch my cheeks, tell me I was a worrier and that I reminded her of her. But now I just can't tell her. The worries feel too big, stuck in my throat, like a boiled egg swallowed whole. She knows, though. 'What's going on in that big old brain of yours, Benny?' she asks, as I'm lying on my back on the tasselled rug, flicking my eyes round the four corners of the ceiling. She pauses her garden show and comes down on to the rug with me. She pinches her fingers to her thumb like a little mouth and then press it to my forehead, making a sound like a cow drinking from a straw (*shllllluurrrp*), and moving her hand back, telling me she is sucking all my worries away. I guess it helps a bit. Kind of.

Mum tells me she has made me chicken, rice, sweetcorn and peas. She puts it on the table and ruffles my hair with her left hand four times, but she is looking at something in the distance that I can't see, and she seems a bit space cadety. I wonder if she has been drinking. Normally I would start doing lots of routines to try and make her come back, but today I just rush through them tapping my feet on the floor sixteen times and saying *Mum will be OK* four times in my head so that I can go back to thinking about the note.

I finish my tea as quickly as possible, zooming my fork round chicken, rice, sweetcorn and peas like I'm on fast-forward. I must always go round my plate having one mouthful of each of the four things until everything is gone. Each of the four foods must be finished at the same time, because otherwise there would be a point where the mouthful rounds would stop being in fours. This means I have to calculate how big each mouthful of each particular food should be, so that all the foods run out at the same time. For instance, if your pile of rice is bigger than your pile of peas, then your rice mouthfuls will need to be a little bigger than your pea mouthfuls. The proportion calculations usually take me about thirty seconds to work out, but today I don't care, I'm spooning this food into my mouth like my life depends on me finishing this plate as soon as humanly possible.

I rinse the plate in the sink, turning the tap on and off four times so quickly that I spray my school shirt with water. I chuck it in the dishwasher, changing its position four times, and open and close the dishwasher door another four times, before sprinting out of the kitchen (door open and closed four times) and into my room (repeat) and diving on to my bed.

When I have something big to think about I always get into bed and stare up at my solar system mobile that Mum made for my tenth birthday. It took her ages to get all the clay planets the right sizes. I sat next to her in her shed watching her press sludge into a perfect ring for Saturn and scrape holes into the Earth's tiny moon with the end of a piece of wire, until it looked like the pockmark-holed cheeks of Kyle's friend George. Technically, Uranus, Neptune and Jupiter also have rings, but it is true that they are harder to see, and Mars, Jupiter, Saturn, Uranus and Neptune also have moons, but I definitely didn't say anything. When she finally fired the finished version and took it out of her kiln she said it was her favourite thing she had ever made. I love lying underneath it with the window open so that they drift round in circles. My favourite is Jupiter, which she glazed yellow, orange and white, all swirly like the inside of a marble cake.

Who sent that note? I haven't made a single friend – I don't even think anyone knows my name. Mr Montague seems like a total geek, but I don't think he's going to start putting secret notes in some kid's backpack. That said, I *did* wonder whether he was an alien rather than a normal teacher. But what kind of alien is going to give themselves away by making reference to a TV show *about* an alien?

I am trying very hard not to let myself think a silly thought that can only lead to disappointment. I have always dreamed that one day the Doctor will come for me. The TARDIS will materialise into my bedroom with a *vworp vworp* and the Doctor will step out and lean against the door, give a shrug and say, 'Are you coming or not, Ben?' and I will say, 'Am I coming, Doctor? I've only been waiting for this moment my entire life.' Of course I'll sound much cooler than I normally do, because this is a line I've prepared, but even if I didn't it wouldn't matter because the Doctor really does not care if you are cool or not.

But things don't normally happen exactly how you imagine them, so what if, instead of coming straight to get me, the Doctor might send a note ahead, like a clue, so I know to expect him?

The Doctor can be very sneaky, so maybe he zipped in and out while I wasn't looking, or perhaps he got someone else to put it there.

Every time I let myself think this thought I can hear Kyle's voice telling me to grow up and stop being a baby. But is it really so unlikely? I can't think of anyone else who could have put it there. Sherlock Holmes says that once you eliminate the impossible, whatever remains, no matter how improbable, must be the truth.

Maybe the Doctor really is going to come for me soon, and we'll travel through time and space fighting monsters and saving worlds. Mum and Dad won't have to worry, because having a time machine means that you can travel for years and get yourself back to the moment you left without anyone knowing you ever went anywhere. And if I never wanted to come back at all . . . well, I'm sure the Doctor could sort something out.

Tomorrow morning I will solve this once and for all. As soon as I get into the classroom I will sit down at my desk and not stop staring at my bag until I see who's putting the notes in.

And just in case I don't see them, I'm going to send a reply.

I think about replying with another *Doctor Who*

quote, but I can't think of anything where all the words have the right number of letters. So I just write: *IDENTIFY YOURSELF* on a piece of paper torn out from my exercise book, because each of those words has eight letters which together makes sixteen, and that is what you get if you times four by four.

I hope the receiver doesn't notice how wobbly the letters are, because my hand is shaking like mad. I roll it up and put it in my bag, ready for tomorrow morning.

1.4

Mum seemed good this morning at breakfast. She was already in the kitchen when I came down, wearing her pottery outfit: clay-stained brown tracksuit bottoms and an oversized black sweater, hair in a high bun. Her eyes were kind of glittery, and she was going on about this series of German gnomes she's started working on that she thinks will bring in 'significant revenue'. I didn't see Dad or Kyle. Dad's work shoes were not in the hallway, meaning he must have already left, and I could hear Kendrick Lamar blaring through the ceiling, so Kyle must have still been upstairs in his room.

Mum was poring over pictures in one of her ceramics books on the counter and humming a tune I didn't recognise. She doesn't have her garden shed any more like she used to in Essex, but she's rented some studio space really close and is planning to start working again. It's in the same direction as school so we left together this morning, but I turned down her offer to walk me all the way.

When I get into the classroom, I make sure the note is poking out of my bag where the two zips meet so that the note sender can't miss it, and hang it up on its normal peg.

I stare hard at the pegs, so that if someone puts another note in my bag I will see who they are. So far so good, but then there's a massive surge of kids all arriving at the same time, which obscures my peg, and I can't tell exactly who's hanging what up or putting what where.

Mr Montague takes the register, and I keep staring hard at the pegs just in case someone comes in late and puts something in, but no one does. Then he tells us to file downstairs to the sports hall for drama. Today is our first drama lesson, which I have been seriously dreading. As soon as we get into the sports hall, I discover that I had good reason to. Our teacher is called Miss Valentine, but she tells us to call her by her first name, Adore, as soon as we sit down. Miss Valentine has extremely long pointy black nails, and is wearing a tie-dye dress and sparkly boots. She talks very sloooowly with the sort of croaky voice that women in old movies sometimes have, which Kyle told me is supposed to be sexy, but I really can't understand how. She tells us to find a space and that we're going to do an exercise where we walk around the room, pretending to be different things and characters when she calls them out.

We start off as just ourselves, and then we have to be a tree, an Egyptian and a soldier. Mostly everyone is just charging around and bumping into each other. I am trying to walk quickly and spend a while tying up my shoelace, repeating in my head: *invisible, invisible, invisible, invisible*. Miss Valentine is now shouting random job titles over the noise and her voice is getting less croaky and more car alarm. *Teacher! Waiter! Prime minister!*

Dylan crashes into Michelle, who starts wailing that she thinks he has broken her skull, and Miss Valentine shushes her and tells her to take a friend and go and see the nurse, and Michelle picks Aliya and seems much better already.

Rhiiiiino!

Bradley runs at April and headbutts her in the chest. April wastes no time in stamping her massive black boot (so she wasn't joking) on his foot. Bradley screams a rude word at her, and Miss Valentine asks what in the world is going on, and April says, 'In fairness, you did tell us to be rhinos,' and then they both get sent to stand in the corner.

The whole class is complete mayhem, until Miss Valentine says she needs to leave ten minutes early because she has an audition for a very major film, so we all get to go to break early.

Everyone else heads towards the playground, and I walk back upstairs to the classroom, peek through the meshed window in the door to make sure Mr Montague isn't in there to catch me, and grab my backpack. Even from a few steps away I can see that my note isn't sticking out of the bag any more. I unzip the bag, throat going *gulp gulp*, heart going *bang bang*, and—

Nothing.

Nothing?! I'm so disappointed I feel tears stinging in the corners of my eyes and I have to bite my lip hard to stop them rolling out.

I go and mope in Music Room 4 and try to read my comic but keep rereading the same page over and over because it doesn't feel right, and finally I give up and wander back for maths.

Mr Montague is writing out an equation on the board and showing us how to balance it, and Bradley yells, 'Balance this!' and pings his rubber at Sophia's head using a catapult made of a pencil and an elastic band. I think Mr Montague is going to freak, but what he actually does is manage to turn round in time to CATCH the rubber before it hits Sophia in the face, pop it in his pocket and say, 'Thanks, Bradley, I've been needing a new rubber.' And Bradley is just staring at him with his mouth hanging open like nothing this confusing has happened to him ever before.

Mr Montague turns back to the whiteboard and I hear someone cough. I don't think much of it, until it happens again, and this time I know it's deliberate. It's one of those pretend coughs someone does when they want to get your attention. I flit my head slightly to the right, and as soon as I do, April, lightning-quick, stretches her arm out across the gap between our desks.

The sleeve of her school jumper has rolled up her arm slightly and I see a flash of a silver bracelet jangling with tiny moon and star charms. She has a folded piece of paper between her thumb and index finger, the nails of which are painted a pearly white colour. I look at her like, 'Er, hello, are you sure you're passing that note to the right person?' and she raises her left eyebrow and nods at me to take it like, 'Er, hello, are you stupid or something?'

I take it and open it:

I'M APRIL, THE ORIGINAL, YOU MIGHT SAY.

Basically, when the twelfth doctor (Peter Capaldi) doesn't want to regenerate, he is visited by the first doctor (but not *actually* the first doctor, because the actor who played him died a long time ago, so it's a lookalike), and the first doctor says this to the twelfth Doctor to introduce himself, except he says 'Doctor' rather than 'April' . . .

Anyway. The point is: April is the Doctor!

OK, well, obviously April *isn't* the doctor, but the thing is, it's witchy-named-after-the-fourth-month-girl *APRIL* who's been sending the notes!

I can't even look back in her direction. I feel my face getting hotter and hotter. It's so boiling that the air in front of my eyes seems to be waving and shimmering, like when you look into the distance on the hottest day of the year.

I try to focus on the whiteboard, but X and Y are wiggling round, and nothing Mr Montague is saying seems to be in English. Which is weird, because no one else seems bothered, so either they are so bored they don't notice Mr Montague start speaking in his alien mother tongue, or I've briefly stopped being able to understand English. The second scenario seems more likely.

I practically sprint out of the room at lunch, I don't even go and get my bag because I'm scared that will give April time to intercept me at the pegs. As soon as I get out of the classroom I do sprint, all the way down the long corridor and up the four flights and through the green door, bursting into Music Room 4 and slamming the door shut. I sit on the floor leaning against the back wall, screwing my eyes shut so hard I see rainbow dots and lines fizzing in the blackness.

I count to sixty-four and open my eyes, then start to move my eyes round the four corners of the room, whispering, 'One, two, three, four,' over and over and trying to get my heart rate under control. I know it's pathetic, but I'm so disappointed that the notes aren't from the Doctor that I'm crying horrible baby tears and my face is getting all snotty. And why is this girl sending these notes anyway? Is she making fun of me for being a geek because of my backpack? Or is she a . . . *Doctor Who* fan?!

She *does* seem to know a lot of classic quotes.

I can hear footsteps out in the corridor. I really hope it's just Clarinet Boy coming to start practice, but they sound like they're getting nearer. I'm still so on edge that all I can think to do is close my eyes tight, like when you're little and utterly rubbish at hide and seek because you think that if you can't see anyone because your eyes are shut, then they won't be able to see you. Oh my god, oh my god, the steps are really close now. I'm forgetting to breathe! I can feel the gulps coming . . .

I hear scratchy noises at the door. Oh, man, it's like I'm in a horror film. I crack my right eye open just a few millimetres. There's a piece of paper slipping under the door.

Jeez, she's followed me here.

I crawl forward and grab it, snatching my arm back like April is a poisonous snake who might also slither under the door and bite me.

GERONIMO! says the note. This is something the eleventh Doctor says when he's about to do something exciting.

I look up. The door handle to the room is moving down. The door is opening!

April stands in the doorway, her left eyebrow raised slightly, just like it was in the classroom.

'I thought you might at least wait for me,' she says.

I don't say anything – I *can't* say anything.

'I mean, I went to quite a lot of effort. Finding the right quotes and stuff. Making sure everything was spelled right.'

Nothing. She shuffles her feet and sighs.

'Do you have a voice?' She moves her arms round like people do in music videos when they're doing the robot dance. 'ARE-YOU-FROM-THIS-PLANET?'

'Yes,' I say to the floor. 'Just don't get why you're sending me those notes, that's all.'

'Why? I thought it would make you smile. I saw your TARDIS backpack.' My lower lip is wobbling and I'm terrified that I'm about to cry in front of April. 'Oh, god, I just thought you'd think it was fun. I wasn't trying to bring on some kind of personal crisis. Are you . . . crying?'

'No!'

'This always happens. I try and do nice things for people and they take it the wrong way. I was just trying to cheer you up, OK?'

'Cheer me up?'

'Yeah. You look sad all the time.'

Oh, fantastic. Me not saying anything has resulted in people thinking I'm miserable. I guess I'll just have to figure out how to make my face look more . . . neutral? At peace? Maybe I can practise in the mirror when I get home . . .

'How did you know I was in here?' I say.

'I noticed you slip away and upstairs at break time. I wanted to know where you went.'

'You sent me notes. You followed me.'

'Don't say it like that, you make me sound like a stalker.'

'All because I looked sad?'

'Yeah. Also I thought you might let me read your comics with you.'

'My comics?'

'Don't pretend you don't have any. I can spot a geek like you a mile off. You smell of screen time. Also, I saw them in your backpack when I put the notes in.'

'You – want to read comics – with me?'

'Yeah. I brought your backpack.' April pulls the bag out from behind her back. 'What do you have today?'

'Do you like *Doctor Who*?'

'Yeah, enough. My older brother Thomas is the major fan. He made me watch them all with him.'

'You have an older brother who likes *Doctor Who*?!'

'Yeah.'

'That's so cool. My dad liked it – he collected all the classic DVDs which means I can watch them all now. It's really hard to get every episode otherwise. I wish my brother liked it. I mean, he used to like it, and we'd watch it together . . . but then he kind of . . .' *Stopped wanting to do anything with me.*

73

Got annoyed that I took all the attention from Mum and decided he hated me. Shut up, Ben. 'Um, grew out of it.'

'I used to find it a major pain when I wanted to watch my own stuff,' says April. 'But I got used to it eventually. And now I sometimes even watch them by myself. They remind me of him.'

'Why do you need reminding of your older brother?'

April looks down at the floor and I immediately feel awful for asking. Probably she will tell me that he died in a horrible plane crash and how can I be so insensitive, and then this, whatever this is, will be over as immediately as it began.

'He's a medic. He works for Doctors Without Borders, helping people who have lost their homes and are injured and need emergency help. Which is amazing and everything. I just miss him sometimes.'

'You can read my comics with me, if you like.'

April laughs. 'You geeks. You're all the same. You show sympathy by allowing others to touch your merch. Cool.'

April passes me the backpack. I take the comic out and April comes and sits next to me. I have no idea what to say to her, so we just read the comic together in silence. I am a fast reader so I am sure

April will take longer than me and I say, 'Tell me when you've finished and I'll turn the page.'

'Oh, I just look at the pictures,' she says, like it's the most normal thing in the world. To me this is beyond strange – think about how much important information you would miss. I don't say this. Instead I say, 'Cool, well . . . I guess they're the best bits,' while wondering why I am saying things I don't believe.

We sit there for the rest of lunch, flipping through pages, not talking. It should be capital-A awkward, but somehow, it's not. Actually, I think it might even be nice.

*

On Monday, April moves to the desk next to me! I came back after the weekend and she'd moved her pencil case and notepad over here and slung her jumper over the back of the chair. Like it was no big deal or anything.

I stare straight ahead, trying to buy some time to figure out how to react. In some ways, it's pretty amazing that she's sitting there. I liked reading comics with her over lunch and she's probably the coolest girl I've ever met. And for some reason *she's* speaking to *me*.

But not sitting next to anyone meant people were less likely to spot me darting my eyes round the room or flitting my hands back and forward. I've been trying hard not to do anything super-noticeable, like tapping my feet or opening and closing my Dalek pencil case in fours, but sometimes it happens before I realise I'm doing it. Having someone sitting close to me makes them more likely to notice, and then they'll tell everyone. But April doesn't really seem like that kind of person. Does she?

I sneak my eyes to the right slightly. April has a pencil case covered in beads and little pictures of bats outlined in silvery thread. Her hand darts inside and she grabs a black pen. I think she's going to start copying Mr Li's notes on how rivers erode rocks to form waterfalls, but instead she hunches her head over the notepad and starts doodling something. I'm trying to see what she's drawing while definitely not *looking* like I'm looking, when I hear someone behind us making kissing noises. I turn round and see Michelle miming a smooch with the back of her hand. April has also turned round.

'What are you drawing, April? Your new boyfriend?' says Michelle. April puts her middle finger up and turns back round to carry on her doodle. She seems unbothered, but I am capital-B bothered, because this is exactly the kind of attention that will make my invisibility plan fail.

I try to look like I am copying Mr Li's waterfall diagram and am not interested in anything Michelle has to say, or the noises that she's still making and that Lauren and Aliya have now joined in with. April nudges me with her elbow and pushes the notepad in my direction. She's drawn the twelfth Doctor accidentally landing his TARDIS in the middle of a waterfall and getting drenched when he opens the door, which is quite funny, because it is true that the Doctor isn't very good at landing the TARDIS in a safe spot.

In April's drawing, the Doctor looks quite annoyed about how wet his jacket has just got. It's an amazing drawing; it looks super-professional. I actually laugh out loud.

'That's really cool,' I whisper, and April winks.

'Do you draw?' she asks.

'No.'

'You could learn, with me. Miss Ruiz from Hilltown Primary runs art club after school on Tuesdays and Fridays. She brings these cute Year Fives and Sixes to use our art room, and anyone in secondary can show up too. She's cool, you'll like her. She used to teach me in Year Four.'

'No, thanks.'

'Why? It could be fun. Come on!' she says. 'My parents are always having to work super-late and it's boring being at home by myself in the evenings.'

'I'm not sure I can,' I say quickly. 'They're probably really expensive, and I won't be any good at anything so guess I'd better not.' I shrug and try to smile, like, hey, just one of those things, no problem, but the truth is I would love nothing more than to hang out with April after school. I just don't think I can leave Mum by herself in the evenings.

'Actually, they're free, and you don't have to be any good. You learn how to do stuff, that's the point.'

'I suck at art.'

'Will you just think about it?'

'OK.'

*

April texts me all the way home about art club. She says stuff like, **MISS RUIZ IS NICE U'LL LIKE HER PROMIS X** and **IT CLD B FUN!!!!**

It's hard to explain to April by texting only four- or eight-letter words that while it could be fun I am too worried about what Mum will do if she's home alone.

I'm walking fast so I can get home and tell Mum all about April. She's always going on about how I need to make friends and I know she's going to be super-excited. But the flat is in darkness when I open the door, and I feel the slugs lurch in my tummy. Is Mum home? I flick the lights on and off in the hall and then the sitting room, sixteen times each because I need the luck, but no more in case Mum isn't here and I need to act fast.

Oh. I see a lump on the sofa wrapped in a blanket. She's home.

'Mum,' I say, peeling the throw away from where I think her head is. 'Come on, stop it, please.'

Her face is all red and shiny, her eyes crusted together.

'You should get up.'

She grumbles something.

'You need to make me dinner,' I say, realising I sound pathetic, and also knowing from past experience that this is not the sort of thing you should say to encourage Mum out of a duvet mound. It is, however, true.

'I don't needa do anything,' she slurs, pulling the blanket over her head.

'Please,' I say. 'I want to tell you about my day. I . . . think I made a friend.'

The mound doesn't move. I wish I could make her get up. I think about yelling, 'I'll tell Dad on you!' but we both know I wouldn't.

Out of nowhere I have the most awful thought: *I wish Mum would disappear!*

Noooooo! I clutch the sides of my head. Why did I think that? I'm upset with her but I definitely don't want her to disappear.

I wish Mum would disappear! I'm going to MAKE her disappear! screams my head.

I run out of the sitting room and up to my room, Bumble scampers after me. I dive on to my bed, Bumble jumps up and puts his big head on my chest. I flick my eyes round and round the ceiling corners, not even counting how many times, just saying *one, two, three, four* over and over and over, hundreds – probably thousands – of times, trying to undo the bad thought.

I didn't mean it! I plead with The Thoughts. *I would never hurt Mum.*

I badly want to call Kyle. But I'm pretty sure he'll just get angry and say it's not his problem. I also have no idea where he is right now. He never seems to be around after school any more.

My phone pings.

U DONT HAV 2 B NY GD AT ART!! CLASS

TOMOZ??

Fine. I text back. I don't know if it's just because I'm angry and I'm going to regret it, or if I really mean it.

YAAAAAAS, replies April immediately, with a row of seven fist-pump emojis.

Bumble gives a soft whine because I guess he hasn't had dinner either, so I go downstairs and pour more Pedigree Chum than he normally has into his bowl, and bring it up to my room for him to eat there. Double treat.

I realise I forgot my orange squash, so I go downstairs again.

Mum is in the kitchen, but her back is to me and she is facing the kitchen counter. She is tipping liquid from a bottle into her cup of tea. She is staring out into the steam rising from the kettle, pouring without even looking. Her hand is shaking. I creep out of the room – I can't bear to listen to her beg me not to tell Dad, to tell me that this is 'a secret'.

I'm sick of secrets. But Mum is good at secrets. She's so good that even when I creep down twenty minutes later to find the bottle and hide it, she's already thought to hide it somewhere herself.

If she hadn't become a potter I think she could

have been a secret agent. If she wasn't sloshed, obviously.

At 9.48 p.m. I hear the front door open and close, and the low tone of Dad greeting Mum. I lie very still, trying to hear what they are saying, but the doors between us make their voices sound underwatery, and I can't quite make it out.

Then Dad is raising his voice, and I can't hear Mum saying much in reply. He must know she has been drinking. I hear stomping upstairs and someone walking around in their bedroom and the banging of cupboards and drawers opening and shutting rapidly for a period of nine minutes and thirty-four seconds. The footsteps go back downstairs again, and the front door slams. Then the house is entirely silent.

2

2.1

April is antsy all day because she just wants it to be time for art club. I am antsy all day because I am not sure about art club. More importantly, I am almost certain that Dad did not come back again last night, and that he was not home in the morning. I want to tell April about it for pretty much every minute of the day, but somehow I think that if I say it out loud that will make it real, and right now at least I can hope I might be wrong. I flick my eyes round the corners of the room all day, and absorb precisely zero per cent of the information imparted by Mrs Williams and Mr Montague.

April puts her hand to her mouth and pretends to radio me on three different occasions in an American accent: 'Control to Ben, this is Commander April, do you read me?' but I can't even fake a smile. I just focus on telling myself that even if Dad *didn't* come home last night, he'll definitely be back tonight – maybe he'll be there when I get home from school.

Because *he* was the one who kept going on about London being our fresh start – so he'll be sorry for whatever happened between him and Mum, and want to fix things, won't he?

Won't he?

A little later the class is rustling – everyone is trying to pack their stationery and folders away without Mr Montague noticing. Ezinne seems to think that if she moves in verrrry dellliibbbberattte slow motion he won't see her. I don't know why they bother, because he always sees and tells them that he has special ways of making home time a lot further away.

Definitely alien.

But maybe he has a galactical event or something today, because for once he winks and says, 'Oh, go on then, off with you.' Everyone sprints for the pegs, and before I've even put my pencil case in my bag, April is dragging me out of the door and down to a basement I never even knew about.

There are five other kids sitting round three rectangular tables that have all been pushed together. Four look younger than April and me, and they've got newspaper laid out in front of them, stuck to the table with masking tape at the corners. Miss Ruiz is grabbing PVA glue sticks from the cupboard above the sink and putting them in the middle of the table next to a group of cardboard animal models and a pile of colourful paper with different prints all over them, like the kind you see on wrapping paper at a birthday party.

There's one guy at the far end of the table with headphones on, who looks way older. He could even be in Year Eleven – I wonder if he knows Kyle, or if they have any lessons together. He's completely focused on the sketchbook in front of him, where he's drawing buildings in charcoal. Even from over here, looking at them upside down, I can see they're incredible. It looks like Gotham City over there.

Miss Ruiz sees April come in and calls, 'Whassup!' and for a second I think I might have misheard, but April grins and says, 'Whassup yourself! This is Ben.'

'Hi,' I say, looking at my shoes.

We grab seats at the end of the table and Miss Ruiz says, 'OK, guys, so I thought we could do a thing today called decoupage. It's pretty chilled; you don't have to concentrate too hard. You've got these pieces of paper and you can choose the ones you like and just tear or cut small bits off them. Then you PVA them on to whatever cardboard animal you like. When you've covered the animal,

86

you PVA the whole thing, and when it dries it looks nice and glossy. Like this . . .' She holds up a bunny covered in polka dots, stripes and stars.

She hasn't even finished explaining everything but the younger kids are already choosing their animals and reaching for paper sheets and glue pots. April dives in too and picks a bat, and some midnight-blue paper sprinkled with gold stars.

I look at the stuff on the table. All the sheets I can see have colours I don't like on them, and I'm worried that even if I cut the paper it will still be hard to make sure all the pieces are the same size, and what if I lose track of how many bits I've stuck on? *I'll make an evil bat, a bat that makes Dad definitely not come back.* The other kids have started gluing.

Miss Ruiz comes over and asks if there's an animal I think I might like to do. I shake my head. I'm worried she will tell me I have to pick one, that I can't just sit here, and if I don't want to join in like I'm supposed to then I can just get out.

'No prints you like the look of?' she asks.

I shake my head again.

'Or something else you might like to do? I've got some clay – if you want to make a sculpture I could whack it in the kiln for you after.'

87

'NO!' I say. Suddenly all I can see is Mum at home by herself on the sofa wrapped in her blanket. I shouldn't be here. 'I think I'd just like to watch.'

'Sure, that's fine,' says Miss Ruiz, which shocks me, because I thought she would tell me off for shouting.

'Ben, you can watch me do mine and join in if you want to later,' says April.

I nod.

'Scooch over here then,' she says, and I drag my stool closer to hers.

Miss Ruiz brings us all cups of orange squash and puts a plate of biscuits in the centre of the table, and the younger kids dive on them. Then she sits down at the table too. She starts tearing bits of the green paper with the leafy print and sticking them on a cardboard giraffe. I watch April tear and glue, tear and glue, her fingers dancing like a magician's. Her pieces are stuck perfectly with no bumps; it's weirdly calming to watch. After, she coats the whole thing with such an evenly spread layer of glue that it looks like a decoration you might buy in a shop. The younger kids' ones are messier, with paper not stuck down as neatly and gloopy finishes, but they still look cool.

'What do you think?' says a girl at the end,

proudly waving a sticky pink-and-yellow horse at me and April.

'Pretty cool,' I say.

'Thanks! I'm Priya.' She's beaming. 'What year are you guys in?'

'Eight,' I say.

'Cooooool!' she replies, and then adds sadly, 'I'm only in year four' – like it's her own fault she wasn't born sooner. Then all the other kids want my opinion on their animals. It's pretty weird, being de facto cool just because you're older. Not that I'm complaining.

'Are you guys going to come every week?' says Priya.

'Uh, maybe,' I say.

'Awesome, because Rhys doesn't talk to us,' says Priya, rolling her eyes at charcoal dude.

April starts to make another bat, this one with light-blue paper with silver swirls on it.

Tear and glue, tear and glue.

Mostly we're quiet, but Priya asks what everyone's favourite animal is, so we talk about that, and then Miss Ruiz asks us what we would choose to be if we could be any animal we wanted, and why. She even *joins in* when we've all given our answers. She tells us she would be a cat, because

89

they get to skulk around exploring and doing their own thing all night, but still come back to a warm bed and food. And best of all, they don't have to work because their human pays the bills.

'But I would miss painting,' she says. 'And you lot. I'd miss you guys.'

I thought Rhys couldn't hear us with his headphones in, but I see him give a slight smile.

Somehow the hour and a half is up in what feels like no time at all, and I actually wish we had longer. It's weird. I'm dreading getting home in case Mum's in a state, but I'm also desperate to go and check she's all right. Maybe Dad will have come home early from work to make up with Mum and they'll be sitting at the table talking and everything will be *fine, fine, fine, fine*.

'Which bat would you like?' asks April, as we're walking out of the main doors. I hadn't realised one of them was for me. I seem to always be the last one to realise everything.

'Uh, the starry one, please,' I say. The midnight blue creeps me out a bit. I think if I touch it then maybe I'll come home and Mum will be sad, but it's preferable to the lighter-blue one, which might make us all really, *really* sad for ever (if faced with two blue options, always go with the one closest to dark, TARDIS blue). Miss Ruiz has attached a string to the back of each bat. I don't want to offend April so I let her give me the midnight bat and decide I will throw it in the bin on the way home.

April spots her bus pulling into the stop down the road and sprints towards it. 'Byeeee!' she is calling. 'Text meeee!'

I turn and walk home in the other direction. Every time I see a bin I tell myself I will throw away the bat, but I can't seem to do it. It feels too bad, like I'm chucking away something that's really alive. I take a few steps from the bin, and then I think, *No, I must chuck this, it's totally dangerous*, so I go back, but I can't do it, it's wrong, April made it! Walk away, go back, away, back, away. Both options feel terrible; I can't win. I'm sweaty and feel like I'm going to be sick. I'm still holding it by the time I get home. Actually, I'm basically cradling it.

I open the door slowly, scared of what I will find and whether Dad will be here. I quickly then shut it and open it another three times for luck. The lights are on; I hear Mum in the kitchen. Bumble is curled up in his basket, snoring quietly, but he gets up and stretches when he hears me coming in, claws skittering along the tiles, and gives my hand a lazy lick.

'Hey, Ben,' she says. 'Made you supper.'

She has a funny look on her face; it's hard to explain exactly. I immediately know as soon as I see her that Dad isn't here, and I think she may have been drinking, but not so much it's completely obvious. The curve of a smile, but only on the left side – the look of a challenge, like there's a deal to be made. You get to hang out with your friend, it says, I make you dinner and do *my* thing, and we'll just agree that this is how it's going to work.

But maybe not. Maybe I just imagined it. I really hope so.

'Thanks,' I say, taking my plate. Sausage, beans, mash and toast, all with the perfect amount of white porcelain space between them.

I want to ask her where Dad went last night, and whether he'll be back soon, preferably tonight? But the words jam in my throat. After dinner I go to my room and try to stay up and listen for the sound of Dad coming home, but it doesn't come; there's just the tinny sound of Mum's programmes on the telly drifting through the ceiling. I open and close the curtains repeatedly in sets of four. I tell myself that if I can get them in exactly the right position, Dad will definitely come home. Standing by the window also has the added benefit of seeing the porch and the road, so I can watch for him. I'm feeling sleepy, so I allow myself to get into bed, but keep myself awake by pinching my upper arms and forcing myself to look around all the corners of the room forty times, four hundred times, four thousand times . . .

*

I am angry with myself when the red light filtering through my eyelids tells me I fell asleep, and now a new day has started up like everything is normal and something awful isn't happening. I run downstairs hoping to see Dad's coat and shoes by the door, but there's no sign of them. I try to tell myself that he could have come back late and left early, and I just didn't hear, but I know it's not true. I feel the creep of *more* anger – and I don't think it's just at myself, which is . . . unusual. I think I might be . . . kind of angry at Dad? Because yesterday I guess I thought he hoped Kyle and I didn't hear him leaving and was planning on coming back in the evening and acting like nothing had happened.

But now it's the *next* morning and he's still not back, and he hasn't even sent me a text, or tried to call to tell me where he's gone. Has he really not thought at all about how worried that would make me?

Mum isn't awake yet, and even though maybe it's cowardly, I can't bear to face her and a) pretend everything is normal, or b) ask her what's going on. (So maybe I *don't* want to know? Argh, it's all so confusing.) I dash back upstairs and get dressed as quickly as possible (although I get stuck with routines at my bedroom door and the stairs) and manage to leave for school without seeing her.

Today it's really cold, like winter might be on its way, so I wear my black scarf for the first time since last year. I'm walking down the road to school, moving my arms subtly in fours pretty quickly, when I realise the wool on my scarf around my neck is getting damp. I am sweating in the cold. I get to the classroom twenty-five minutes early, so early no one is here yet, not even Mr Montague.

I concentrate on moving my eyes round and round the four corners of my desk, and gradually people start to trickle in. The room fills with gossip, gum and Snapchats, and I want to shake it like a snow globe and wait for it to go still.

'What's up?' says April, plonking herself down next to me with a minute to spare. 'You seem sad,' she says. 'I mean . . . sadder than usual.'

I should be happy. Someone is sitting next to me wanting to be my friend, a thing that has never happened to me before. Also, that someone is April, and before, when I thought about this, it seemed like a brilliant sparkly dream.

'Did you bring a comic for lunch?' she asks, which is annoying, because now my desk routine has been interrupted and I'll have to start from scratch. I shake my head and mumble, 'Forgot.'

'Wow, you must be *really* sad.'

Mr Montague, who has been sitting with his feet on the desk reading *A History of Gingerbread Men*, clears his throat and stands to take the register. The time is 9.01 a.m. We have physics with him first, and we're learning about the order of the planets in the solar system. He tells us to push all the desks to the corners of the room to clear 'performance space'. Then he blows up ten different-coloured balloons and we have to get into ten groups of three or four per balloon and stand in different parts of the room orbiting the sun – played by Mr Montague standing in the middle of the room in a yellow inflatable ring coordinating us all.

Mr Montague says it's very important that we get the proportions between the planets right so that our model is to scale. April and I are in a group of four (good) with Ezinne and Sophia (bad) playing Uranus, because unfortunately we were last in the balloon queue. Sophia points a plastic pink fingernail towards me and says to April, 'What's his name?'

She's talking about me and I realise two things at the same time: 1) Being invisible worked. 2) I'm not actually sure I like being invisible.

'He's called Ben, and he can actually talk for himself!' says April.

'Oh! Like, wow!' says Sophia sarcastically. She and Ezinne have a brief struggle over the balloon, before sighing and agreeing to hold it together. Now they are bumping into Saturn and Neptune and generally screwing up its trajectory. April and I trail after them.

'I thought you'd love this stuff, geekazoid,' April whispers to me.

'Don't call me that,' I say.

'Sorry, I was just . . . Yeah, you're right, sorry.'

Now April looks sad too, and I immediately feel bad but don't know what to say. We march behind Uranus in solemn silence.

At break I leave immediately for Music Room 4. I stride out of the class as quickly as possible and power-walk up the stairs to avoid April, but when I finally get there and shut the door I realise that, weirdly, the only thing I want to do is *be with* April. My brain is being very confusing at the moment.

I hear footsteps. This time April swings through the door without knocking.

'Wanna come to mine?' she says.

'It's the middle of the day,' I say, confused.

'Yes, I am aware. But we have drama after break and Miss Valentine doesn't really strike me as the type to keep adequate records of student attendance. Also, my parents are at work.'

To be honest, the idea fills me with pure horror. I feel my eyes inching to bounce round the corners of the room, and I tap my toes rather than my feet in fours so April doesn't notice.

'What are you saying?' she asks.

'Nothing! I'm not saying *anything at all*!'

April is just standing there not saying much because I think I accidentally shouted this. I didn't mean to. I just wish I didn't do all this stuff – I wish I wasn't such a loser. I wish I could wake up in the morning and smile and laugh and really mean it, like other kids. I wish I knew how to have a friend. I wish I wasn't me.

'OK,' she says. I stare at the floor. 'Well, shall we go then?'

'Fine,' I say.

I think I just decided not to be me.

It's the weirdest thing, walking downstairs and

buzzing ourselves through the red double doors with our key cards and no one noticing. Being out on the street with April in the middle of the day, bunking school like in a film, wondering if the buildings will fall over like a cardboard set if you touch them.

We have to get a bus to April's, and that's when the real me comes back. I don't say, 'Hey, April, I can't get on this bus because it's red,' because I don't want her to think I'm a total weirdo. So I tell myself, *You can do this, you can get in a red vehicle with your new friend, it's no big deal.*

April pulls me along the aisle and into the back row and I dart my eyes round the bus's four corners, over and over, to magic away any red anger between Mum and Dad that this journey might create. April says, 'Why d'you do that?' and I say, 'Do what?' and she says, 'That thing where your eyes go round and round, over and over. What's it *for*?'

Kids have laughed at the things I do, but they've never actually asked me why I do them. It's a good question, I guess. I could lie and be angry, like earlier, or . . .

'Um . . . I think it just . . . makes me feel better,' I say. April nods and chews a pearly thumb nail, thinking over this new information.

98

'Is that why you do that stuff with your hands too? And your pencil case? And the tapping with your feet?'

Oh. I feel so embarrassed. I thought I'd been careful enough not to let anyone see.

'Um, yeah.'

'Do you do it a certain number of times?'

'Yeah, four, or a multiple of four. Do we have to talk about this?'

'No. Of course not.'

So we don't talk about *anything* for the next few stops, and then April rings the bell. An old man with a tartan shopping trolley in the priority seats shakes his head and says we should be in school, and April waggles her tongue at him. The man looks disgusted and says the country has gone to the dogs, but April just shrugs like she couldn't care less.

We hop off the bus and take the first left. April says her house is just a few doors down, overlooking the park. She points to a grey door with the number 82 on it.

'This is us,' she says. It's the door to a massive block with ninety-four individual buzzers.

April is rummaging in her shoulder satchel for keys and I'm standing there thinking, *Don't gulp, don't gulp, don't gulp, don't gulp.* Maybe I could handle a red bus because I've been on them before, but a grey door with numbers on it that aren't even multiples of four is another thing entirely. I am sure that if I walk through that door something horrendous is going to happen.

Grey is the colour of stormy clouds and swirling smoke. It is the colour old people's hair goes in the years before they die. It is the colour of the T-shirt I was wearing the time in Essex that Dad left for three days and no one knew where he had gone.

If I walk through that door Dad will never come back. He'll never come back, and it will all be my fault. Because grey is the colour of the end of everything.

I've been pushing the gulp down but it's coming up my throat like a tidal wave and I know it's going to happen – *gulp, gulp, gulp, gulp* – oh, no, April is going to think I'm a fish boy or something – *gulp, gulp* . . .

April has her two hands on my shoulders, her keys in her left hand, slung down my back.

'Hey, Ben? Ben, what's up? Are you scared?'

I shake my head.

'Really? Because you kinda look like you can't breathe.'

She squeezes my hand.

'Come on, it'll be fine, promise. And if it isn't, I'll buy you a comic.' She's still holding my hand, and she leads me through the door. If Mum or Dad were here they'd probably collapse with shock because it's been years since I agreed to walk through a grey door, and I have absolutely no idea why I'm doing it for this strange rebel girl.

Dad's never coming back! scream The Thoughts. *Never. Coming. Back!*

I feel like I'm going to be sick, but we get the lift to the eighth floor, so that's something. From the outside of the building, I could only imagine a flat inside being dingy and cave-like, but when April opens the green door (which feels pretty neutral since green means vegetables – phew) it's like . . . well, it's like art.

There are no walls or door between the hallway, sitting room and kitchen; it's all just one huge room with massive bookshelves across the two tallest walls, and the other wall is jam-packed with posters, paintings and photos in every kind of frame you could imagine; ornate gold antique-looking ones, rainbow-coloured plastics, knotted wood and plain old IKEA grey. There are beanbags instead of sofas and a hot-pink rug in the hall and a yellow sheepskin in the sitting room. They don't even have a kitchen table

– just four swivelly red leather chairs at a counter, like at a restaurant bar. In the middle of the room, for a reason I don't understand, is a fat concrete pillar from floor to ceiling, like in a car park.

'Oh my god,' I say. 'April – what do your parents *do*?'

'They're doctors, like Thomas. Surgeons, actually – Mum's a neurosurgeon, so she operates on brains, and Dad's a vascular surgeon, which means he fixes people's veins and arteries . . . Don't ask me what they do all day. I'm the stooooopid one.'

'You're not stupid,' I say.

'Shut up,' she says. 'So, cereal and TV? What do you think? Or do you fancy something else? Mum always leaves me food for when she's not here. I can offer you –' April opens the fridge, revealing a tower of neatly labelled Tupperware boxes – 'macaroni cheese, fish pie or what looks like . . . some chicken stew?'

'Just cereal is fine, thanks,' I say.

'Good choice!' April gets on a stool and starts grabbing bowls from a high-up cupboard. 'I love cereal for lunch! You can pick what we watch, by the way.'

She gets out two bowls – thankfully they're yellow, which is the colour of the sun, making it the colour of happiness. I know this sounds a bit babyish, but I have always thought this, and I can't change it now. She fills them both with Coco Pops and milk, pretty much to the brim – a few drops slop over the side as she brings them back over. I can see nearly all the classic *Doctor Who* DVDs in the DVD cabinet, but I remember April said she watched them with her brother, so I don't pick them in case they make her sad. I choose *Star Trek* on Netflix and wonder if April will pull a face or tell me I'm tragic, but she nods very seriously and says, 'Good choice.'

We sit on the beanbags spooning Coco Pops into our mouths and watching *Star Trek: Deep Space Nine*. I am thinking how much better this is than drama with Miss Valentine, when April says, 'Hey, Ben, what did you think of art club?'

'Yeah, it was OK. Miss Ruiz seems nice.'

'But you didn't make anything?'

'Yeah, well.'

'Why didn't you make anything?'

How can I tell her? She'll think I'm mad.

The colours and the patterns, they all seemed so wrong. I worried bad things would happen if I touched them. If I didn't glue something the right number of times it might stop you wanting to be my friend. If I cut paper and the corners weren't all equal maybe I'd get home and Mum would be gone for ever too.

What would April think if I said that?

But maybe it's *my* turn to ask April a question.

'Why are you asking me so much about the stuff I do? Or don't do?'

'Because . . .' April doesn't say anything for a few seconds, which weirds me out because April *always* has something to say. 'Because I think it might have a name.'

'A name? What are you talking about?'

'I remembered something. Something my parents were talking about last year. One of my mum's cases. A woman who had to do certain things repetitively. Except her number was three. She . . . she couldn't leave her house.'

'Well, my number is four.'

'Yes, but, Ben, that's not the point. It's a . . . a way in which your brain can go funny. They called it OCD. I'm not sure what that stands for, but I remembered it because Lauren always says she's OCD about her pencil case. It sounded different to the way Lauren says it, though, because Lauren made it sound kind of cute, but this . . . well, it wasn't cute.'

I have never been less sure of what to say, and that's coming from me, the most awkward person in the world. I am wondering if this thing April is talking about is the reason I had to go for that assessment back in Essex? The one that we still haven't heard anything from. Or at least no one's told me about it. Hopefully that means there was nothing scary or important to say . . .

'Do you like doing it? Does it make you happy?' April interrupts my thoughts.

Well, at least I know the answer to that one. 'I hate it.'

'Well, maybe you should do something about it.'

'Like what? Get a new brain?!'

I try to laugh, because I just want everything to be OK between me and April. I don't want her to stop being friends with me because I have a funny brain.

'No, because then you'd lose all the stuff that makes you Ben, and that would be sad.'

'Yeah, I guess,' I say, but really I am thinking: *That doesn't sound so bad.*

We watch a couple of episodes. I can't stop thinking about what April just said. Mum and Dad call it 'Benny stuff'. They always tell each other I will grow out of it, and I don't think they were very

105

happy about having to take me to the assessment centre. There was one time when Kyle actually screamed at them both that they needed to 'sort him out!' That I needed to see a head doctor – or 'whatever you call them'. It was the time where I took so long to leave the house that we missed *Spider-Man: Into the Spider-Verse* at the cinema, because they don't let anyone in once the film starts. I don't think Kyle ever forgave me for that actually. Dad told Kyle calmly that I was 'just going through a phase'.

But April was talking about a grown *woman*. So what if Kyle had a point? What if there's actually something wrong with my brain, and it's not just a phase?

I'm not so scared on the bus on the way back, and I think it might show because April smiles at me and says, 'See, you're a rebel really.' But there's one thing April said earlier that I can't get out of my head – and I hear her words over and over, even though I'm not sure I want to: *Maybe you should do something about it.*

We use the fire escape round the back of the building rather than the main stairs to get back to our classroom. No one seems to have noticed we were away, so we scuttle to our desks and exchange a victory smile. Halfway through maths, April tells me that she's going to come back to *my* house after school today. I try to explain to her, without actually explaining, that it is a bad idea for her to come to my house. But she tells me there is nothing I can say that will convince her not to, because now I've seen her house, so it's only fair she comes to mine.

'I won't stay ages,' she whispers quickly, her breath warm and tickly on my ear. 'Just show me your stuff and maybe we'll watch something and then after I'll head home.'

Five minutes later: 'Come on, don't be mean, I've already told you there's no one home and nothing fun to do at my house.'

Eventually I give up, and my stomach fills with the slugs. All through the rest of maths, and then through French with Mrs Dubois, I can picture them slithering slowly over one another. If Dad still hasn't come back (I tap my feet on the floor under the desk sixteen times to cancel out the thought), then I'm even less sure what Mum will be like.

I had hoped April would change her mind, but she automatically starts walking home with me. Actually, it's more like marching, and I give up any pretence of being a normal kid, and step in fours all

107

down the road to make things OK. It takes us a very long time to get home.

When we finally get to my door, I open my mouth one more time to try and ask April not to come up, but she just puts a hand up for me to stop and says, 'Keys.'

I take my house keys out of the inner pocket of my TARDIS backpack and unlock the front door. The hallway and stairs are in darkness, so I flip the light switch four times. At the top of the stairs I unlock the door to our flat. The lights are on, which is a good sign. Bumble comes running to the door and yelps in excitement when he sees I've brought someone with me – Bumble is a total sucker for new people. In seconds he's lying on his back demanding tummy tickles from April. He would be utterly useless if we ever got burgled.

'Mum?' I call. 'Mum? I'VE BROUGHT APRIL WITH ME.' I call as loudly as possible, hoping that she'll catch on and cease any weird or inappropriate behaviour immediately. I hear clattering sounds in the living room.

I follow the noise and find Mum sitting upright on the sofa, rubbing her eyes. The TV is on with the sound down low, and there's a magazine on the floor by her feet. She looks surprised. I'm trying to do a speedy assessment of what sort of mood she is in. Sofa usually means bad, but at least she wasn't in one of those sleeps where she won't wake up for anything.

April pushes past me and extends her hand for my mum to shake. 'Hello, Mrs Hardie. I'm April, Ben's friend from school.'

Mum is staring at April's hand. It takes her a second to realise that April is going for a handshake. Then something clicks on in her mind and suddenly she's in full Mum-of-the-Year mode.

'April! How lovely it is to have you over! Can I get you anything? Squash? Tea? Water? Or do you prefer fizzy drinks? I'm not sure we have any. But I could go to the shop if you like?'

The change is so rapid I feel like I've been teleported somewhere and my head's been left behind. Mum is smiling so wide her face might split. Her forehead and eyes have gone shiny. She doesn't look entirely human.

'Oh, don't worry, Mrs Hardie,' says April happily. 'I just came to introduce myself.'

How is April so confident with grown-ups? Maybe it's having an older brother. Wait, *I* have an older brother.

'Please! Call me Leila!'

'OK.'

'Do sit down, April!'

April sits on the armchair opposite Mum. I study her face. I need to know what she thinks of Mum. Whether she is weirded out and doesn't want to be my friend any more.

But April is very good at not letting her face give things away when she doesn't want it to, and I can't tell a thing. I hover in the living room awkwardly. I don't want to sit on the sofa with Mum, but there's no space on the armchair with April. So I just sit on the rug between them.

'April is a pretty name,' Mum is saying.

'Thanks,' says April. 'I was born in April. Hey, those are cool!' She's looking at the queue of tiny ceramic sea creatures crawling and swimming across the mantelpiece. 'Did you make them? Ben says you do pottery.'

'I did! You can take one, if you like them.'

'Cool! Thanks.' April picks out a glossy red lobster and holds it up to the light, studying it. Then she grins, pockets it and sits back down. 'I love it. I'll look after it, Mrs Hardie — sorry, Leila.'

'So, drinks! Should I go to the shops?'

'No, I'm OK actually.'

'Oh, no, you must have a drink, you'll be all thirsty from school!'

'OK,' says April neutrally. 'Water would be good.'

'Water! Sure, sure!' Mum disappears off into the kitchen.

'Sorry,' I whisper. 'She can be a bit weird.'

'Don't worry,' April whispers back. 'She's fine, Ben.'

Mum clatters back in with a tray with three glasses of water on it. She's put some custard creams in a bowl. Custard creams are the Doctor's favourite biscuit, and Mum gets them for me sometimes as a treat. But I know those custard creams are stale, because I tried to have some the other day. Oh, god.

There are four things on the tray; everything will be OK, OK, OK, OK.

Mum pushes her piles of paper, magazines and books off the coffee table and on to the floor in one sweeping motion so she can place the tray there, and sits back down.

'So what did you guys get up to at school today?'

April tells Mum about our day (except for the skiving) and also art club yesterday, and reaches for a custard cream. She takes a small bite, realises her mistake, and tries to put it back subtly, but of course it's the one time Mum notices anything.

111

'Oh, gosh, April – are you hungry?' She disappears into the kitchen before April can reply. There's some banging and I can hear drawers being rifled through. She reappears a couple of minutes later, holding a crumpled Chinese takeaway menu.

'Takeaway?' she smiles shyly.

I glance at April, worried she will think it's a weird suggestion, but April looks like she's about to implode with delight and says, 'Oh my god, Mrs Hardie-sorry-Leila, you are the *best*.'

We order way too much food on the Deliveroo app, and totally stuff our faces while watching *Star Wars: The Empire Strikes Back* (I have FOUR duck pancakes and FOUR helpings of sweet and sour chicken, and April can just eat and eat). April and I are so full we are lying on the rug clutching our bellies, and every time we laugh at the situation there seems to be a very real chance we might be sick. I realise I haven't thought about the Dad Situation for at least thirty minutes, and then the stomach slugs immediately come back because how can I possibly forget something as major as that?

I feel like April will have to go soon, but then Mum says to her, 'Oh, April, it's getting late. Do you want to stay the night?'

I'm a bit embarrassed, because this is not the sort of thing a normal mum asks on a school night. I absolutely know there is no *way* she would say this if there was a chance Dad was coming back tonight (stomach SNAKES). I'm about to give April an apologetic look, when April replies:

'Sure, that would be GREAT!'

'But what about your parents?' I ask.

'It's fine, they're on their shifts, they wouldn't be back till later anyway,' she shrugs. 'I'll text them, I'm sure they won't mind.'

Which is how I come to have MY FIRST EVER SLEEPOVER – with a *girl*. Mum gives April a new toothbrush, and I tell April she can borrow any of my pyjamas. She picks my Darth Vadar ones from the very back of my drawer.

We decide to read comics with my torch, so no one will see the light under the door if they check, and start laughing and laughing, because suddenly everything seems funny, and I have to keep telling April to '*shhhh*' even though I can't stop laughing either. Every time we giggle like this I immediately feel bad that I'm laughing, and then I think about telling April about Dad. But it feels like that would spoil everything, so I don't.

We sneak downstairs at 12.04 a.m. to get a giant

bar of Cadbury's Dairy Milk Fruit & Nut – Mum always hides chocolate under the sink with the cleaning products. She thinks I don't know, but I do. I have to tell April which steps creak when you stand on them, so we don't wake anyone. There's a moment on the way back up with the chocolate when April accidentally stands on the seventh step and it goes *eeeeek* and we both freeze and stare at each other, looking scared but also covering our mouths with our hands so we don't burst out giggling because everything still feels very funny.

We make it back up without waking everyone and I shut my door very slooooowly and I go to open and close it three more times to make four but April says, '*Shh*, you can't do that! You'll wake everyone. Come and sit here and you'll forget about it in a moment.'

I *really* want to do it again but April does have a point. It would suck if we got caught with the chocolate when we're so close to eating it. So I sit down on the floor with her and tell myself if it still feels wrong when we have eaten the chocolate, I can go back and do it and then if anyone comes up I'll just say I went to the loo.

I eat eight squares and April eats eight too.

We read twelve comics cover to cover. April

teaches me how to draw Matt Smith in comic-book style. Mine doesn't even look that bad. It starts to get light outside and I can hear the first few birds starting to chirp.

We must fall asleep at some point, because now Mum is calling up the stairs for us to get ready for school, but I don't remember the point at which it happened.

I realise I had so much fun I forgot all about the door.

2.2

April and I are so tired at school we move through our lessons like zombies. We can't even talk properly and just grunt at each other all day, caveman-style. I'm even too tired to think about the Dad Situation clearly, and April actually FALLS ASLEEP in history with Mrs Williams this afternoon. Mrs Williams is doing her wonky pacing (argh!) towards us from the other side of the room. She is squinting at April through her half-moon spectacles. I think her eyesight must be pretty bad because I have time to elbow April and she jumps awake with a tiny snort.

Mrs Williams keeps walking and droning on and on about the Tudors. I honestly can't tell you a single thing she said.

So I guess the two of us aren't on top form. But it was worth it.

*

Mum is in a good mood when I get back from school.

We eat tea together, and then she curls up on the sofa under the blanket and watches her garden show while I sit on the rug and read my comic.

Except I'm not really reading. I'm thinking I really need to know what's going on with Dad. Also, why haven't either of them *told* me what's going on? Why are Mum and I just sitting here learning about common garden fungi like nothing's going on? I guess if Dad doesn't have the guts to tell me himself, then I'm going to have to hear it from her. I decide to wait until the programme ends and the twinkly violin theme tune starts up again, getting more and more anxious, and when it does I burst out, 'Mum, where's Dad?'

Mum doesn't say anything for what feels like ages, and the violin music just seems to be getting louder, drowning out every noise in the world, until I have to get up and switch the TV off. Dad gets annoyed if you switch the TV off at the box because then you can't switch it back on with the remote. *But Dad isn't here, is he?* say The Thoughts. I clutch my head.

'He's not here,' says Mum slowly. Oh, *great*.

'Well, where is he?' I snap back.

'He's . . . away for a bit.'

'Where's he staying?'

'At your Uncle Jay's. In Plaistow.'

The other side of London.

'Is he coming back?'

I have so many other questions, like why didn't Dad tell us he was going? Does he really not care about us at all? Maybe I'm just not getting his messages?

And, worst of all, the question Mum would never be able to answer: is he not coming back because I went through the grey door into April's house?

'I don't know,' she says.

It's because of you, I want to say. It's because you were drinking again even though things are supposed to be getting better now we're in London, but you're not even trying—

Mum drinks because you didn't do the right four routines to stop her, The Thoughts interrupt. *Mum drinks because of* you. *Because you're not normal. So when you put it like that, Dad left because of you.*

You are tearing this family apart.

'STOP!' I yell, clutching my head. I kind of wish Mum would get up from the sofa and do the thought-slurping thing to my forehead. But she doesn't move.

I get up and go to my room. Every pair of pyjamas

118

I put on feels unlucky, and like wearing them will mean Dad never comes back. Eventually I've changed so many times I'm covered in a thin layer of cold sweat, and I decide to just sleep in my boxers, even if it's a bit gross. I check my phone; there's still nothing from Dad. He didn't message the last time he went away either. I start writing different texts to send him (**COME HOME, WHEN BACK????**), but each one feels wrong – like the way it's written is unlucky and sending it will *make* him not come back. So they stay in my drafts.

I open and close the curtains in fours, looking out over the street for him.

'Where are you?' I thump my hand angrily against the glass, and then have to do it another three times for luck.

*

On Friday, April squeezes my arm as soon as I sit down. 'I'm so excited for art club tonight,' she says.

'Same,' I say, but my throat is scratchy because I'm thinking about all the things Miss Ruiz might suggest making, and all of them sound scary.

Mr Montague takes the register and says there's something we're going to spend half an hour doing before biology.

'We're nearly halfway through the term,' he says, 'and to celebrate that I thought we'd all go round the room again, like we did at the beginning of term, but this time we'll say something we like about the person we sit next to. If you sit next to two people you can say something nice about both of them.'

Mr Montague starts in the left-hand corner of the room. People seem pleased to be getting out of some of biology, but no one seems bothered, or like this might be a hard activity. People just say things like, 'I like Isiah because he's really funny,' or, 'I like Niesha because she always thinks of good things to talk about at break time,' or, 'I think Jules is great because she's always there if you're worried about something.'

WHAT AM I GOING TO SAY ABOUT APRIL?!!!!!!

It is not that I can't think of loads of things I like about April, I just don't want to say something stupid. Time is doing a weird thing where it seems to be going very slowly and quickly at the same time, and finally, or suddenly, when it gets to me, I hear myself saying, 'I like April because she isn't scared of anything.' I look round the room quickly, worried that everyone will be smirking or saying, 'What a stupid thing to say,' but no one actually seems that interested.

Then April looks up from her sketch of this four-headed lizard thing and says loudly, 'Ben is my best friend because he's clever, and always kind, and he has excellent taste in TV.'

Mr Montague grins at us, but he keeps going round the room, like something totally life changing hasn't just happened. I can't take in any of the other answers people give. I literally wouldn't care even if someone said they liked someone else because they'd learned how to fly or discovered time travel.

I am April's best friend.

*

This afternoon Miss Ruiz says we will be doing origami. Origami!

She says she thought we could learn to do cranes, but if there's something else we want to do we can just ask her. Rhys isn't joining in – he's preoccupied with his charcoal city. But everyone else seems pretty excited.

Miss Ruiz demonstrates how to make the crane. I actually think it looks pretty easy, but everyone else is like, *whoooooaaa*, mind blown. She hands out instruction sheets for everyone to follow and says we can ask if we aren't sure. I thought I liked the crane at first, but that was when she was folding the square paper equally on all sides and making it into a rectangle. Then she folded it into a kite and started opening out sections for the neck and wings, and I thought, no, this is all wrong, I can't make this.

I guess I should have known, it being a crane.

I decide to watch April. She's pretty good, twice as fast as everyone else. Priya has already given up and is sitting on the table cross-legged eating biscuits. There are moments where April forgets what comes next. I could tell her, but isn't that similar to making a wonky shape myself? So I don't.

'Origami not for you either, Ben?' says Miss Ruiz.

I shake my head.

'Is there anything you would like to make?'

I can't think of an animal that's all squares, so I shake my head.

'Why don't you make a box?' says April.

'Would you like that, Ben?' asks Miss Ruiz.

I feel like everyone is looking at me. Actually, that's probably because everyone *is* looking at me. I guess I don't want to be the weirdo art creep who just comes to watch.

'OK, maybe,' I say. 'Can you make it and I'll see then?'

'Sure,' says Miss Ruiz, pulling out the chair next to me and tucking loose strands of hair behind her ears.

She grabs a square piece of card, spinning it round in her hands and folding bits in and out, creasing it into different shapes – triangle, rectangle, pentagon, rectangle, and then, finally, box.

'Do you want to have a go?' asks Miss Ruiz.

'I'm not sure,' I say.

'What would make you want to do it?'

'If it didn't have the triangle and pentagon inside.'

'What's wrong with the triangle and pentagon?'

'They aren't squares.' *Shoot*. If I were in a movie I would cover my mouth with my hands. Miss Ruiz's voice is kind of soft and relaxing, and I think I forgot where I was for a moment.

At exactly the wrong moment.

April is looking over.

'Hey,' she says. 'Make it for me. Like I made you the bat. Then triangles and pentagons will be in my house and they won't be able to hurt you.'

I don't want to I don't want to I don't want to I don't want to.

'You owe me a present,' she grins.

123

'Fine,' I say. 'I'll make the stupid box.'

I whizz one out just like Miss Ruiz showed me – fold flip spin, fold flip spin.

'OMG,' say the girls who sit with Priya. Priya herself is gawping, a biscuit suspended halfway into her mouth. I turn to April – her forehead is creased like she's trying to understand something complicated, and then she cracks up, laughing really hard.

'I knew it. I knew you were a genius. Hey, thanks for helping with my crane, *not*. Guess you didn't want to share your smarts around? Oh, awesome. Make more, please, please.'

'Pleeeeeeeeasssse!' says Priya. 'You're quicker than Miss Ruiz. It's like a magic trick.'

'OK,' I say, and I make another, and another. Soon everyone wants a box.

So I make everyone a box.

And it feels pretty great.

*

When I get home I can hear Mum talking in the living room. I rush in, thinking Kyle, or even Dad, must be home. But she's just on the phone.

I can hear her saying, 'Uh huh,' and, 'I see,' into the phone in a quiet voice, like she's in trouble. She's twirling her hair in knots round her pointer finger.

'Well, that's great news,' she says in a frightened voice that doesn't sound like whatever it is is anything like great news. She puts the phone down.

'That was the woman from the mental health team. She says they're following up on the assessment you did in Essex. They've made a London referral. They said . . . you need to go for an appointment next week.'

So I guess I was wrong that not hearing anything meant that I'd passed the crazy test, or they had forgotten about me. I want to tell her I'm fine, that they've made a terrible mistake, that I don't need to go.

But I remember what April said. *Maybe you should do something about it.*

So instead I just say, 'Fine.'

I eat dinner and go upstairs to read my comics. I hear Mum coming up the stairs to my room at 9.54 p.m. and I dive on to my bed and screw my eyes tight shut because I don't want to talk to her. She pulls the covers over me and strokes my head.

'I'm not sure how long your dad's going to be away for. He's angry about a lot of things. I hope he decides to come back. We'll have to see.'

I'm not sure whether she's talking more to me or

more to herself. Either way, I don't reply.

She pats my duvet and says, 'Well, good night then, Benny, my love', before switching off my light and shutting the door behind her.

I lie very still, staring into the dark.

He's angry about a lot of things.

Is he angry about me?

*

April and I are now texting pretty much constantly, especially at the weekends, although I still haven't explained about the Dad Situation. Kyle is all raised eyebrows and, 'Who are you texting, Benny?', craning over to try and see my screen, because I don't usually ever use my phone. I just say, 'Oh, my friend April,' casually, like it's no big deal, and Kyle pretends to pass out in surprise. Which is a bit mean but I can't say I blame him. It *is* pretty miraculous.

'She had a sleepover here,' I say quickly. 'You'd know if you were ever home. Hey . . .' I say, trying to sound casual, 'do you have any news about Dad?'

'No,' growls Kyle, 'and we're better off without him.'

I hold my breath, waiting to see if he'll tell me anything else about it, but he quickly changes the subject back to April: is she popular, is she pretty, who does she hang out with, what is she *actually like*? I tell him she's into *Doctor Who* and he howls with laughter before saying, 'I knew she couldn't be real.'

Then I briefly wonder if April actually *is* real. But then she texts, saying, **HEY WLD U RATHA HAVE HANDS THT KEEP GROWIN AS U GET OLDA OR FEET?** so I know that she really must exist.

I reply:

FEET

Having April texting me at home has been really great. It's nice to sit upstairs and distract myself from everything by texting her, rather than wandering round the house for hours by myself tapping and opening things.

My phone pings again and I lunge at it. It's weird, I've never been into my phone before. Now I can't stop checking it.

R U FREE 2DAY? WANNA COME OVER?

The answers are yes and yes. I'm actually shaking with excitement and I run around my room hooting. I know that's a bit sad, but I can't help it. No one's ever asked me over to their house on a weekend before, and I know Mum's meeting her old school friend Tina this afternoon, so I don't even have to worry about leaving her home alone. Although . . . what if Dad comes back and none of us are here? It *almost* makes me think I should stay, but then I think about the fact he has still made a grand total of zero attempts to speak to me and I remember that I'm angry with him.

Mum says it's fine for me to go, as long as I plan the route and text her when I'm there. Getting there involves walking for ten minutes, taking a bus for twelve minutes and then another four-minute walk. I want to get to hers as soon as possible, but choosing what to wear takes ages. Normally I always wear a black or white T-shirt and jeans, because they are strong and clean colours, so when you wear them nothing much can happen (thankfully our school uniform is a white shirt with black trousers and a blazer, or who knows how I'd ever get dressed and out of the house). But today I don't want to be black or white – I don't want to be boring for April. Mum stopped buying other colours years ago, but Kyle slammed out of the front door a few minutes ago, so I can probably steal one of his.

Kyle's floor is so covered in dirty clothes you can't even see the carpet – it's like some gross quilt. His window is closed and the Lynx he covered himself in before he left somehow makes the teenage boy smell even *more* noticeable. His T-shirts are balled up on all the wrong shelves, and most of them smell pretty musty and have red or blue on them, which I just can't do. I find a yellow one right at the back that I've only seen him wear a few times and put it on. It doesn't smell too bad and has LEGEND stitched on it in green felt. Yellow and green are fine (sunshine and vegetables), so maybe I can wear this and April will think it's cool?

But immediately The Thoughts shout: *NO, it's too risky not to wear black or white, and you must take it off RIGHT NOW or today will go badly.*

I pull the shirt off over my head double quick.

Are you kidding? Do you really want to be boring?

So I pick the T-shirt up and put it on again. *Risky.* T-shirt off. *Boring.* On. *Risky.* Off. *Boring.*

What should I do?

Risky. Boring. Risky. Boring. Risky. Boring.

I take the T-shirt on and off sixty-four times. My arms ache and I'm covered in a glossy sweat. I feel dizzy.

Risky. Boring. Risky. Boring. Risky. Boring. Risky. Boring. Risky. Boring. Risky. Boring.

'AHHHHHHHHHH!' I roar, my heart beating so fast it just feels like one long throb, and I scream so hard my throat feels clawed at from the insides.

129

I throw the T-shirt across the room and punch the cupboard. One minute I'm standing and the next I'm on the floor lying in Kyle's smelly clothes. I open my eyes and see Mum come running through the door. She sits down on the floor with me, wrapping her arms around me and rubbing my back like when I was small. She whispers into my hair that everything is OK, and says we will get plasters for my poor knuckles.

'Can I still go to April's?' I ask through tears, because I'm sure she won't let me now. But Mum says that getting worked up and having a bad moment doesn't mean the whole day is ruined, and of course she will still let me if that's what I want. She says she thinks getting the bus by myself probably isn't a good idea, and I'm embarrassed that I feel mostly relieved.

'We'll get a taxi,' she says brightly. 'I'll take you and then come back in it!'

I must look horrified, because she looks at the ground, chewing her lip. 'Don't worry, I don't have to see April.'

'What about the money?' I whisper. 'A taxi is expensive.'

'It's not like Dad's here to notice,' she says sadly, and squeezes my shoulders.

Too true, I think, and the whole thing is so upsetting I can't think of a single thing to say back.

*

I wait for the taxi to disappear round the corner before ringing April's door, feeling a bit guilty for being worried about Mum being weird in front of April, when she's been so nice to me today. I am wearing my black T-shirt and jeans and hoping that I will still be fun. The buzzer sounds and the door unlocks.

I'm nervous about meeting April's parents as I walk upstairs, but when April opens her door, still wearing her pyjamas and spooning Coco Pops into her mouth from a blue (!) striped bowl, the flat looks pretty empty.

'Weekend shifts,' she explains through chomps. ''S just us.'

I'm seriously starting to wonder if April actually has any parents. I feel a pang that makes me want to ask April if she thinks *my* dad will come back, but it seems an unfair thing to ask, given at least my mum's home most of the time.

'Come look,' she says, putting her bowl down on the counter and leading me in the direction of the bathroom. There's a note stuck to the mirror that says: **Baby girl – turn the tap off!!!** with a little heart and *xxx* underneath. April sees me looking at it and pulls a face. 'That's from my dad,' she explains. 'Because *once* – or maybe twice – I forgot to turn the tap off.' She's opening the cupboard above the sink and pulling out a carton labelled *Nice'n Easy* with a picture of a smiling woman with short red hair on it.

'What is it?' I ask.

'What is it?! It's hair dye,' says April, lifting up a chunk of her own red hair.

'But your hair is already red.'

'Because I dye it!' April flips up her fringe and points at her eyebrows, which are black. 'You don't seriously think my hair naturally grows cherry red, do you?'

'I . . . hadn't really thought about it.'

'My hair comes straight outta a bottle,' she says in an American drawl, staring at the woman on the carton dreamily and swinging her legs over the bathtub. 'I thought you could help me; it's a total pain doing the back by myself. I just need to do my roots. But you have to use this dye –' she rummages round in the cupboard under the sink and pulls out another box marked PLATINUM BLONDE – 'to bleach it first, and then wash it out and then put the red on top.'

'Why?' I ask, now totally confused.

'Because my hair's so dark. You can't just dye Indian hair red and expect it to hold.'

'You're Indian?'

'Yes – well, half. No one ever notices until they see me with my dad; he's Goan.' She pauses. 'So can you do it?'

'Um . . . can I see the boxes?'

'Sure,' says April, handing them over. I read the backs of them. I don't recognise most of the ingredients, but I can see that the blonde one has PEROXIDE in it, which I know is a pretty hardcore chemical.

'Er . . . are you sure we should be messing around with peroxide?' I ask. 'Where did you even get these? I didn't realise kids were allowed to buy hair dye.'

'Amazon,' says April with a wink. 'But before you get all stressy about it, my parents *do* know – I mean, it would have been kind of hard for them not to notice. I've done it loads of times *and* I've never had a reaction before, so can you pleeeease just accept I know what I'm doing?'

'OK, I guess,' I say, though I still don't feel a hundred per cent sure.

'Cool . . .' April seems to be thinking. 'You know

what, there'll be loads left – you could dye yours too! I don't even think you'll have to bleach yours first, since your hair's such a light brown.'

RED? The colour of blood, the colour of arguments and rage, the colour of accidents that can't be undone! NO WAY. No, no, never going to happen, never in a million years, no thank you—

'I mean . . . only if you want to, of course.' She smiles at me hopefully.

April has red hair and there doesn't seem to be anything bad about her at all . . .

'OK,' I say, trying to sound like I often change my personal appearance and it is totally no big deal at all. Oh my god, what am I doing? 'What about if we just do a few strands?' I suggest.

I think Mum's eyes will probably fall out of her head, literally.

'You mean, like a streak?' asks April thoughtfully.

'Yeah, whatever it's called,' I say.

'Really? Oh my god! Yay!' April is bouncing up and down and I don't think I can take it back. 'OK, we'll do my bleach, and then your streak, and then we'll wash my bleach out and put the red on mine.'

I think I'm nodding. April passes me a pair of plastic gloves from one of the boxes, which she says will protect my hands from any dye, and takes the pair out of the other box for herself. She stands over the sink, unscrewing the cap of a small white bottle from the PLATINUM BLONDE box marked COLOUR BLEND FORMULA into a larger bottle marked DEVELOPER. She screws the top of the DEVELOPER back on and shakes the bottle hard and counts thirty Mississippis out loud. Then she does the same thing all over again with the bottles in the red box. She places an old scratchy blue towel with peach-coloured stains over her shoulders and leans over the sink, and tells me to take the bottle and dab it along her roots, and the hairs behind her ears and at the top of her neck. I check four times that I've got the blonde bottle in my hand before I start, to make sure I don't do it the wrong way round.

My hand is shaking a bit, and thankfully she doesn't notice that I'm dabbing it on in lots of fours, or if she does, she doesn't say anything. It's actually done pretty quickly because I only have to do around her parting, so then she passes me another old towel and says, 'You're up!'

Before I know it, *my* head is over the sink, and she's squirting the red dye on, parting my hair with her fingers to mark out the section for the streak. We don't talk, apart from April saying, 'I'm not hurting you, am I?' twice. The silence feels

135

OK, though, not awkward like when you don't talk to someone because you don't know what to say. It's . . . weird. I've never had anyone's hands run through my hair that aren't my mum's. I've never been this close to someone for so long who isn't my mum. Maybe I should be worried, though – I feel like *Benny* would be worried . . . When April says, 'We're pretty much done. How are you doing?' I just smile a bit nervously and say, 'I'm feeling good,' and I almost entirely mean it.

'My turn again!' she says, switching places with me.

The dye has to stay on my hair while I wash April's blonde out and put the red one on, and this time, when I'm done, she grins and says, 'Cheers, you're pretty useful actually,' and we go and watch *Star Trek* on the beanbags with the towels over our shoulders, waiting for it to 'develop'.

'It's itching,' I say. 'Is that normal?'

'That means it's working. Pain is beauty, dahling.'

'So, uh . . . my hair's not going to like . . . all fall out or anything?'

'No! You're not the first person to home-dye their hair, you know.'

April says it's time to get the dye out after one episode, and we take it in turns to lean over the bath while the other one uses the shower head to rinse it out, and the dye swirls down the plug, turning the water purple.

'Is—'

'No,' says April, cutting me off. 'I didn't get the wrong dye, no, your hair is not going to be purple and, yes, it is normal for dye to go that colour.'

I laugh. 'OK then.'

We towel-dry our hair and stand looking in the mirror. My hair's sticky-uppy and slick with water, but you can already see a streak about five centimetres wide on the left of my head that is bright, flaming red.

'You look older,' says April. 'And it brings out all your bony angles and your big eyes.' April sucks her cheeks in. 'Look at your cheekbones! You look great!'

'Do you really think so?'

'Yes.'

I look at April in the mirror, properly. I wouldn't normally, but it feels OK since mirror gazing seems to be our current scheduled activity. I've never thought about it before, but her hair does look pretty awesome red.

'You look good too,' I say. 'Like a vampire, you know, uh, a pretty one.'

'I look like I always look,' April laughs. 'You've just never noticed it before.'

2.3

I'm nervous on Monday morning about what people at school will think of my hair — Kyle took one look at me when he got back last night, laughed and said, 'Well, *that's* a choice.' (I think the implication was that it wasn't a very good one.) Plus, I've got my first appointment with the new mental health team at 4.30 p.m. — Mum's going to take me after school.

My stomach has the sluggy feeling when I walk into the classroom, and I stare at the ground and try not to catch anyone's eye as I hang up my backpack. I hear someone say, 'Nice hair, Ben,' and I look to my left and see Niesha putting her anorak on her peg, which is next to mine. I scan her face to work out if she is joking, but she gives me a thumbs-up and says, 'Really suits you.'

I smile and say, 'Thanks,' and head over to sit next to April.

'So,' she says, not looking up from her biro

drawing, which seems to feature some sort of highly detailed dog-fish hybrid with long rows of razor-sharp teeth. 'The moment of truth. What did your parentals think?'

'Mum says it's good to have a change every now and then. And Dad . . .' I think about what I know Dad would have said. 'Well, Dad thinks I'm a bit too young to dye my hair.'

Liar, liar, liar, liar.

'Hey, April,' whispers Aliya, as she takes her place behind us next to Michelle and Lauren. 'How's the clone?'

April doesn't respond.

'Is it fun making a double of yourself?' hisses Lauren. 'Ben, what do you think of having April play Barbie with you?'

I wish I was brave enough to say, 'Actually, it's awesome,' or, 'I'd much rather have April as my friend than a bunch of total cows,' but instead I feel my throat start gulping. April is staring down at her drawing and you wouldn't think she cared at all. But then I notice how hard her fist is clenching her pen, and that she is scribbling in the same spot and a hole is forming in the paper.

'Hey, Ronald McDonald, I asked you a question.'

Luckily it's 9.02 a.m., so Mr Montague puts down

his book and takes his feet off the desk and says, 'Righty-ho, here we go, happy Monday, one and all,' and starts to call out the register, which thankfully means I get out of having to reply to Lauren.

*

April and I were going to skive drama today, but Mr Montague said he had to have a word with Miss Valentine about something, and basically ended up shepherding us all in there. I think he was trying to make sure we all went. Probably his alien senses told him that people had been skipping it.

Today we have to get into groups of four and create a three-minute horror play to perform at the end of the class to the other groups. 'To get into Halloween spirit', Miss Valentine has powdered her face white, making the wrinkles on her forehead look like the ice crevasses I saw on *Blue Planet*. Her long nails are painted black, with red varnish dripping from the tips to look like blood.

'Ew,' I whisper to April. 'She looks like she's been rummaging around in someone's body.'

'Maybe she attacked a casting director to make them finally give her a role,' replies April.

Ezinne practically sprints over to me and April, dragging Sophia behind her.

141

'Do you guys wanna be a group?' she asks.

'OK,' says April. 'But I'm directing.'

'Sure. Hey, did you hear, there's going to be a Halloween disco in a few weeks. It's gonna go on until 11 p.m.!'

'Yeah,' says April. 'I heard about that.'

'What are you going to go as?' asks Sophia.

'Huh?' says April.

'What are you dressing up as? We're thinking . . . bunnies.'

'Bunnies?' I say a bit uncertainly, because I wasn't aware this was a go-to costume choice, but Sophia and Ezinne either missed it or don't care.

'I didn't know it was fancy dress,' says April, chewing the pearly nail of her pointer finger thoughtfully. 'Awesome. We'll have to think of something. In the meantime, I have a play to direct.'

April says she has an idea based on this fear her older brother used to have. She wants Sophia to be the main part. It's about a girl who wakes up one day thinking it's just a regular day, but when she gets into the kitchen she sees that her family are frozen – not like ice, but more like if you pressed pause on a film. She waves her hand in front of their faces and tries to shake them, but she can't get them to unfreeze. Her mum (played by Ezinne) is still as a statue stirring her porridge on the stove, and her dad (April) is frozen sitting at the table with his arms outstretched, reading the newspaper. Her little brother (that's me) is frozen on the other side of the table with his arm holding a spoon full of cornflakes, and his mouth open.

'It's totally silent,' commands April. 'Apart from the occasional drip of milk from Ben's outstretched spoon.'

'Oooh! It's super-creepy,' giggles Sophia.

The girl runs out into the street but it's just the same there. April, Ezinne and I become the people on the street: frozen in their cars, or mid-step on their way somewhere. The girl tries and tries to unfreeze them, shaking them and yelling, but she can't. Then she turns to the class and says slowly:

'What if they never wake up? What if I'm the only one left?'

And then the lights go down, which April says in a real theatre would make this look all dramatic, but when we actually perform it for the class it is just Jia standing by the light switch, which we've asked her to turn off right after Sophia says, 'What if I'm the only one left?' This is called a cue.

Still, everyone claps and whoops, and says it was the best one, which wasn't that hard since the other groups just wrapped themselves in toilet roll and stumbled round moaning like zombies, or shouted a lot and pretended to kill each other. Miss Valentine tells April in her husky voice that she is an artiste. I'm thinking that it was clever of April to give me a role where I didn't have to speak in front of everyone, because I would have found that scary. And better still, there were three of us not speaking, so I didn't stand out as the loser who had been given the dud role. In fact, Miss Valentine says we were *integral* to the performance.

Afterwards, when it's just April and me walking down the corridor to break, April says, 'Guess what? That wasn't my brother's fear. It was mine. Still is.'

And I have to try not to gawp because I didn't think April had any fears.

'But you're not scared of anything, ever,' I say.

'Everyone is scared of something, Ben,' she says, wafting her arms around. 'It's allll a matter of presentation.'

*

Mum picks me up from school for my appointment (I made her wait down the road, rather than right outside school), and then we get the bus together. We have to go to the local children's mental health centre. I thought it would look like the GP surgery or like a hospital, but actually it is an old-fashioned square white house with balconies and wide windows and a bright-blue door.

When we walk up the steps to the door I want to say that I can't walk through the blue door or we will all get sad, but then I realise we're probably already as sad as we can be, since Dad has left. So I take a deep breath and step through.

The lady at reception tells us to sit down in the waiting room, and that I will be collected shortly by my counsellor. The waiting room is a safe rectangle shape, but there are eleven plastic blue chairs. I try sitting on the fourth chair from the door, and then the eighth, but they both feel wrong. The Thoughts say that if I sit on those chairs, Dad will never come back, and Mum might even leave too. I've hopped up from the two chairs like they're burning my bum or something, and a teenage girl wearing headphones and chewing gum is staring at me from across the room like I'm a freak. So I just stand by the door, even though Mum tells me that nothing bad will happen if I sit down.

The wall clock is one of those white plastic ones like we have in school, and I watch the minute hand count four minutes. There is an abacus on a low table, and a couple of plastic dinosaurs with most of their tails chewed off who look like they have been through some rough times. I want to stroke the dinosaurs and play with the abacus. I would like to sit quietly and sort the coloured beads into fours, but I feel like I'm too old, and the girl will stare even more. The minute hand says there are twelve seconds until it is 4.30 p.m., when a man with a neatly cropped black beard and checked shirt comes into the room. He is holding a massive ring binder folder with paper coming out of the sides at all angles in his right hand, and another fat paper wallet clutched under his left armpit.

'Benjamin Hardie?' he calls out with a grin. He seems slightly out of breath. I stand up. 'I'm your counsellor, Dinesh. Come this way!'

I nod. I am staring at the file and the wallet, wondering how there can possibly be so much writing about me from the assessment five months ago. It is really freaking me out.

Dinesh must notice me looking, because he says, 'Don't worry, it's not all about you! I've just rushed over from my appointments at one of the other centres. They like to keep us busy!'

Phew, I think. Then I start thinking about all the other children Dinesh might have been talking to.

Children like me? I find I want to ask him about them.

Mum stands up to come too, but Dinesh says he'll just need me for now. I feel a relieved feeling I wasn't expecting. I thought I wanted her there. It's all very confusing.

Dinesh takes me up to a room on the top floor, and I'm feeling so nervous that my routines are getting out of control and I have to go up the last set of stairs SIXTEEN TIMES before I can go into the room. He does something no one has ever done when I'm doing my routines. He waits patiently WITHOUT STARING and when I'm finished, he just says, 'It looks like things are difficult for you at the moment,' and I don't know what to say, so I just stare at the floor and say, 'Yeah.'

The walls in the room are painted light yellow, the colour of sherbet lemons. There are eight pictures on the walls, cartoon cats and dogs playing with bouncy balls and sausages, which I guess is nice. There are two black (phew) chairs opposite each other and he takes the one nearer the desk, which is good because then I don't have to choose my chair. The room has six corners because of the way the wide window slopes out, so I sit and start counting them. I tell myself I will get to a multiple of four and stop, and concentrate on what Dinesh is

147

saying, but twelve, twenty-four, thirty-two and thirty-six have come and gone with no luck yet—

'Benjamin? What do you like to be called? Benjamin? Ben?'

'Ben,' I say. 'Well . . . my family call me Benny but I prefer Ben.'

'OK, Ben it is,' he says, and starts to explain that we'll be together for fifty minutes, and he's going to ask me some stuff about me, if that's OK.

I say that's fine, and he asks me what I like and who I'm close to, so I tell him all about *Doctor Who* and April and Kyle, and even Miss Ruiz, because he asked if I had any hobbies and I said art club, even though I'm not really arty, but still I do go and now I even quite like it, so I don't think it was a lie. I think about saying Mum and Dad, but then I think maybe it's a bit loserish to list your parents as people you're close to, Also, I definitely *do not* feel close to Dad at the moment. Not that I'm exactly close to Kyle, but, you know – at least I *see* him (sometimes).

I'm just thinking that this is nothing like how I expected a counsellor to be, and that maybe it won't be as scary as the Essex assessment, when he starts asking about things I find difficult, and I have to say, well, basically everything (apart from maths). Then he asks why and I say, 'Because of The Thoughts.'

'What are the thoughts, Ben?'

'The Thoughts say that something bad will happen if I don't do things right.'

'Something bad? Like what?'

'Like . . . like that my mum will get . . . hurt.'

'OK.'

'I worry about Bumble, my dog. And my mum, dad, Kyle and me, and whether I'll be happy, and the world ending, and also my friend April, and whether she'll always want to be my friend.'

'Are there any other thoughts?'

That I want Bumble and my mum to die. That I made my dad leave.

'Not really,' I say.

Liar, liar, liar, liar. My eyes start flicking round the corners in fours, trying to make the lie go away.

'OK, well, I'm going to ask you some more questions, but if you think of anything else, we can come back to it.'

He stands up and gets a clipboard from his desk and brings it over to me. It has a tick-box form on it and he asks if I would be OK to sit and fill it in. He tells me he knows I probably had to answer loads of questions like this back at the Essex assessment, but that it would be helpful for him to get an idea of where I'm at now, since that was a little while ago. He tells me that it isn't a test.

'OK,' I say. It's totally a test.

I'm thinking whether it's better to lie on a few of the questions so that I don't get in trouble, or whether I need to answer them all completely truthfully.

My pen is hovering above the page, and I am pointing it round the corners of the clipboard, over and over.

'Ben,' he says. 'There's nothing you can put on this form that will get you in trouble. Nothing at all.'

'OK,' I say.

The following statements are about things that happen to many people in their everyday lives. For each statement, write the number which says best how much it has troubled you **in the last week**.

0 – has not troubled me at all
1 – troubled me a little
2 – definitely troubled me
3 – troubled me a lot
4 – troubled me extremely

I decide to tell the truth, so I really hope he means it. I start scanning the list and rating statements:

I have to wash and clean all the time.	2
I check water taps and light switches over and over, turning them off.	4
I have thoughts that I might want to harm myself or others.	4

???!!!!!

I get upset if things are not arranged properly.	3
I have to follow a certain order in dressing, undressing, and washing myself.	4
I feel I have to count while I am doing things.	4
I need to pray to cancel bad thoughts or feelings.	0
I find it difficult to touch an object when I know it has been touched by strangers or certain people.	1

I need things to be arranged in a certain order. [3]

I have to do things over and over again until it feels right. [4]

I am upset by bad thoughts that come into my mind even though I don't want them to. [4]

How did they know? How did they know?!

Before going to sleep I have to do certain things in a certain way. [4]

I feel that I must repeat certain words or phrases in my mind in order to wipe out bad thoughts, bad feelings, or bad things I do. [4]

I feel that there are good and bad numbers. [4]

When I'm done, Dinesh has a look at my answers and tells me that the assessment team in Essex felt that I was living with obsessive compulsive disorder.

'I know,' I say, without entirely meaning to.

'That's interesting,' says Dinesh, stroking his beard. 'How did you know?'

'Well, my friend . . . April . . . she said that's what she thought it was. She said I should do something about it. It made me want to go ahead with . . . this.'

'Your friend sounds very clever.'

'Yes,' I smile, feeling a little bolder. 'Yes, she's the cleverest.'

Dinesh asks me if it's something I'd be happy to work on with him, and adds that it might be helpful if we get my mum involved too.

OH MY GOD, oh my god, I am thinking. It was all a trick. And now I HAVE WRITTEN DOWN that I have bad thoughts, so Dinesh has evidence and they are going to tell Mum. Will she tell Dad?!

'You're not in trouble,' he reiterates.

'OK,' I say, tapping at the floor again. He walks me to the Family Room across the hall. I can hear Mum coming up the stairs. I can't breathe. Have I forgotten how to breathe? My throat is doing the gulpy thing.

Dinesh gestures to the sofa and Mum and I sit down together.

Dinesh opens his mouth and I'm sure he's going to tell her that I'm going to be taken to children's prison and can never come back.

But what he actually says is:

'I'm confident Ben has obsessive compulsive disorder, OCD. What that means is that he experiences distressing thoughts about bad things happening – "obsessions" – and then he has to do things – "compulsions" – to stop them happening. It's extremely distressing for him.'

'Obsessive . . . compulsive disorder?' says Mum. 'Isn't that when people are a bit of a neat freak, or when they like things to be just so?'

'Well, lots of people think that, but actually it's a distressing condition that can be to do with pretty much anything, not just being tidy.'

'I see,' Mum says slowly, taking it in. 'And if you have it, is it something you can change?'

'Well, actually there are lots of things we can do to help Ben live in a world that isn't run by compulsions.' Dinesh turns to me. 'Ben – how would you feel about coming to see me once a week?'

'I think that would be . . . good,' I say, surprised to realise that I do *actually* mean this, and I think I really would like to see Dinesh every week.

We both turn to look at Mum.

'OK then,' she says, still looking a bit uncertain.

'Great,' says Dinesh. 'Do you have any other questions?'

'Is . . . OCD common?' She fiddles with the ends of her sleeves. 'I mean, are there other kids with it?'

'Yes. Lots of children and adults experience it. About two per cent of adults, and one per cent of children.'

I have to think about this for a moment. That means that for every hundred children, at least one of them has weird and scary thoughts too . . . But I've *definitely* met more than a hundred children in my life, and I never saw any of them behave anything like me.

'Um, OK,' says Mum. 'Will this fix it then? This talking therapy thing?'

'It might not completely fix it, but we can definitely start to make it easier to live with. Was there anything else?'

I notice the corners of Mum's mouth twitch, and I can hear the clock ticking. Finally she asks in a teeny-tiny voice, 'What causes it . . . OCD, I mean?'

'Well,' replies Dinesh carefully. 'We don't entirely know for sure. It may be partly genetic, and partly caused by the environment a person is in; most likely a bit of both.'

'The . . . the environment?' stutters Mum.

'Yes. Sometimes people describe their OCD starting at a time that was stressful in their life. But this is not always the case.'

Tick tock, tick tock.

'So going forward, Ben, I'll see you for your sessions on Thursdays at 4.30 p.m. – does that time work for you?' asks Dinesh when it becomes clear neither of us have anything to say in response. Mum and I nod. 'From now on I'll only need Ben – but you are welcome to sit in the waiting room, or in the coffee shop across the street. Is that OK?'

Mum nods again. She looks terrified.

I feel like the world is ending but Mum leads me out the centre and we go home via the ice-cream shop for four small scoops of salted caramel ice cream in a pot, with chocolate sauce, chocolate buttons, sprinkles and whipped cream, so I guess I'm not in trouble after all.

What I really want to know is if Dad knew I had the appointment today, and if Mum is going to tell him about the diagnosis. I almost ask Mum, but something keeps stopping me. If he *did* know and didn't message me, I'm not sure I could stand it.

'I'm sorry, Benny,' says Mum, reaching out across the shiny tabletop to take my hand. If possible, her voice is even tinier than before. She sounds small and far away, like a person hiding at the end of a long tunnel. 'For everything.'

2.4

When Thursday comes around I can't concentrate on ANYTHING at school. April asks what has got into me and I whisper to her that I've got my counselling session this evening.

'Oh,' she whispers back. 'Fair.'

When it's finally time to walk home from school, April comes too, and says we don't have to talk about anything. She says good luck and presses a folded note in my palm and tells me to open it just before my session. And then she is gone.

Mum meets me at the end of the road from school. She has even put some purple lipstick on and tied back her hair, because obviously purple lipstick totally screams 'responsible mother'. We get the bus back to the waiting room with eleven chairs, where the dinosaurs still look sad and lonely. There are no other kids here at the moment.

'You could play with the abacus if you like, Benny,' says Mum. 'There's no one to see.'

My fingers twinge but I shake my head. I don't want Dinesh to walk in and think I'm even weirder.

I reach into my pocket and unfold the note from April. It is a cartoon picture of the two of us, surrounded by stars and planets. Underneath, April has written:

B IS 4 BEN.
B IS 4 BRAVE.

My throat feels tight – not in the gulpy way. Like I might cry – but not because I am sad. I fold and unfold the note four times and put it neatly back in my pocket.

'Hi, Ben!' says Dinesh, appearing at the door, even more out of breath than last time.

'Bye, Benny,' says Mum. 'I'll be right here.'

I nod.

'We're back up at the top again.' We walk without saying anything to each other. Dinesh opens the door to the yellow room, and I sit in the same black chair as before. I stare at the pictures of the happy dogs and cats.

The Thoughts say, *I want Bumble to die.*

Owwww. I screw my eyes tight shut so that I won't imagine horrible things happening to Bumble.

I repeat, *stop, stop, stop, stop*, in my head. But it doesn't help. The more I try not to think about bad things happening to Bumble, the more I do.

Dinesh starts to explain that we'll be trying things out: different ways of thinking about things and different ways of doing things that will help me to feel less worried.

'How does that sound?' he asks.

'OK,' I say, but my voice is a bit squeaky, because I'm still thinking about Bumble.

'So on Monday we were speaking about some of the thoughts you have that you find overwhelming, and I wondered if you might be able to tell me what you actually do when you have those thoughts?'

'I have to make things safe again.'

'And how do you do that?'

'The fours . . . I do things in fours. Like touching stuff, and eating. And I avoid bad colours. And I say special stuff in my head. To make things go away.' *Bumble is safe. Bumble is safe. Bumble is safe. Bumble is safe.*

'Take me through a normal day in your life.'

'From when?' I wish my voice would stop coming out so high. I stare hard at the floor, hoping that if I can't see the dog and cat pictures, I will forget the thought about Bumble.

'From when you wake up.'

'I get dressed in the right colours, and have my breakfast in the yellow bowl. I brush my teeth for four minutes. I put the toothbrush in and out of the glass four times. All the toothbrushes have to be touching the right way. I pack and unpack my backpack four times . . .'

I trail off, because I'm not sure how much detail he actually wants. People sometimes say I give too much detail. Dinesh helps me out.

'What do you do when you get to school?'

'I hang out with April. I hope that no one else notices me.'

'Ah, April. Your clever friend.'

'Yes, that's April.' I find myself smiling slightly. *My* friend April. I wonder what she's doing right now. Probably she's home on her own. Doing what, though? Maybe drawing. Or watching TV. Or texting me! I want to check my phone. I can hear Dinesh asking,

'What do you do at lunch?'

'I don't go to lunch. I go to the music room with April.'

'Why don't you go to lunch?'

'The dinner ladies . . . don't get my plate right.' I remember the peas and gravy catastrophe and my stomach feels like it's going to fall out of my bum (and I *am* talking literally) all over again.

'What about the rest of the day?'

'Well, we have lessons. But I don't like writing if my words aren't four letters long, or in multiples of four, so I think my teachers think I'm stupid.' *And they're not the only ones.*

'Do you think you're stupid?'

'I'm not sure. I'm good at maths.'

'What do you do after school?'

'Sometimes I have art club.'

'How's that?'

'Well . . . at first I was a bit scared of all the different colours and ways you can make things, but now I join in sometimes.'

'Cool. And what about if you don't have art club?'

'I go home.'

'And what happens at home?'

Mum is asleep. I can't wake her up. My stomach feels like there's a hole in it. I do routines around the house all evening. I still don't know where Dad is. I think it's all my fault.

'I read my comics.'

'DC or Marvel?'

'DC,' I smile.

'Good man,' says Dinesh. 'And at bedtime?'

'I find bedtime quite hard. The things in my room . . . they have to feel right. I can't sleep until they do.'

'What would happen if they weren't?'

'I'd feel like we weren't safe . . . Me and my family . . . I have to do it to make sure we're protected through the night.'

'So it sounds like you're doing a lot of magical thinking throughout the day.'

'Magical thinking?'

'Magical thinking is a thing people do where they act like they have the power to control what happens to themselves or other people by doing or thinking "special" things. So you worry that something bad will happen to you or your family, and then you have to touch things four times, or repeat your special phrase, to "stop" that happening. You are acting like you have magical powers: the ability to change what happens in the world.'

'Oh,' I say. 'Yeah, I guess I am.'

'Do you actually believe that? That you have superhuman powers?'

'Um . . .' Do I really believe I am magic? It doesn't feel like I'm magic when I'm doing my fours. I don't feel powerful, I just feel scared. Of course I'm not magic. I'm just Ben.

163

But it's true – I have been acting like I'm magic. What would be the point of doing this stuff otherwise? But clearly I'm not magic, because if I were, I could have stopped Dad leaving, and Mum being . . . well, Mum. *It doesn't even work.* 'No, I don't think so.'

'So you're not magic. But you're acting like you are. And taking on all the stress and responsibility of an overworked superhero. Isn't that . . . a bit of a waste of time?'

'Yeah, now that you say it like that.'

'What would you rather be doing?'

'Just regular kid stuff. Having fun.'

I want to watch TV without having to count the corners of the screen. I want to text April proper sentences. I want to run with friends without having to retrace my steps. I just want to have friends.

'Well, in our work together we're going to try and make that possible for you. Would you like that?'

Something terrible might happen. But what if it didn't? I take a deep breath.

'Yes.'

'OK, well, we've come to the end of our session today, but that's what we'll be working on going forward. I'll take you back out to your mum now.'

Mum is smiling anxiously at me when Dinesh

takes me back down to the waiting room.

We get the bus home together. When she asks me how the session went I answer, 'Fine.'

But I am busy thinking. My number-one hero, the Doctor, does not believe in magic. He believes in science and logic. There is an episode from 1971 where the third Doctor, played by Jon Pertwee, gets annoyed because his companion Jo keeps going on about witchcraft. The Doctor says everything that *appears* magic can be explained by science. Suddenly it looks like his yellow car, which is called Bessie, is driving itself round the yard with no one in the driving seat.

Jo is all, 'Wow, magic!' But the Doctor takes a remote control out of his pocket and just gives this knowing look, like, 'You *see*? No such thing as magic.'

So why the heck have I spent so long acting like *I'm* magic?

*

April waits until break when we are safe in Music Room 4 to ask my how my session went.

I tell her that I'm *pretty sure* Dinesh likes comics too. I explain to her about the magical thinking, and April says she's had thoughts like that before – a

165

nagging feeling that something bad would happen if she didn't wear her special heart and moon bracelet, but that she guesses the difference between her and me was that she didn't get totally obsessed by it.

'You mean you just forgot it and moved on?'

'Yeah, I guess,' she says.

'*How?* Weren't you worried that something terrible was going to happen?'

'No . . . not really.'

'So HOW then?'

April sighs. 'People are just different, Ben. You can't compare us like that. I'm sure there's loads of stuff I struggle with that you wouldn't get.'

Like what?

'I'm just glad it went well. Listen, I've come up with an idea for our Halloween disco costume.'

She pushes her notebook across the carpet so I can see. At first I don't get it. I see sketches of creepy doll after creepy doll, and after I get through them there are two drawings of perfect old-fashioned outfits, coloured in felt-tip so neatly they look like they've been printed. Then I notice that each one has little square tabs coming off the outside of the arms and legs. I ask, 'What are those?' and April explains that she thinks we should go as paper dolls, because everyone thinks dolls are creepy. Paper dolls require outfits, and in the sets she used to play with when she was younger, the paper outfits had little paper tabs round the edges so you could fit them on the dolls.

'I can't go as a doll!' I whine. 'I'm a boy!'

April tells me to stop being so boring, and that I can go as whatever I want to go as. I tell her I don't mind being a bit boring if it means I don't become the laughing stock of the school, and also that at no point did *I* specify that I wanted to go as a doll. Plus, I'm a bit disappointed, because I really wanted us to go as Cybermen. To me, they are the creepiest of all the *Doctor Who* villains because they are humans who have been 'upgraded' into shiny metal robots who stomp around and want to 'upgrade' any regular humans they find so that they are Cybermen too. The scariest thing about Cybermen is that they see emotions as counterproductive. So when a human gets upgraded they lose all their feelings because the Cybermen say it is more efficient not to feel things like fear and pain.

And even though occasionally, when I'm feeling really, *really* bad, there is a small part of me that thinks that might actually be quite a relief, most of me just thinks it's creepy as hell.

Anyway, April with an idea is not someone to be messed with. She says it would be nearly impossible to make Cybermen that looked half decent in only a few weeks and without a load of metal. So by the time we get to art club the paper dolls are 'our idea' that 'we' can't wait to get started on.

Great.

Miss Ruiz also thinks it an awesome idea and, for what it's worth, Priya and her gang agree. Rhys is, as usual, drowning us all out with his headphones to focus on his charcoal buildings. Miss Ruiz says we can help ourselves to the giant sheets of card, and the paint. She suggests that we use the measuring tape to take measurements of the different parts of our body, and mark them with pencil on the card. We should use those measurements to draw our outfits on the paper, and then we can cut them out. She also says we can use the computer to google pictures of Victorian paper dolls and get ideas for what outfits they might wear.

April and I share the spinny office chair and spend the rest of the hour searching outfits. There are so many options! Well, for girls at least. The Victorians were really into frills, lace and bows. When I say it's not fair that there's way more girl choices, April says (NOT EVEN JOKING) that she doesn't mind going as a guy if I want to be a girl. Or we can both be girls!

'Why would that be so bad?' April says, laughing at how horrified I look.

'Well, everyone would probably die laughing at me!' I say. 'You know, think I'm even weirder than they do already?'

'So?' she asks. 'What do you care what they think?' I sigh – there's no point trying to get her to understand. Still, I guess if I'm honest, there's a part of me that would love it: to really not care what anyone thought of me.

Sometimes I really wish I could Be More April.

In the end, April chooses a green dress with a TINY waist (apparently these women wore things called corsets to make their waists as small as possible, which sounds very painful) and a skirt that comes out in a cone shape. The dress has short puffy sleeves trimmed with lace, and there's lace around the collar which meets in the centre of the chest in a loopy bow. The bottom of the skirt is trimmed with, you guessed it, lace. There's also a closed paper umbrella, and paper bows for the hair. Most of the men are wearing grey suit trousers and jackets, with a white shirt tucked in, and long boots and a top hat. April says she thinks the two will go well together, and before I can start moaning about the colour she says, 'Don't worry, we can paint them black instead if you like.'

April hits print on the outfits we've chosen, and tells Miss Ruiz that these will be our reference images, which sounds very professional. Miss Ruiz says she'll keep them safe in her drawer and that she can't wait to see what we make.

*

'Mum!' I call. I'm unlocking the door to our flat and I can't wait to tell her all about the paper dolls. Mum is always wanting me to 'unleash my creativity' and make things, but fours and colours usually get in the way. When Kyle and I were little, I remember, hazily, that we used to make lots of things together with Mum. The three of us would lie on our bellies and paint pictures on large sheets of paper that Mum fixed down with masking tape on the kitchen floor. Mum would always be bringing home random things she'd found in the road, like someone's old broken wooden chair that they'd put outside their house on the off-chance someone wanted it, and together we'd clean it and make it usable again. Or she'd get something from the recycling, for instance a tin or glass bottle, and we'd paint it and turn it into something else like a plant pot or a vase. It was amazing how Mum could always find a way for us to make a boring old thing into something new and cool.

But I started to find it difficult to make decisions about what to make, and then I'd scream if Kyle used the wrong colour, and eventually Kyle got angry and said he didn't want to make stuff with us any more, because I sucked all the fun out of it, *as usual*.

I guess he was right.

'Mum?'

I push open the door. The house is dark, and there're no sounds, not even from the TV.

'Mum!' I run up the stairs and into the kitchen, thinking I'll find her there making my tea. 'Mum?'

I search the whole house, even though I already know – she's not here. Dad made a rule for Mum, which is that now that I'm walking home alone she absolutely must be around to make sure I'm back OK. I heard him tell her that it is a safety thing.

But I know that it's much more about *her* safety than mine.

And anyway, that was before Dad went away, so who knows if that rule even exists any more?

Maybe Mum hasn't disappeared, I tell myself.

171

Probably she has just gone to the supermarket to get something she forgot for tea. That's not disappearing, is it? People are allowed to go to the shops.

I go round the house turning all the plugs on and off four times, and opening and shutting all the doors and cupboards four times. While I'm doing this, I repeat the phrase: 'She will come back,' even though I think Dinesh might be right about me not really having any special magical powers that can control any of this stuff, and that the Doctor would think I was being stupid. But if they are wrong, and I'm different, and I *really* can control what happens, isn't it better to be on the safe side?

I do the whole thing again and again, and after sixteen times it has been forty-six minutes, according to my watch, and I stop being able to hold back the worry any more. I wish Kyle was here. I get my phone out of my backpack and call him, but it rings out.

When Mum used to be late to pick me up from school I always used to cry, even though I really, *really* didn't want to, in case anyone saw and thought I was a stupid baby.

But now it doesn't matter because there's no one here to see me gulp or cry. So I slump on the floor screaming like a toddler and letting my throat go *flex, flex, flex, flex.*

I pound the carpet with my fists sixty-four times. It doesn't make her come back. I cry and cry. I cry until I'm exhausted by it and think I might have cried out every tear I have, and then I lie flat on my back breathing hard like I've run a race and trying to work out what to do.

I turned my phone on loud, so I should have heard if Kyle had called me back – but just in case, I get up and check anyway. Nothing – I can't believe it. I mean, he *told* me never to call him unless it was a 'total emergency'. So he *must* know I am phoning because it's a LEGITIMATE emergency. And even then, he can't be bothered to call me back. I call him again, but of course he doesn't pick up. I even try Dad, but it goes straight to voicemail.

Where are *you, Kyle? I need you.* Maybe he's at the arcade and that's why he's not replying – I could walk down there and check? But then I have a better idea: maybe I can find Mum *myself.* I know where her studio is, from when we went to school together. I grab my backpack and let myself out of the front door and start off down the road. It is only four streets away and I know that it is number 47 because I asked the door number as soon as Mum told me she had a new studio. I want to do my stepping but I tell myself that if Mum is in a bad state then it is best I get there as quickly as possible, so I power-walk and just move my hands backwards and forwards quickly.

There are lots of buzzers on door number 47, because it's a massive block of shared studios. I ring the one that says, STUDIO 18: LEILA HARDIE. Neither forty-seven nor eighteen are divisible by four, and 4 + 7 does not even make a number that it divisible by four and neither does 1 + 8. I am trying extremely hard to be brave about this fact, but every time I touch that STUDIO 18 buzzer I feel like something absolutely terrible is going to happen. Like Mum might be alive and fine right now, but touching that number with my finger could snap her into a rag doll collapsed on the floor.

I make myself ring it again and again but there's no answer. Maybe she's not here. I really have no idea where else to look, though. A man buzzes himself out of the front door and I sneak past him, trying to look like I just happen to be going in as he is coming out and not like I am breaking and entering.

A block plan on the wall tells me that Studio 18 is on the fourth floor. I breathe out in relief.

I run up the four flights and burst through the door. It's quite a sight.

The studio is chaos. Mum's wooden worktable is on its side by the window. There are bits of smashed-up gnome all over the floor – snapped-off legs ending in little brown boots, torsos studded with little blue button waistcoats, random arms in checked shirts and shards of faces with only one eye or half a mouth left, like they had some kind of mass gnome punch-up.

At first I think Mum's not here, but then I see a leg sticking out from behind the table and I creep round. She's on her side, asleep, snoring slightly. I shake her.

'Wake up!' I shout. 'Wake up!'

She's groggy but she sits up, rubbing her eyes. She has the sour-sweet sweat smell that I recognise only too well, like a giant rotting fruit. She's been drinking. She looks around the studio.

'Oh,' she says quietly. 'Icouldnmake themlook . . . gnomeyenough.'

I find an empty pot in the metal work sink filled with her paint brushes and chisels. I rinse it out and fill it with tap water.

'Drink all of this,' I say. She's shivering, so I grab her parka which is hanging on the back of the door and put it over her shoulders, pulling the fur-trimmed hood over her head. I go round picking up all the gnome parts and putting them in the bin. Then I pick the table up and take her tools and put them back in the centre.

I look back to Mum. She's barely touched her water.

'Drink it all,' I say. 'And then we're going home.'

She nods, wide-eyed, as she drinks it all in one go. Then she puts it down on the floor and tries unsuccessfully to pull herself up using the side of her worktable. I give her both my hands and hoik her up.

She's staggering down the stairs so I put my arm round her waist to steady her and that's how we walk home too. Most of what she's saying makes no sense at all. Then she doesn't want to go into the flat, but I coax her up, telling her I will make her a cup of tea and run her a bath the way she likes it.

She sits on the sofa in space-cadet mode while I run the water, staring at nothing. I make it steamy hot and put sixteen lavender drops in. I help her take off her things and get in. Then I pull the shower curtain across so she can have some privacy, and I sit on the toilet seat with my knees up, reading my comic.

'Benny, youdon have tosit withme likel'msome kindababy.'

'Yes, I do,' I say. She doesn't complain again. 'Wash your hair, it smells.'

She sighs, and I hear a big splosh that means she is taking my advice. Afterwards I hold her hands so she can get out without slipping, and I make her brush her teeth. I help her up the stairs and get her pyjamas out for her. I pick the plainest white ones that hopefully won't make anything bad happen.

I get her another glass of water from downstairs, tell her to drink it all and fill it up again and put it on her bedside table. I pull the duvet up round her. She grumbles something I can't make out and shuts her eyes.

Downstairs, I open a tin of tuna and empty it into a bowl, squirt mayonnaise in and add a can of sweetcorn. I spread it on to a piece of toast which makes the fourth component. I eat it on a plate on the sofa, chewing in fours, watching *Star Trek* on Netflix to distract myself. I check my phone and see I have three missed calls from Dad, as well as a text.

Hey, big man, sorry I missed your call. Hope things have been OK. Is everything all right?

Hope things have been OK. I feel a surge of something hot and wavy shooting around my insides. This is the first time I've heard from him in over a week, and he's not gonna say anything about him disappearing? For the first time, I think I know how Kyle might have felt that time in Essex when Dad came home after three days with presents for both of us, smiling sheepishly, acting like nothing had happened.

I thanked Dad for the action figure of the ninth Doctor. Kyle punched a hole in the wall.

I text back, **Fine**. Then I go to check on Mum.

She's fast asleep. I kiss her on the head four times, because I want her to be protected, even if I am really cross with her. I start to get myself ready for bed, because somehow the time is 9.49 p.m. In my room I go to turn out my main light and flick the switch two hundred and fifty-six times before it feels right. If Dad were here he would tell me that I am going to make the house explode. I see the whole house going up with a cartoon bang, and the words *BOOM* plastered across the picture in comic-book letters.

It should make me want to stop, but it doesn't.

3

3.1

Mum and I don't really talk over the weekend, and, anyway, she spends most of it in bed. Kyle's back briefly on Sunday morning – I ask him where the heck he's been and he says at work, and that he stayed at 'a friend's' for a couple of nights – 'not that it's any of your business'.

I tell him that actually it *is* my business because there was *A Situation* where I couldn't find Mum, AND why didn't he even try and call me back? And Kyle says, 'Well, obviously whatever you did worked because she's home now, isn't she?'

I want to punch him in the face when he says that, but I think he'd probably start punching me back – and I don't exactly need to think about who would win in a fight. He calls to me that he's 'heading out' after twenty minutes. I run to stand in the way of the front door and ask him to stay. 'Please, please stay just a little longer – I'm scared.'

It probably sounds like I'm a massive pathetic baby, but at this point I don't care any more.

'I'm not your dad,' he sighs, pushing me aside gently. And then the door has shut behind him and it's just me and Mum.

'I know,' I say to no one.

*

I can't concentrate on a single thing at school all week because I keep imagining Mum slumped on the floor of her studio. I am snappy to April and even snappier to Mum. On Thursday, when she meets me at the end of the road after school to get the bus to counselling, I wonder if Dinesh will see her and notice that she doesn't seem very well. Because she looks . . . Well, honestly, she looks a mess. Her hair is extra out of control and the bags under her eyes are darker than ever. She doesn't try to talk to me on the bus and I'm glad, because I really have nothing to say to her, so I just focus on moving my eyes round the four corners of the bus (even though I know I'm not supposed to be doing this).

Dinesh is slightly out of breath again when he arrives in the waiting room, and today I notice a tiny drop of sweat on his hairline. Mum tells me distractedly that she's going to get a coffee, but she'll be here when I get back. My stomach gives a lurch. *Will she?*

'Hello, Ben,' says Dinesh, when we've gone into the yellow room and taken our seats.

'How are you doing today?'

I'm terrified that Mum's getting really bad again. I don't know how to make Dad come back.

'I'm . . . OK.'

'What's your week been like?'

'Well, April and I are going to go to a Halloween disco. It's fancy dress, so April's come up with an idea for a costume for us. I've never been to a disco before.'

'What are you going as?'

'Freaky Victorian paper dolls.'

'Ooooh!' Dinesh pulls a pretend frightened face. 'How are things at home?'

'Fine.' *Liar, liar, liar, liar.*

'Ben, can I ask, I was looking at your forms again before we met today. You said you sometimes have thoughts about hurting people you love, even though you don't want to. Would you be able to say a bit more about that?'

My eyes drift over to the smiling pictures of dogs and cats loving life. *I want Bumble to die, I want*

Bumble to die, I want Bumble to die, I want Bumble to die.

I think about Mum on Friday. *I want her to disappear. I'm going to make her disappear.*

'I, uh . . .' My mouth goes dry and I can feel the gulps coming. 'I think maybe I made a mistake. With the scores.'

Liar, liar, liar, liar.

'Well, can I tell you something?'

Oh, god! What will he tell me? Please don't send me to child jail.

'Everyone gets bad thoughts now and then. They're called intrusive thoughts. Most people have had a weird thought like, *What if I hit that person right now?* or, *What if I pushed that person on to the train track?* But when most people have that thought, they just think, *Oh, that's a weird thought*, and then they forget about it, and move on with their life.'

'Really?!'

'Definitely.'

'Even . . . *you?*' I cannot believe that someone like Dinesh, who is a BRAIN EXPERT, has bad thoughts sometimes. He seems so . . . normal.

Dinesh smiles. 'Even me. The problem is that people with OCD tend to be really caring and prone to worrying a lot. So when someone like you has a thought like that, you find it hard to just dismiss it, like other people do. You start to think about it, over and over. You think: *Why did I have that thought? What does it mean? I shouldn't be having that thought.* The more you tell yourself you shouldn't be having that thought, the more you do. It's like if I said to you now, "You are not allowed to think about pink elephants," you would probably only be able to think about pink elephants.'

I smile. It's true. I am picturing pink elephants. And I'm also realising something . . .

'You mean . . . having those thoughts doesn't make me a horrible person?'

'The opposite. People with OCD tend to be some of the kindest people you can find. That's why you find those thoughts so upsetting and can't let them go, whereas other people are able to dismiss them.'

I am one hundred per cent shocked. I don't know what to say. All this time I thought I was a monster. But I'm . . . not?

'Really?' I whisper.

'Truly,' Dinesh smiles.

'So what . . . what do I need to do when I have the bad thoughts?'

Is Dinesh going to tell me the magic fix, so that finally, *finally*, I can feel better?

'You don't need to do anything.'

'Oh.'

I think Dinesh notices my distinct absence of joy at this answer. 'But *that's* the magic of it,' he grins. 'You actually need to do *less*. You don't need to keep thinking about it and telling it to go away. I get that you don't like it. I know it makes you scared. But if you are able to allow the thought to be there, without getting all worked up about it, it loses its power.'

Huh. It's so strange. It's the opposite of everything I've ever done when I've had The Thoughts. It sounds, possibly . . . I don't know – dangerous. Because what kind of person sees disaster unfolding and just chooses to ignore it and carry on going about their day?

'Even if . . . even if it were a really bad thought? Say I thought . . . say I thought . . . I can't say it.'

'Go on, I dare you.'

'I can't. You'll never have heard a thought this bad before.'

Dinesh laughs. 'Try me.'

'Say I thought . . . about . . .'

I must not say. If there's any hope of being sent home rather than to child prison, I must, must, not say.

'About?'

I whisper, 'About wanting my mum to die.'

I wait for the walls to close in like there's been an earthquake. Mum will drop dead in the coffee shop down the street, if that's even where she really is. Dinesh will say that he made a mistake, that I'm an exception to the other children, and that I really did make this happen by saying it out loud.

'Then I would tell you,' says Dinesh, 'that I hear that thought all the time. And that the only reason you hold on to that thought is because you love your mum very much and don't want anything to happen to her.'

I take a deep breath.

'OK?' says Dinesh.

'OK,' I say.

I feel like when you have woken up from a nightmare and start to realise it was only a dream and that really you are safe and everything is OK.

'Think about just letting those thoughts be there between now and when I next see you on Thursday. I'll take you back out to your mum now.'

'OK,' I say again.

*

On Friday, Mr Montague asks me to stay behind after maths. Everyone is filing out for break and I'm standing behind my desk thinking I must be in some serious trouble, even though I have no idea what for. What have I done?

April stays standing next to me, but Mr Montague says, 'I only require Ben, Lady April.' April shrugs like she doesn't care and makes for the door, but she's smiling the tiniest bit and I think it's because Mr Montague called her 'Lady April'.

'Don't look so terrified, Ben,' says Mr Montague. 'I just wanted to check in.'

Oh, right, it's just another person who wants to talk about my feelings.

'I was told that you'd been referred for some counselling. They contact your school so we know what's going on, but they don't tell me any more than that, because it's confidential. I just wanted to see you for a moment and see how you're doing.'

'OK,' I say.

'You don't have to tell me anything if you don't want to – it's just so you know that I haven't forgotten you, and I'm here if you need me.'

My throat is feeling weird again – not in the

187

gulpy way. Just tight. It's strange – everyone caring so much.

'I'm seeing a counsellor. He's . . . nice.'

'That's great. I'm happy to hear it. Is there anything we could be doing at school? To make things a bit easier for you?'

I think about this for a second. I'm about to say no when I think about how excruciating the story subjects can be.

'Actually, there is something.'

'I'm all ears.'

'It's about . . . writing. I want you to know that I know how to write sentences. I just don't like writing with words that aren't four letters long, or a multiple of four. I want you to know that I can do it, I just don't. I'm not . . . stupid.'

'I never thought you were. I thought maybe you struggled with writing, and that's fine, lots of kids do. But this is helpful to know. You don't like writing unless it's in fours or multiples of four . . . Wow!' He shakes his head, amazed. 'The human brain – it never fails to amaze me! I'll keep it in mind. Anything else?'

'Nope, just that.'

'All right-y, well, off you go then – I think a friend of yours is probably waiting for you.'

April and I are going to 'realise our ideas' (April's wording) in art club today. I'm still a bit sulky about the fact we aren't making Cybermen.

We get the pieces of extra-large card, but even then we need to stick two sheets together so it's the length of our bodies. Once we've taped the backs together (with four lines of tape, not for OCD reasons but just because they need to be firmly taped together . . . Well, OK, a bit of both), April tells me to lie on the card. She tells me to stay as still as possible and traces around my upper body and legs with a black marker.

Priya and her crew are hovering over April, and nothing Miss Ruiz says can convince them that making clay pots would be more interesting that watching April trace around me.

'Guys, step back, I can't see what I'm doing with you lot leering over me,' sighs April. But I think she secretly likes the attention.

Then we switch over and I trace round April. I'm scared Priya and the others will jog me. I want my line around April to look as neat as the one April did for me, even though April says it doesn't really matter, since for her it's more about getting the length of her body down, as the dress will puff out at the bottom. I realise I haven't taken a breath.

When I'm done, April says it's great. She uses the lines to draw a paper dress her size, and tells me to do the same. Next she grabs two pairs of scissors from the pot and we cut them out. Finally, she tells me to use the print-out to sketch in the details of the suit. 'And for god's sake, do that bit in pencil,' she commands, 'because knowing you, you'll think it's not right and want to do it again.'

She's not wrong. I draw some buttons on and keep having to rub them out because they don't look like perfect circles. I think maybe it's the pressure of having Priya and everyone watching and commenting on *everything*, but The Thoughts are coming faster and faster.

What if I punched Priya to make her go away?

No!!! I don't want to think that. I really like Priya. Sure, she's kind of annoying, but what self-respecting Year Four isn't?

Then I remember what Dinesh said. *It's just an odd thought. Everyone has them sometimes and it doesn't mean anything about me.*

So I don't have to panic. I guess I can . . . just let this thought be there? Would that be OK?

April holds up her fully sketched-out dress.

'What do you think?' she asks.

'It's great,' I say.

Priya says it looks sick (as in awesome, not unwell). The sound of Priya's voice makes me realise I had forgotten the bad thought about her. I had 'let it be there' and it had gone, just like Dinesh told me it would. But now her voice reminds me of the thought, and I'm thinking it again. I tell myself it's just brain noise, and it can stay if it wants, but *I* have stuff to do. It worked a second ago, and I don't feel so scared this time.

'Yeah, I'm pretty happy with it,' grins April. 'Well, we can't be here all night. Shall I help you finish those buttons?'

I smile. 'Sure. Thanks.'

*

It's weird, but I find myself almost looking forward to seeing Dinesh again. It's been such a relief to find out that having bad thoughts doesn't make me mad or wrong. And I guess I feel kind of warm towards Dinesh, because he was the one who let me feel like I wasn't a criminal. Which is a pretty low baseline for feeling OK, I realise. But, hey, you've got to start somewhere.

On Thursday Mum takes me on the bus again,

191

and waits in the waiting room, while Dinesh walks me back up to the yellow room and asks me how my week has been.

'OK,' I say. 'It helped, what you said. About just accepting The Thoughts rather than pushing them away. I'm not completely OK with them, and I still feel like I need to do things in fours to make them go away. But it did help.'

'Good.' Dinesh strokes his beard again, looking like he's thinking. 'I'm glad you've jumped straight in there, because that's what I wanted to talk about today. So, when you do something in fours, or repeat a special phrase or words in your head, do you remember me saying that that's called a "compulsion"?'

'Yes . . .'

'So what does that mean to you?'

I think hard, wanting to get the answer right, so that at least Dinesh won't think I'm stupid.

'Maybe, like . . . they're the things I do to make the bad thoughts, um, my obsessions, go away. Sort of like a spell? But, um, over and over.'

'Good. And do you find that when you do those things, they help make the bad thoughts go away?'

'Um . . . sort of . . . but . . .'

'But?'

'But they always come back.' Like boomerangs, I think. Annoying, bad thought boomerangs.

'OK, I see. I'm going to draw something for you.'

Dinesh reaches for a piece of paper and places it on a clipboard on his lap. With his biro, he draws a circle made of arrows.

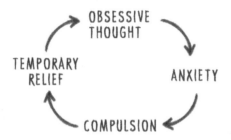

'So you might have an obsessive thought that something bad is going to happen to your mum. And that makes you feel anxious. And your brain thinks you need to do something to get rid of that anxiety. So it tells you to perform a compulsion, you know, like when you look round all the corners of the room in fours. That might make you feel better for a second, but the problem is that by doing that compulsion, you've given power to the original thought about your mum: you've made it seem like it was something you needed to do something about. And once you give a thought power, the more likely it is to come back, and then – *BAM* – you're back experiencing the bad thought again.'

'So what should I do?' I ask.

'Think about it like this. If a bully came up to you in the playground and asked you for money, what would you do?'

'I don't carry money on me.'

'But if you did.'

Honestly, I'd probably give it to them. 'Hand it over and beg for mercy?'

'And what might that make the bully do tomorrow?'

'Um . . . come back again? For more money?'

'Exactly! If you don't stand up to a bully, they'll always come back. Giving the bully money would be like doing a compulsion. It solves the problem for a bit, but the problem always comes back.'

I seriously think Dinesh's grasp of bully protocol is a little loose if he thinks a bully would even flinch at me standing up to them. Still, I get the point. (For once!)

'So . . . to make the bad thoughts and the compulsions go away, I need to . . . not do the compulsion?'

'Exactly!'

Wow. Why have I never thought about just not doing them? 'It sounds so simple.'

'It sounds simple,' says Dinesh. 'But it doesn't

feel easy when you try not to do a compulsion. Have you ever not done a compulsion before? When you really felt like you needed to?'

I think about this. There have actually been a few occasions where I didn't do a compulsion, even though I really wanted to. They were all with April. The time I walked through her grey door, and the time I took the bus. The time I dyed my hair. The other week, at my first and only ever sleepover, where I came into my room and didn't open and shut the door four times. I don't remember ever being able to go to bed without doing my door and light checks, and I did it, that night.

'Yes,' I say. 'With my friend April.'

'And what did you think would happen when you didn't do what the brain bully said?'

What did I think would happen? I thought I'd never feel calm again. I thought I was going to be sick and that the terrible things I was trying to protect everyone from would actually happen. 'I felt . . . pretty stressed.'

'And what did happen?'

'Well . . .' I now feel a bit silly that I hadn't realised this before. 'I forgot about them. They bothered me for a bit, and then I did forget.'

'Good. So that's what happens when you resist

a compulsion. Initially, you feel more stressed than you would have felt if you'd just done the compulsion. You may, as you say, have the feeling that you will never be calm again. But over time, your stress fades away, and you start to escape that OCD loop of feeling like you always need to respond to bad thoughts.'

'OK,' I say, and I'm nodding because it's true, that was what happened.

'So I have a mission for you, between now and next Thursday. Pick one of your compulsions for me. One is fine – we don't want to be overloaded, because this is stressful work we're doing, and it's hard – reversing habits you've had for years and years.'

'Um, opening and shutting doors four times or in multiples of four,' I say, because that was the one I resisted before.

'OK, great. Let's see you try and not do the door thing. And if you accidentally do it, because it's something you've been doing for years, that's fine. Just mess it up by making it a number higher than four, so it doesn't "feel right" to you.'

'OK . . .' I say, because Dinesh is right – a lot of the time I do seem to just do my fours automatically.

'And if you end up giving into the compulsion

and doing it, that's OK too. You won't have failed or anything. It's just something I'd like you to try so we can talk about what happened and how it felt. How does that sound?'

'Scary,' I say. 'But I want to try and do it because I want to get better.'

'Good man,' says Dinesh. 'I'll see you next week.'

3.2

Thinking about 'the cycle' is actually pretty helpful. Because it's true – I always *think* compulsions will make me feel better, but I still get anxious again pretty quickly after I've done one. The idea that the way to make them get better is just to not do them is . . . kind of exciting. I'm definitely in a better mood today than I have been in the last couple of weeks, and April notices. She's been calling me 'chuckly cheeks' all day, and I don't even really care.

'What are you guys going as to the Halloween disco?' asks Sophia in RS on Friday, our final lesson of the day before art club, playing with the toggle on my Dalek pencil case, zipping and unzipping it. She has done this seven times. I am trying hard not to get worked up about it.

'Pap–' I start to say, but April claps her hand to my mouth, the stars and moon of her bracelet dangling against my chin.

'Secret,' she says. 'You guys?'

'Secret also,' says Sophia. 'If you won't tell us yours.'

'Go on,' says Ezinne. *Zip, unzip. Zip, unzip.* 'Tell us.'

I never thought I'd say this, but we are saved by Mrs Williams, who bustles in right at that moment.

'Places!' she calls, clapping her hands.

We've been learning about Hinduism, which Mrs Williams says is the religion practised in India. I wonder if April's dad is Hindu? Or even April? I nudge her. 'Hey, April – is your family Hindu?'

This makes April snort. 'No – didn't you notice all the crucifixes my dad had put up round the house?' she whispers back. 'There's lots of religions practised in India – not only Hinduism. There's no way I'm gonna correct Mrs Williams, though.'

'Oh, OK,' I say, feeling kind of bad that I *definitely* don't have the guts to say anything to Mrs Williams, who is pacing around the board explaining that Hinduism doesn't just have one god – it has thousands of them. So many that you can't even count them all.

And they look *incredible*. She's getting some pictures up to show us but I wish she'd stay on them for longer rather than clicking through so fast.

Sometimes they have more than one head, or eight arms. Some of them can change from one thing to another, and most of them have a special companion, like a pet, that follows them around. For example, Ganesh, the elephant god, has a pet rat, because most people don't like rats, so this shows that Ganesh is a friend to all creatures. AND the reason Ganesh has an elephant's head is because his father came home from a trip away and his wife had had a baby (Ganesh) that had grown up in the time he had been away. He thought his wife was having an affair, even though Ganesh was his OWN SON. So he CUT OFF HIS HEAD. Obviously, Ganesh's mum was very angry about this and said he had to go and find himself a new head – the head of the first thing he saw.

The first thing he saw was an elephant.

So as you can see this religion is super-exciting. But somehow Mrs Williams is finding a way to make it super-not-exciting.

We are supposed to be answering ten questions on the whiteboard in our exercise books.

In traditional representations, which Hindu goddess has four arms and brandishes a spear dripping with blood, and a severed head?

Kali
(Four letters, perfect.)

How many chapters are in the Hindu holy book, the Bhagavad Gita?

Eighteen
(Eight letters, perfect.)

Hanuman is known as the . . .?

The answer is 'monkey god'. But that would be nine letters. Shoot.

I look over at April's exercise book. She has not answered a single question. She has drawn Kali, though, equipped with her spear and severed head, and a bowl to catch the dripping blood of said severed head. Kali is the destroyer of evil. She's pretty awesome.

I hear Mrs Williams before I see her – her rasping breath behind our backs as she approaches our desk.

'Why have you only answered two questions?' she rasps. 'And . . . what's this?' She's holding up April's drawing.

I cannot understand how Mrs Williams can hold up April's drawing and not a) think it's a work of

ART and b) know IMMEDIATELY that it's Kali.

She scrumples it up and throws it in THE BIN.

April looks like she did when Michelle and her gang were giving her a hard time. She's just staring straight ahead, like she doesn't have a care in the world, but her left hand is steadily scribbling a hole through the pages of her exercise book.

'When are you going to start paying attention?' drills Mrs Williams.

No answer.

'I asked you a question!'

No answer.

'Speak when you're spoken to!'

'No law against silence,' says April through gritted teeth. Mrs Williams sends her out of the classroom. I can hear Lauren, Aliya and Michelle sniggering.

I just sit staring hard at my exercise book. I realise that if I write *the monkey god*, that will be twelve letters, which is 4 x 3, so that's OK.

I feel something light hitting my back. When I turn around, there's a crumpled piece of paper behind the legs of my chair. I reach down and open it, even though every part of me is yelling, 'Don't open it, it will only upset you!' But I have to know what it says.

I unfold it and smooth it out across the desk.

FREAKS

I couldn't tell you what happened for the rest of the lesson. I just sit there, whizzing my eyes round the corners of room, counting in fours, trying to stop the drumming of words:

FREAKS, FREAKS, FREAKS, FREAKS.

I go straight to art club when the lesson is *finally* over, expecting to find April there.

But there's no sign of her.

Priya looks sad and says, 'Won't April be here today?'

And I say, 'April will most definitely be here. I'll just go and find her.'

I think about where I would go if I wanted to feel safe around here: Music Room 4. So I leave the glass basement and head down the main corridor and up the four flights, through the green door with the laminated sign and into the music department. I take a deep breath, and breathe in the smell of this corridor. It's musty – but not in an unpleasant way. At the end of the corridor, bright sunshine filters through a floor-length window. It is so bright that it makes the flecks of dust moving slowly through the air visible. Hardly anyone uses these rooms. When there's no one playing, and the green door shuts behind you, it feels like the quietest, most still place in the world.

I peep through the window into Music Room 4. April is there, staring blankly into space, her sketchbook open and a pen on the floor beside her.

I open the door slowly and look round.

'Hey,' I say.

April grunts.

I look at her sketchbook. 'Can I see?' I ask.

I think she nods.

I pick up the book. April has drawn herself sitting at our classroom desk, with her mouth open in a scream. The inside of her mouth is an open cash register, with notes and coins organised in various compartments, and a lot of the money is actually spewing out of her mouth/the till and on to the page.

She has titled it:

PAYIN ATENTION

'Cool,' I say. She grunts again.

'It's art club. I know Mrs Williams was horrible, but you love it and it always cheers you up, AND we

204

need to finish our outfits.'

She nods, but not like she means it.

'And Priya was asking after you. She was sad you weren't there.' I only say this because I'm not sure what else to say, but it actually makes April smile a bit, even if it's only for a second, and she quickly returns her face to a scowl.

'OK,' she says, standing up slowly and getting her things together. We start to head back down to the basement. April stops on the way to go in the girls' loos and wash her face. I stand outside, petrified that Lauren, Michelle or Aliya will come out of the toilet or down the hall and tease me for waiting outside the girls' loos. Which is silly really, because it's now fifteen minutes after home time, and this toilet isn't even on the same floor as our classroom. But still.

FREAKS. FREAKS. FREAKS. FREAKS.

April emerges and says, 'Well, come on then, we've got work to do.' I have to say, it does weird me out a bit when April goes from upset zombie back to April again in five seconds flat, but I'm still glad she wants to go to art club now.

She's power-walking down the flights of stairs to the art room, saying, 'Come on, Ben, we don't want to waste any more of our art-club time,' which I feel is what Kyle would call 'a bit out of order', but I don't say anything.

'April!' says Priya, getting up from her seat and running over when we come through the door. 'What are you guys doing today?'

'We've got to paint our dolls' outfits,' says April, dragging out a stool, standing on it and reaching up to the top shelf to drag down our sketched outlines.

'Holy cow, April,' says Miss Ruiz. 'Get off that stool before I have a health-and-safety-related freak-out.'

April hops down. Now she's sorting out a palette with our paints. Bottle green for her dress, white for the frills and black for the outlines and buttons. She gets me one with some black for my outlines, white for my shirt, and is about to squirt some grey on for my suit, but then says, 'You won't want to use grey, will you?' and looks back at the paint wall and chews a strand of her hair. 'I could make a slightly lighter black?'

I think about what Dinesh said about standing up to the bully in my head if I want to get better.

'It's cool,' I say, feeling my stomach go slimy. 'Grey works fine.'

'You sure?' I nod. 'Wow, awesome,' she says, squirting out some grey.

We sit down to paint. April's looks super-neat, you can't see the brush strokes and she doesn't go outside any of her outlines. Mine looks . . . Well, it looks OK. I do the grey of the suit last. I feel like I might be sick, but I want to fight the bully.

'BEN!' says April. 'OPEN YOUR EYES WHEN YOU PAINT.'

I realise I've been closing my eyes as I do the lines so I won't see myself painting in grey. Priya giggles.

'You guys are so funny,' she says.

I do as April says for the rest of the outline, even though my heart is beating very fast. It was good advice, though, because it turns out painting *is* a lot easier if you can see what you're doing.

Miss Ruiz says we'll be packing up in two minutes. April has finished hers, and Priya abandoned her egg-carton castle as soon as April arrived so she could watch what she was doing. They help me finish off the last of the lines, and then Miss Ruiz helps the three of us cart the massive, soggy pieces of paper over to the drying rack to dry.

'We'll cut them out at next art club,' April tells Miss Ruiz.

We were working so fast we didn't have time for any of the custard creams Miss Ruiz had put out, so she says we could each take a handful for the way home. Priya takes a handful too, and Miss Ruiz says, 'Not you, Priya! You've been scoffing them all club!'

Priya waggles her tongue at Miss Ruiz, like a mini April.

'I didn't see that,' she smiles. 'Now, go on, off with you, you raggedy bunch! Out you go!' she says, herding us to the door and shutting us out of the room.

I look back through the window in the door and see her walk over to the paint wall. For the first time ever, I wonder what Miss Ruiz does when we're not around.

*

Mum is hiding under her duvet on the sofa when I get home.

I know I should eat something, but the sight of her there when I've just used grey paint makes me feel all wrong. I start to think, was it my fault? Did I make it happen? But then I remind myself that that's magical thinking, and I am not a superhero. I cannot control events.

If I try to make something to eat I'll probably get stuck at the fridge – opening and closing it over and over, and not being able to find food that will make

Mum OK. Dinesh would say that I'm acting like I have superpowers about things that aren't actually in my control. And it made so much sense when I was in the yellow room.

I accept I'm not a superhero.

So I don't have to act like I am.

It feels different now, though, seeing Mum like this, and I can't help thinking: but *what if?*

I don't want to look at Mum on the sofa, so I traipse up to my room. I open and shut the door four times, even though I know I'm not supposed to.

I've been on my bed reading my comic for thirty-three minutes, when I hear the door slam and Kyle's footsteps on the stairs.

'Hey, are you OK?' he says, poking his head round the door.

'Yeah,' I say, without looking up. 'Why wouldn't I be?'

'Because Mum's –' I can tell he's rubbing his face hard, and that he's annoyed – 'doing her space-cadet thing and you're in bed and it's still early.'

'It's fine.'

'Fine?'

'Well, it's pretty normal for her. I thought it *wasn't your problem.*'

Kyle doesn't say anything for a bit, and I try hard to look like I'm reading.

'Have you eaten anything?' he asks.

I shake my head.

'Come on, I'll take you to KFC. My treat.'

'Cool,' I say, placing my comic under my pillow and grabbing my hoodie from the chair.

Mum doesn't stir when we walk past the sitting room. I try to be good and not do the stepping thing on the street because I know Kyle taking me to get food is a treat and I don't want to annoy him, but I still do it once just to make sure Mum will be OK. Kyle keeps walking and doesn't say anything, and I jog to catch up.

KFC is a couple of blocks away, on the high street, between the post office and this other weird shop that sells everything from plastic old-lady wheelie shoppers to carrots and lightbulbs. It has a sign outside that says *EVERYTHING UNDER FIVE POUNDS!* which is a lie because I can also see a pink plastic garden chair in the window with a luminous yellow tag on it that says £6.99 in black marker pen. I start to tell Kyle this but usually he doesn't find this sort of thing very interesting, so I stop. We walk in to KFC and Kyle goes up to the counter and orders us a ten-piece chicken bargain bucket. We sit at a plastic red table with four white chairs, and Kyle has six pieces and I have four. I eat every bit, apart from the hard fatty white knotty bits, and then I lick the bones until they are all shiny and clean.

I realise we haven't been talking, just munching, and it's nice and everything, but I start to think that if only I could make good conversation then maybe we could get on better and Kyle might take me out more often. I think about what April would do. She would probably make some jokes, but I am not very good at making jokes. She'd ask Kyle something about himself.

'Um, so how's things at the arcade?' I say.

Kyle looks like he's going to choke on his fries, and raises an eyebrow. 'Have you been taking a social skills class?' he asks warily.

'No,' I say. 'Just interested.' Offhand, like April.

''S OK,' he says, chewing. 'Got a new manager who's a bit of a nightmare. Always wanting to check exactly how much money is in the till at close – to the penny!'

I look at him blankly. To me this sounds like a very sensible request.

'Before we used to just look at all the pennies and make a guess,' he explains. 'Now I have to count every one, two, five, ten and twenty p – and there are *hundreds* of the things.'

'*Total* bummer,' I say.

Kyle is giving me a weird look and I don't understand what it means.

'How's theraaaapy?' asks Kyle in an American accent.

'Fine. Helpful,' I say, hoping Kyle asks me something else quickly, because Kyle is probably the last person on the planet I want to talk to about therapy. He already thinks I'm enough of a freak.

'Been talking about your *mummy issues?*'

'My *what*?'

'Mummy issues – you know, that's why people always go to therapy in films – "oh, your mother, she just didn't care, she made you feel so *bad*, and that's why you're all muddled *inside*," etcetera, etcetera.'

My throat starts going all scratchy. I stare hard at my food and see a tear plopping on to my chicken bones. I realise it's mine and grab a paper napkin and pretty much punch myself in the face with it.

'Oh, Benny, I'm sorry – I didn't mean to . . . oh, god.' Kyle rubs his forehead like a stressed cartoon character. 'I was just messing with you. Oh, please don't cry, mate.'

'No, I'm fine, I'm fine.'

'No,' sighs Kyle. 'It was wrong of me. I just get so annoyed when Mum is a jerk. Well, and Dad too, actually.'

Now it's Kyle's turn to look down – he is shredding his paper napkin ferociously under the table.

'I actually don't even know if Mum told Dad I'm going to therapy.' I sniffle. 'Have you heard anything from him? From Dad?'

Kyle shakes his head sadly. 'Not really. I texted him a few days after he left and told him he was a douchebag for just going without saying anything. He replied all formal, like, "You're understandably upset, but I thought it would be easier if you heard it from your mother. I felt, on balance, that you might be too angry to hear from me. I had asked her to explain the situation." *Blah, blah, blah.* Right, like Mum's going to explain anything to us. *On balance*,' he sneers. 'They're just cowards. The both of them.'

'What *is* the situation?' I ask, not sure I'm going to like the reply.

'The *situation* is that Dad finally got fed up of Mum drinking. So he doesn't want to live with her any more. They're having a *break*. Unfortunately for us, we can't do that yet.'

I want to tell him it's not unfortunate, that *I*

213

want to live with Mum, and for Dad to come back too, but I feel like it's not something we're going to agree about, so I just nod.

'Yeah,' he says, seeming relieved that I don't want to talk more about it. 'It's a mess. Hey, we could go to the arcade if you like?'

'What, now?'

'Yeah, if you want. We could play on some of the machines.'

'OK,' I say. 'But I don't know if I'll play anything. I might just watch.'

Kyle says that's fine, and we stack our trays on the tray shelves and I don't even move my tray into the perfect position that makes everything OK between Mum and Dad because I don't want to annoy Kyle and make him rethink the arcade. The arcade is a few shops down, and as we go in the bouncer on the door looks me up and down and says, 'Over eighteens only,' but Kyle winks and says, 'He's with me, mate,' and the guy shrugs like, *Oh, go on then*, which doesn't make sense because even Kyle is only sixteen, but they probably have special rules for people who work there.

Kyle has some change in his pocket, and he slides two pounds into the slot for the machine where you pull three levers to try and get pictures of all the same fruits. Kyle gets pear, banana, strawberry, and strawberry, apple, apple. Then he says it's my turn. I don't want to pull only three levers but I really, *really* want to make Kyle happy, and I also remember that I am supposed to be challenging myself, so I think, *What would April do?*

So Kyle puts another two-pound coin in and I close my eyes and pull the levers and when I open them the machine is making lots of *ding-ding* happy noises, and I see three raspberries all lined up, and money is flying out of the bottom of the machine.

'Yaaas!' yells Kyle. 'Yaaaas, my man!' He goes for a high-five and I don't even miss. The security guard looks over and tells us to *shh*, but he has this teeny-tiny smile on his big broad face.

Kyle says what do I want to do now, and I say we should go home and put the money somewhere safe, and Kyle laughs and says we will always be very different. Then he spends *ALL* of the money having goes on the different machines, and he says I have to do them all too, the ones with treasure and rainbows and four-leaf clovers, because I am lucky. Kyle does them once, and then I close my eyes and do them all too.

And what happens is we lose all the money.

And I don't even really mind.

3.3

Back in the yellow room, Dinesh asks me how I've been. I'm exhausted from school today. It feels like this has been the longest week ever, and Michelle and her gang were sniggering behind our desks all day. April tries to look like she doesn't care, but I know she does. Plus, Mr Montague reminded us that it's non-school uniform day tomorrow and to bring in a small donation if we can (to raise money for our school charity). I'm worried everyone is going to think my clothes are boring and weird if I show up in black jeans and a big baggy white T-shirt.

I want to tell Dinesh about the *FREAKS* note, but I also don't want him to think I'm a loser. I've been excited about my breakthrough in the arcade, so I decide I'll start there today.

'Pretty good – I wanted to tell you that I went to the arcade with Kyle and played on a game that only had three levers.'

'Amazing!' Dinesh grins. 'What was it like?'

'Hard. I was worried something bad was going to happen. But I wanted us to have fun. And then we played even more games after that.'

I try not to look too pleased with myself when I say this. So that maybe Dinesh will think I'm just a regular kid, and my big brother thinks I'm cool enough to hang out with him. 'Yeah,' I could say. 'We, like, hang out all the time.' But that would be a lie.

Dinesh says it's amazing that I was able to challenge my fours at the arcade. He says that if I want to get better, that's exactly what I need to do: keep challenging compulsions and finding out what happens.

'Maybe,' he says, 'we could do something with the colours, since you already had a go with the grey paint. Do you think you could try using different coloured bowls to eat this week, maybe wearing some different coloured T-shirts, and not avoiding using things if they're the "wrong" colour? What do you think?'

'I think that sounds . . . scary. But OK.' Then I have an idea: 'We actually have a non-uniform day at school tomorrow – I could maybe start then?'

I have no idea why I am volunteering this information. It's *almost* like I want to make my life as hard as possible.

Dinesh grins and says that sounds like a great idea. I guess there's no turning back now, because our session is over before I know it – Dinesh is saying he can't wait to hear how the T-shirt challenge goes, and walks me back to the waiting room to find Mum.

Mum asks me how it went and I say, 'Fine.' I think it might even be true, because I'm feeling pretty good when I'm on the bus with her on the way back, but then I realise that I'm not sure I'll be able to do the challenge tomorrow, because all my T-shirts are black and white. Mum stopped trying to buy me any other coloured ones years ago, when she realised I was never going to wear them.

Part of me feels relieved: well, I simply can't do the challenge then. But part of me . . . was sort of excited about the challenge. Like I wanted to do it? I could borrow some of Kyle's, but I'm sure he'd get annoyed. Also, most of his stuff is kinda big . . .

'Why so serious, Benny? What are you thinking about?' asks Mum, stroking my hair behind my ear.

I don't say anything.

'Was it something about your session?'

'Sort of,' I mumble.

'Was there something that was hard to talk about?'

I shake my head. 'Not really.' I am thinking, I could tell Mum about the T-shirt problem. She might know what to do. But then Mum will know that I'm supposed to challenge compulsions rather than go along with them if I want to get better.

And Mum always lets me give in to my compulsions because she thinks it's for the best. And if she knows what I know now, then she'll stop doing that . . .

But I think I must be getting a bit stronger against the brain bully, because I hear myself saying, 'Dinesh set me a challenge: to wear different coloured T-shirts. Not just black and white. But . . . I haven't got any and I didn't tell him that and now I don't know what to do.'

'But wouldn't that just make you really stressed? Wearing a "bad" colour?'

'Dinesh says . . . that the way for me to get better is to challenge the things I'm scared of. Until I'm not scared of them any more. That doing all the stuff according to my rules only makes the stuff stronger.'

Mum is silent. Maybe she didn't understand what I was saying.

'But . . . but I always thought it was *better* to go along with your rules. That that would make you less stressed,' she says quietly. 'Oh, Benny, I feel like I can't do anything right.'

Mum being sad makes me feel all funny inside, and I feel my eyes instinctively start to flick round the corners of the bus ceiling. I wish I was better at making her happier.

'I know!' she says, sitting upright and dinging the bell for the bus to stop, even though we are nine stops away from our house. The bus comes to a halt with a lurch, because we were only a few metres from the stop. The bus driver shakes his head and tells Mum not to stop the bus two seconds before the stop if she doesn't want to cause an accident. But Mum isn't listening; she's practically dragging me off the bus.

'Shopping trip!' she says, marching me across the road to the massive red-block and turquoise arches of the Lewisham shopping centre. Shopping centres are my kryptonite. So many colours and decisions to make. Even when Mum asks me to get something in the supermarket I end up picking up and putting down items so many times. I'm always sure that *that* bunch of bananas will be the one that makes the world end . . . She's stopped asking me now.

Mum heads for the boys' section in H&M. She says we will buy four new T-shirts, and then she looks confused and says, 'Or, wait, maybe we need to buy five? If we have to challenge this thing?'

And I say, 'Yeah . . . I guess.'

'OK,' says Mum, nodding fast and flicking through the T-shirt rails. 'See anything you like?'

She picks out a top that says *SK8 CREW*, which makes no sense because I've never skateboarded, and another one with an arrow that says *TO THE BEACH*, which also makes no sense, since we live in London now. There are ones that say *EPIC VIBES 4EVER* and *PEACE OUT*. The sort of tops Kyle could maybe get away with, but definitely not me.

I feel a bit sick, because I know that even if I choose a T-shirt and pick it up, I'll probably worry that it's not the right one and have to search for a few others in the same size and spend ages making and unmaking my decision. I'll walk away and think, *Finally, it's over*, but then my tummy will lurch and The Thoughts will say, *What if . . .* and I'll have to go back again . . .

There's a *Super Mario* top I quite like, even though the shirt itself is blue. I also like this other one that starts orange and fades into white, which has little green cactuses on it. Then there's a pack of three BASICS – a red, blue and green shirt: anger, sadness and vegetables.

Dinesh said the best thing to do in this situation is to make one decision, stick by it and walk away, even if your head is screaming to go back, and that in time you'll feel OK again . . .

I decide to grab them all once in my size, give them to Mum and not look back.

'Go!' I say, flinging five T-shirts at her. 'To the till!' I'm hot and freezing at the same time. My fingers are tingling like they're numb with cold, but I can feel my shirt sticking to my lower back with sweat.

We both rush over to the till. My brain is SCREAMING to go back and change them, but I tell myself, *Wait it out, wait it out*.

The guy at the till rings up the shirts: 'Fifty-three pounds.'

Firstly, not a multiple of four; secondly, *very* expensive.

'What will Dad say?' I whisper, pointing at the flashing turquoise digits on the reader. I immediately feel like I've been punched in the stomach, because I remember Dad isn't around to say anything. Mum gives me a weird, kind of sad, look.

'Sorry,' I whisper. She squeezes my shoulders and gives the man behind the till a too-wide grin. He takes Mum's card and passes me the T-shirts in a large white paper bag.

'I love *Super Mario* too,' he says with a smile.

'Ice cream, Benny boy?' asks Mum.

'OK,' I say. We leave H&M and head towards the ice-cream parlour. Mum is holding the bag. As we walk along the main part of the shopping centre, I feel a teeny bit better about the shirts than I did in the shop. By the time we get to the parlour, I feel another teeny bit better. It's still there while I'm eating my four small scoops of salted caramel ice cream in a pot, with chocolate sauce, chocolate buttons, sprinkles and whipped cream, and while Mum eats her three chocolate scoops, and I am thinking: maybe I can do this.

But you haven't had to actually put them on yet, say The Thoughts. *That will be when something bad happens.*

'I'm very proud of you, my love,' says Mum.

I don't know what to say, so I just keep eating my ice cream.

'Thank you for my new T-shirts,' I say eventually, and she ruffles my hair. And then, maybe because I'm feeling pretty proud of myself for picking all those T-shirts and actually making it out of the shop with them, I ask something I've been wanting to know since the first time we ever went to see Dinesh.

'Does Dad know – you know – about me having

OCD? And . . . going to therapy for it?'

Mum takes another spoon of ice cream and chews it slowly (who chews ice cream?), playing for time, probably.

'No,' she finally says, quietly. 'I haven't told him.'

I feel my stomach sink – because even though I've been embarrassed and worried about what Dad would say if he knew, I think I also sort of . . . want him to know? Cos I've been working really hard – challenging the annoying things I do, like he always used to go on about.

Maybe if he knew I was getting better, he'd be more likely to come back. Maybe he'd even be, you know, proud.

'Why not?' I say, trying not to sound too annoyed.

Mum sighs. 'I guess . . . I guess I thought he might blame me – for you struggling. I mean – sometimes *I* blame me. For not being a good mum.'

'You *are* a good mum,' I say fiercely – which surprises me a bit, since, yeah, I love Mum, but she hasn't exactly been a normal mum. Whatever that would look like. She shakes her head sadly, prodding at the dregs of her ice cream with her small plastic spoon.

'You *are*,' I repeat.

*

I wake up with a terrible feeling in my stomach –
like some creature in my belly is trying to claw its
way out.

And then I remember: the T-shirts.

Today I am going to wear a different coloured
T-shirt to school.

I open the door to my cupboard, where Mum
helped me hang the five new T-shirts up last night.

I'd decided I would just grab the one nearest to
me, but the nearest one is red! The one I'm most
scared of wearing. I guess at least if I wear that one
first then nothing after can be so scary.

I reach in and grab it. I put it on and try to
breathe like a normal human and not do the gulpy
thing. I stare at myself in the mirror. It doesn't
look too bad. Maybe even looks good? But then I
hear The Thoughts:

*If you wear this top, Mum and Dad will be
angry with each other for ever, and Dad will never
come back.*

I pull it off over my head before I can even think
what I'm doing. It's next to me, crumpled on the
floor. I sit still and breathe hard, pressing my teeth
into my knees so deep they make deep angry marks.

225

I have never wanted and not wanted to do something so much.

Come on, I tell myself. *You're not a superhero. You have no control over anything Mum and Dad do. What would Dinesh say?*

Wear the top, Ben.

I slowly put it back on. This time instead of looking in the mirror I get out of the room as soon as possible. Kyle is eating cornflakes and checking his Snapchat at the table in the kitchen, and I think Mum is still asleep. I also think she might have told him about the T-shirt challenge, and not to say anything, because usually he just says, 'Morning,' or nothing at all, but today he looks at me for a little bit longer than usual and smiles a tiny bit, and normally Kyle doesn't smile before midday.

The Thoughts are screaming to go back and change.

Instead I grab a BLUE bowl and fill it with Coco Pops. My hands are shaking and I spill the milk a bit. But it's OK, I've done it, and somehow I manage to sit and eat it. And by the time I get to the end it doesn't feel quite so bad. In fact, I feel, kind of . . . powerful? It's weird.

I grab my TARDIS backpack and head for the door. Kyle follows me into the corridor and grins.

'Mum told me not to make a huge deal about it, but it looks good, mate.'

Now MY FACE is red too. I'm happy Kyle likes it. It actually makes me feel better about the whole thing. I just don't know what to say. I give him a thumbs-up and set off for school. I turn around to head back home and change the T-shirt a few times on the journey, but each time I manage to make myself start walking back to school again.

I'm running late now, and I get into the classroom as Mr Montague is halfway through the register.

I spot April immediately; she's wearing a long black dress with the same boots she always wears. She's staring at me, her mouth wide open in surprise. It's funny, because at that moment I realise that's exactly the kind of reaction I wanted.

'Whoa,' she whispers as I take my place next to her. 'Rock on!'

*

I pass Kyle and a group of his friends in the corridor on the way to Music Room 4 at lunch break. I think he might smile at me, or even say, 'Hey, bro,' given how I know he's impressed with me for wearing the scary shirt, *and* now he can see I've actually made it to lunch break, but he doesn't even look at me.

'Wasn't that your brother?' says April.

'Yup,' I say.

'Why didn't he . . .' But she trails off, watching Kyle put his arm round high-ponytail girl, like she answered her own question before she could get to the end of it. I suppose it was silly of me to think that wearing a different colour would be enough to make Kyle acknowledge me in public. *Dream on, Benny.*

'How does it feel?' April says when we make it to Music Room 4, and she's pulling a bag of Doritos out of her backpack for us to share. For a horrible second I think she wants to have a heart-to-heart about Kyle ignoring me, but then she gestures at my T-shirt and I realise that what she means is how it feels to be wearing a scary colour.

'Well . . .' I say, thinking about it. 'It's weird – I can't believe I'm saying this, but I actually keep forgetting.'

The more I think about this, the stranger it seems – I wouldn't have believed I could 'forget' about anything this scary. But somehow it really is happening. Throughout the morning, every time I realised I'd forgotten, I'd get stressed, but then I'd forget again eventually. Even the time when I *tried* to keep remembering it, something came along to distract me.

For instance, I finished the sheet of algebra questions Mr Montague had handed out, and it was only when I got to the end that I thought, *Oh, shoot, I forgot I'm wearing the T-shirt*. And then when he was explaining simultaneous equations on the board, he made a mistake and I thought, *He's got that wrong*. A few seconds later he said, 'Sorry, I mean X = -4, not 4,' and then he WINKED at me, like he knew I would know, but didn't publicly out me as a geek. I don't think anyone noticed, so I kind of liked it, and then I thought, *OH, SHOOT, THE T-SHIRT*. But the fact that I had that thought meant I had forgotten about it . . .

In our final class of the day, April draws all kinds of Hindu god incarnations all the way through the lesson. It's like she wants Mrs Williams to see her drawing and get cross. I swear, sometimes April *tries* to get in trouble. I nudge her and tell her to stop, but she ignores me. Miraculously Mrs Williams hasn't noticed yet.

Then I think, *OH, SHOOT, SHOOT, THE T-SHIRT*, and I realise I've gone for about half the lesson without thinking about it.

Mrs Williams drones on and on, and RS seems never-ending. I'm thinking about how it's weird that sometimes, like in Mr Montague's maths class, or art club, an hour can whizz by in a flash, and other times an hour can feel like a whole day, even though it's the same amount of time. If I had a time machine like the Doctor I would definitely NEVER stick around for RS.

Finally, Mrs Williams sets us homework ('Summarise chapters five–ten of the textbook,' WHICH IS FORTY-EIGHT PAGES OF TINY TEXT WITH NOT MANY PICTURES) and says we can pack up for the day.

April has been desperate for the day to be over since the moment she walked in the door so that we can get to art club and finish our outfits, so her stuff is packed up and ready to go. She stands up slightly before me and as she turns round to grab her grey knit cardigan off the back of the chair, I see a luminous flash of a yellow Post-it note on her back, and my stomach gets the slimy slug feeling.

She walks to the door ahead of me and I get a clearer view of it:

KICK ME.

Phew. That's not actually that bad. Just the most uninventive and predictable Post-it note a kid can write. I'm not sure why I expected any more from Michelle and her crew.

I don't think April will be too upset by it, but I want her to be in a good mood since she's been so excited about finishing our outfits. I also don't want Priya to see it, because then she'll know that April gets teased. I have this quite strong feeling that that would embarrass April so much she might do something really stubborn, like never come back to art club.

Without really thinking about it, I reach out and whip it off her as quick as possible. I cough at the exact moment I pull it so she doesn't hear the sticky rip noise. I scrunch it up and put it in my pocket.

Sorted. Michelle is ANNOYING.

We're the first people to art club, and April pulls our giant sheets of paper off the drying rack and takes them over to the table. We draw these little white tab things sticking out of the shoulders and legs – these are the bits that secure the outfit to the paper doll. April says we are going for 'realism', which means making something look as real as possible. Cutting the outfits out only takes ten minutes, and then we just have to glue some string

231

to the waist and neck parts of the outfits, so that we can secure them to our bodies.

We're finished so quickly there's still forty-two minutes left of art club, and Priya says since we've finished our project, pretty please can we draw round her and Maisie and help them make their own paper doll outfits so they can wear them for Halloween too? I'm pleased Priya's asked, because I'm thinking about my T-shirt again and I really, *really* need something to distract me from it. April's all, 'Ugh, what an effort, can't you do it yourself?' but I can tell she likes it really.

April says we should take the outfits back to my house so that we can get ready for the disco there together. I don't want April to come over: she's been trying to get another invite ever since the sleepover. She keeps saying how much fun she had and how awesome it is I have such a cool mum (which is weird, because I've *never*, not once, thought of Mum as cool).

And it's annoying, because, yes, Mum was on good form that one time she came over, but the whole point is I never know what Mum's going to be like on a certain day, as evidenced by the last few days. And I'd rather it was like: cool, April has met my mum, she knows she's nice enough, and she can just carry on thinking of her that way.

If she comes over again then obviously I have to risk her seeing . . . Other Mum. And what if she stays over again and starts to wonder what's happened to Dad? Not that her parents are exactly around much. I tell April we should get ready at hers: it will be way cooler because her parents probably won't be there and we'll have the whole place to ourselves.

'That's not cool. That's just lonely,' April says. 'And anyway school is twenty-five minutes from my house, whereas your house is just down the road. And we're not going to get the bus with our Victorian paper dolls, are we?'

It's annoying, but a good point.

'Fine,' I say, because it's not like I've ever won an argument with April anyway, and I guess it *is* usually pretty boring when it's just me and Mum all evening. And it's true that April does tend to be quite good at distracting me from my head.

We walk back to mine with the dolls tucked under our arms.

The closer we get, the more I feel like my throat's going to start doing the gulpy thing.

I'm wearing a scary T-shirt. I'm wearing A SCARY T-SHIRT.

The house is dark when we get in. Oh, no.

'Isn't your mum home?' asks April.

'I don't know,' I squeak. I step into the sitting room and see a blanket mound on the sofa. I whirl round, trying to take April back into the kitchen, but it's too late: April has flipped the light on.

The blanket mound starts to rise, like a sleeping sea monster waking. At the foot of the monster is a bottle, on its side, empty.

I see Mum squinting in the bright light, rubbing the sleep out of her eyes. And I see the vein in her forehead start to throb like an angry snake as her confusion turns to rage.

It's all my fault. I caused it by wearing red, the colour of anger and fighting.

The following conversation occurs:

APRIL: 'Oh, hello, Leila. How are you?'

MUM (slurring): 'Why're you in my house?'

APRIL: 'I'm dropping off our Halloween costumes.'

MUM: 'Getout, what's ya name . . . June . . . this is my house.'

April drops the costumes and whispers, 'Oh,' and, 'I'm sorry.' When our eyes meet I can tell she really is, and also that she finally understands everything.

April is down the stairs and I hear the front door slam before Mum can even get to her incoherent next sentence – something about no guests on Wednesdays, even though it's Friday – out of her mouth.

I'm so upset with Mum I just leave her there and go upstairs to my room. I open and shut my door sixteen times, and then I stop, wondering why I'm even bothering, because Dinesh is right, it clearly doesn't work. It doesn't stop bad things happening. Otherwise Mum wouldn't behave the way she does. And Dad would still be here.

I lie on my bed, feeling sticky in my red T-shirt. I want to go and open and shut the door more, just for something to do that might make me feel a bit better, but I resist the urge. I also just feel too sad to move. I hope April will still want to be my friend.

My phone pings.

IM SO SORY BEN I SHLDNT HAV COME OVER WHN U DIDNT WANT ME 2

I can't think of a way to tell April what I feel using only four- or eight-letter words, so I send her four sad-face emojis.

R U ANGRY WIV ME?

Nope

SHE LIKE THAT LOTS?

Yeah

WHOA.

I don't say anything back. I'm not angry with April. I do wish she hadn't come over today, but I know she didn't mean for anything like this to happen. She just didn't know. Why would she? No other mums seem to be like my mum. My phone pings again.

POOR YOU ☹

I decide I don't want to talk to April any more. I just want to go to sleep and wake up and for this all to be a horrible dream. I turn off my phone and switch off the light. Good night, world.

3.4

I wake up and for a few wonderful seconds I forget about last night. And then I remember.

I also realise the reason I've woken up is because my door has opened, and Mum has padded in and is standing by my bed.

I roll over. I definitely do not want to talk to her. She crouches down and strokes my head. I swat her hand away. I don't even feel bad.

'Benny . . .' she starts. Her voice is shaking. She's nervous, like a child in trouble. 'Did April come over last night?'

I don't reply.

'It's just . . . I think I remember her being here. But I . . . don't remember properly.'

I'm not going to help her. If she can't remember, then lucky her, because I do, and I wish I didn't.

'I think I might have . . . said some mean things . . . but I'm not sure. It's fuzzy.'

'IT'S FUZZY BECAUSE YOU WERE DRUNK.'

Mum jumps back from the bed. It's not a word I've ever heard said out loud in front of her before.

'You told her to get out of our house, and now I'm telling you to get out of my room.'

'Benny, I'm sorry, I'm so sorry, I—'

'You're always "sorry"! But you're not, not really, because if you truly were then you would DO SOMETHING about it.'

Mum nods and rushes out of the room, hunching over herself, like Bumble when we tell him off for eating something he shouldn't and he tries to make himself smaller and runs off.

Well, good. I don't care.

I turn my phone on and see one new message from April, sent twenty-two minutes ago, at 8.35 a.m.

MY HOUSE 2DAY? I CAN COME GET U ON THE BUS IF U LIKE?

The idea of staying home with Mum is unthinkable. I send back:

☺☺☺☺

She replies two minutes later.

GR8. ILL COME GET YA.

I pull the orange T-shirt with the cactuses out of my cupboard and pull it over my head. Then I have the thought: *Changing my T-shirt made Mum bad yesterday.*

I pull the T-shirt off. And then I try and tell myself to get real. *Stuff it, Mum's wobbly all the time and it does not depend on what T-shirt I wear. She's been like this since I can remember, and I've been wearing black-and-white T-shirts since I can remember, and it didn't change a thing.*

I put the T-shirt back on. But I'm shaking, and I know: I can't do it.

I find a black T-shirt and go downstairs. Dinesh would want me to 'experiment' and use a funny coloured cereal bowl. But I don't even attempt that one. I eat breakfast out of my usual yellow bowl.

I flick my eyes round the room twenty-eight times while repeating in my head: *Mum will be fine, Mum will be fine, Mum will be fine, Mum will be fine.*

April texts me while I'm brushing my teeth:
OUTSIDE
I notice that she doesn't ring the doorbell.

It takes me sixteen attempts at going up and down the stairs for it to feel right enough for me to leave, and so I'm covered in a cold sweat and feeling dirty before I've even left the house.

April is loitering a couple of doors down rather than swinging on the gate like Usual April. I guess she's scared of Mum now. Can't say I blame her.

Before I can say anything, she says:

'We're going to the Peckhamplex. We're going to see *Toy Story 4*. In 3-D. My treat. And I'm going to get us a large mix of salty and sweet popcorn and Coke combo, also my treat.'

'You don't have to—'

'I know. But I want to.'

'Um, OK.'

We have to get two trains to get to Peckham. April doesn't say much on the train to Catford Bridge, apart from reminding me to look out for the Peckhamplex sign when we get there (apparently it's in pink graffiti writing that's somehow jagged and bubbly *at the same time* — April wants to learn how to do it). So I think maybe I've escaped the conversation about What Happened With Mum, and to be honest, I'm relieved. But then on the second train from Catford to Peckham Rye, April turns to me and before she even opens her mouth I know that, uh oh, we're having it, right here, right now.

When most people are going to say something serious, they ease into it. Like, maybe they make some small talk, ask you how you are today, and then maybe they even warn you that they're about to tell you something serious. But April doesn't do that. She just delivers what she wants you to know, as it is. I guess I quite like that. I do really suck at small talk.

Anyway, she just dives right in with:

'Your mum is an alcoholic.'

I'm not sure I've ever heard this word said out loud. I've found it, online, when I've asked Google the things I need to know about my mum. Nine letters, four syllables:

alcoholic

/alkəˈhɒlɪk/

1. a person suffering from alcoholism.
synonyms: drunk, drunkard, heavy/hard/ serious drinker, problem drinker . . .

I don't say anything.

'How long has she been like that?'

'A long time,' I say quietly, like a cartoon mouse.

'What does your dad think?'

'He thinks . . . He thinks . . .' I stare hard at the ground, scuffing my toes against each other in fours and wishing I'd just told her about it all from that start. 'Well, actually he left because of it all about five weeks ago. He's staying with his brother.'

April gives me a look which I think means, *I can't believe you didn't tell me this before, and it's a good thing you've got so much going on right now otherwise you would be so dead.*

'I can't *believe* you didn't tell me about this before,' says April. 'He just . . . left? Is he coming back?'

I shrug. *Scuffety, scuff, scuff, scuff.*

'Have you told Dinesh? About the drinking?'

'No.'

'Are you going to?'

'Maybe. I don't know.'

'You need to think about it carefully.'

'Why?'

'If you tell Dinesh, he'll have to tell social services. And they'll have to take you away from your mum.'

I gasp. 'April! Why would you say something so horrible?'

Honestly, I really feel like if one more stressful thing happens, my brain will explode.

She sighs, in that way she does when she's frustrated that I don't get something she thinks is totally obvious.

'It might be horrible, but it's true. Once you tell a responsible adult, they have to tell social services, and once social services know, they have to separate you from your mum, at least until she can parent again responsibly.'

'She *can* parent responsibly!'

April raises an eyebrow. 'Can she?'

I think about all the missed meals, the shouting, and then just the hours of lost time – when her body is there, on the sofa, but *she* isn't, not *my* mum.

And then I have a weird thought: do I *want* to get taken away from Mum? I mean, it would be nice, maybe, for a bit, not to have to worry about her . . . all the time. But at the same time, she's *my mum*. I need her.

'OK, it's like this. If you want to be taken away from your mum – and I know she's your mum, but no one would blame you, you're just a kid – then you should tell Dinesh. If you don't, then you should never ever tell Dinesh. No matter what. So it's actually quite simple, really. Except that it isn't.'

This is very brand-new information. I never knew I even had the power to get taken away from my mum.

'How do you even know all of this?' I ask.

'Netflix,' she says, totally seriously.

I tell her I don't know what I want, and she says,

she knows it's hard, but guess what, we don't have to think about it for a few hours, because our train is pulling into Peckham Rye and *Toy Story 4* is going to be awesome.

And the popcorn is cheap, so we can always get another bucket if we want it.

*

Toy Story 4 was good, but I couldn't concentrate that hard because I was thinking about the social services thing, and my eyes were going *flick, flick, flick, flick*, all round the cinema, rather than concentrating on the film.

When I get home I think about whether it would make a difference if Dad came back. Is that the issue, that they need another responsible adult around, or does Mum being drunk cancel out all the responsible adults around, even if there were ten of them? I wonder if April would know.

Maybe it wouldn't even matter. I don't even know what he's *doing* at Uncle Jay's house. I guess he's probably still going to work every day – or maybe he gave that up too? Uncle Jay's always lived on his own without a family – so maybe the two of them order pizza every day and play video games all night. Maybe he likes it way more there without the

244

stress of all of us, and he wouldn't come back even if social services wrote him a very serious letter telling him that he had to *right now*.

I continue to think about it for the next few days, and when I'm not thinking about it I'm opening and shutting my bedroom door in fours, or staring round and round my desk in fours if I'm at school, not able to take in a word Mr Montague says. I keep feeling like if I can just make everything feel right enough then maybe I will know exactly what to do, and everything will be OK.

When I see Dinesh on Thursday, I find myself worrying that I will just shout out: 'My mum is an alcoholic!' and 'I don't want to live with my mum!' even though I don't think I *want* to tell Dinesh about it, and I'm pretty sure I *do* want to live with her.

Dinesh says I look like I am worried about something. I don't say anything. He tries again: 'What are you worried about?'

'I used different coloured things, and I wore a red T-shirt,' I say quickly.

'Amazing!' says Dinesh, beaming, like he really means it. 'How did it go?'

I wore the red T-shirt and Mum got bad. I think I made it happen.

I don't know how much to tell him.

'Something bad happened, when I wore the red T-shirt.'

'What happened?'

'I . . . think . . . I made someone . . . mad.'

'Who?'

'Do I have to say?'

'No. Do you mean angry-mad or mad-mad?'

Both? Neither? I watch the yellow clock tick by sixteen seconds. 'I'm . . . not sure.'

'Can I ask, this person you made "mad" . . .' says Dinesh in a quiet voice I haven't heard him use before. 'Have you seen them "mad" before?'

I nod.

'And on those occasions were you wearing a red T-shirt? Or were you sticking to your rules and wearing black or white?'

'I would have been wearing black or white.'

'OK, well, let's look at this logically, since you seem like a pretty logical guy, Ben. It can't be that wearing red causes them to be angry, because previously this person has become angry even when you stuck to your rules. Therefore, would it not seem logical to conclude that this person may become angry whatever colour you wear, so wearing red would make no difference either way?'

I like it when Dinesh says things like 'therefore'

and 'it is logical to conclude' because it makes me feel like we are detectives trying to solve a mystery together, even though Kyle would say he talks like a dork.

'Well, that's kind of what I said to myself at the time. That she – this person – has been angry before even when I've stuck to wearing safe colours, so I guess I *can't* have superpowers,' I say.

'Correct,' says Dinesh, pretending to draw an invisible tick in the air with his pointer finger. 'Even if the thing we worry about happening happens when we are challenging a compulsion, it doesn't mean that it was us challenging the compulsion that made it happen. It just means that sometimes bad things really do happen: they're still not within our control.'

'OK,' I say.

'This person who got angry with you – do they get angry with you often?'

I shrug.

'Are you frightened when they get angry with you?'

You have to be careful what you say, April said. *If you don't want to get taken away. They'll ask you questions, like they're being nice and just want to get to know you, and then – BAM – before you know it, you're being taken away in a white van.*

I told her I think that's just for dogs when they go to the pound and not for actual children, and she shrugged and whispered all dramatically, 'Yeah, but do you really want to find out for sure?'

I thought about whether I *did* want to find out for sure, and really, I don't think I do.

Because even though living with Mum hurts, and sometimes I really *have* had the thought that I wish I didn't have to see her again, I *know* I love Mum more than I want to be away from her.

Which is why I look up and say to Dinesh, 'No, no, it's not like that.'

Even though the truth is I *am* very frightened. And I am wondering whether I really do want to challenge any of this OCD stuff, because Dinesh is making lots of good points that make total logical sense, but there's a part of me that says, *What if he's wrong?*

What if it really *is* my job to keep Mum safe and bring Dad back? And what if I'm the only one who can?

*

April is antsy at school all day on Friday, passing me urgent notes about whether I'm free after school, and throwing me looks I don't understand but that

248

seem to presume I'm in on 'The Plan'.

She keeps saying she's got something to show me that will cheer me up, but is apparently unable to offer any description as to the nature of this something. In art club, Miss Ruiz says that today is a 'freestyle' day, so you can make whatever you want with any available materials. Rhys is obviously still making his charcoal city, since he never does any of the themed stuff Miss Ruiz sets anyway, so it's always 'freestyle' day for him. April makes a voodoo doll of Mrs Williams. I just watch, because I'm really not feeling it, but also, I've been working up the courage to ask Rhys about Kyle for *weeks*, and I'm pretty sure if I don't just go ahead and do it, it's never going to happen.

Miss Ruiz has conveniently placed the biscuit tray in fairly close proximity to Rhys, so I pretend I'm just ambling over to grab a couple of custard creams, and slow my pace so it's like I'm cruuuuuising by — totally normal . . . nothing to see here! But Rhys looks over his shoulder and seems kind of surprised by how close I am, so I guess I haven't really pulled off the whole chilled-spontaneous-chat thing.

'What?' he asks, sounding a bit annoyed to be interrupted.

'Are you in Year Eleven?' I ask.

'Yeah,' Rhys sighs and restarts shading a spindly clock tower with a chunky charcoal stick.

'That's the same year as my brother.'

'Yeah.'

'Don't you want to know who he is?'

'Not really, but I guess you're going to tell me.'

'He's called Kyle Hardie. Do you know him?'

'I know him.' Rhys stops shading, then stares round back at me. 'Wait, Kyle's your *brother*?'

'Yeah!' I say hopefully. 'So . . . what's he like?'

'Honestly?' says Rhys, looking like he's just tasted something nasty. 'He's up himself – probably thinks I'm a loser like everyone else.'

'I don't,' I say, before I can stop myself. 'I think you're pretty cool actually. I mean . . . I wish I could draw like you and not care so much what anyone thinks of me.' I think maybe I've embarrassed him, because he turns away from me and back to his drawing. But then he gives a tiny laugh and says, 'Thanks, that actually means a lot.'

'Yeah,' I say, a little awkwardly, because he flips the paper round and starts attaching a bridge to the tower, and I immediately know he's not going to say anything else.

'Well . . .' I pocket a couple of custard creams. 'See ya.' Rhys grunts and I scuttle back to April, who restarts her whispering about this thing she wants to show me, but I'm finding it hard to listen because I'm distracted by the thought of Kyle not being friendly to Rhys – why does he always have to be so arrogant?

I probably should have tried a bit harder to listen to April at the same time as worrying about this, though, because by the time art club ends, apparently I've agreed to go 'there' (where?!) with her, even though I don't remember saying yes at any point. I also feel momentarily guilty about not going straight home to Mum, thinking, *What will happen if I'm not there tonight?*

But then I think about how mean Mum was to April, so I guess that's why I let her lead me towards a bus stop on the corner of the high street that I've seen but never used before.

April says we have to get two buses, and that we're going in the direction of New Cross, which is where she lived until she was eight. She doesn't say where we're going once we get there – she's being very secretive. On the bus she offers me a headphone and we listen to David Bowie, because she says that, firstly, he is inspiring and, secondly, I need to be musically educated. This music helps, but I still need to keep my eyes going round the four corners of the bus to distract me from The Thoughts. By the time we get to our stop on the second bus, David Bowie is singing about an astronaut called Major Tom going up into space. It's going well and everyone thinks he's awesome for going up there, but then the circuit dies and ground control can't get hold of him any more. I don't know what happened to Major Tom because April yanks the headphone out and rushes to the front to get off before the bus has even stopped. I'll ask Google when I get home.

We turn off the high street and walk down a long road. We go past a block of flats that looks pretty similar to where April lives now, and April points up and says that that's where they used to live. We take a cut-through path between that block and the one next to it, which takes us to the open wrought-iron gates of a small park. As soon as we go in April starts walking faster, dragging me along behind her. She's beaming and singing the song about Major Tom. To me it looks just like a regular London park with litter everywhere and a couple of teenagers snogging on a rusty climbing frame, but April is thrilled.

She wants to take a turn off the main tarmac path and on to a smaller mud one. It's already quite dark, and the street lamps stop once you go off the main path. Which is scary enough, but worse still, I've been counting the street lamps, and the turn-off to this smaller path is right by lamp number six – my ultimate bad number.

'Come on,' says April. 'Let's go.'

I want to be brave. I want to be brave for April like I've been before.

If you go down that path, Dad will never come home.

'No,' I say, shaking my head. 'I don't want to go down there.'

'What?' says April. 'Oh, come on. For me.'

Last time you tried to be brave, look what happened to Mum.

'No. It's . . . too dark. We might get lost. There might be someone bad in there. It's not safe.'

'I really want to show you. It's this place . . . where Thomas and I used to go.'

You'll get back home and Mum will be DEAD.

'No. I'm sorry. I can't.'

April kicks at the grass with her boot.

'But that's not the real reason, is it?'

'What?' I say, my voice coming out like a squeaky scratch.

'It's not because it's too dark. It's because something in your head says you can't.'

April stomps off ahead down the path. I don't want her to go. I don't want her to leave me here with The Thoughts.

'So what if it is?' I shout after her, trying to sound like I couldn't care less. Like my throat isn't burning. Like the tears in my eyes aren't making everything wobble. Like I'm *fine, fine, fine, fine.*

April turns round and stomps back.

'You need to sort it out. This thing in your head. It's stopping you doing things you want to do.'

'No, it's stopping me doing a thing *you* want to do.'

'OK, fine. But this thing is important to me, and you're my best friend, and that should mean something – it should mean more than these invisible rules. Anyway, a lot of the time it *does* stop you doing things you want to do. Normal things that every other kid gets to do without thinking about it – like wearing a red T-shirt. Don't you think that's really unfair?'

I don't say anything.

'I thought the whole point of you working on stuff with Dinesh is that you would be able to start doing stuff like this?'

'I think it . . . takes . . . time . . .' I say pathetically.

'Right. Well, it didn't take you very long to wear that red T-shirt. But this thing is important to me and all of a sudden that's where you draw the line?'

'April, please . . . You're being . . . like . . .'

'Like what? *Selfish*?' Her face is close to mine and she is shaking, even though I never used the word 'selfish'. 'Because for once I want things to be about me rather than *you*?'

I've never seen April like this, and I don't know what to do or say to make it stop.

'You're not the only one who finds things difficult, you know. Yeah, I know.' She puts her hand up, as if to stop me from whatever it is I might be going to say. 'Your dad's been gone a few weeks. Guess what? Thomas's been gone for *years*. If you could get out of your head long enough to be interested in anything other than your own problems, maybe you'd see that.'

It feels like I've been punched in the stomach. And, honestly, I think I would have preferred that. What I want to say is this: 'I know what it's like, maybe not completely, but definitely a bit. Because even though my brother's here, and we live together and everything, he's not really *here* here, if that makes sense. Sometimes I feel like I haven't seen him for years either. I know it hurts.'

But maybe then April will say I'm making it about me again. And maybe that would be true.

'I'm sorry,' is what say instead. But April is spinning around and starting to walk away, back down the path towards where we entered the park. I wonder if I should chase after her.

But something seems to be stopping my legs moving.

So I just stand there and watch her go, until I can't see her any more.

It takes me ages to get out of the park – I end up walking up and down the path sixteen times. I tell myself that if I can get my steps *just right*, then I can fix everything: Mum will be all right, and April will text me and tell me everything is OK.

When I finally do get out of the park and check my phone at the bus stop, there are no messages from April. I want to text her and sort things out. But it is very hard to resolve conflict using only four-letter words. So I hit *CALL APRIL*, even though I never call *anyone*, because I freak out too much about saying the wrong thing, and the idea of speaking to someone when I can't see their face gives me the creeps.

But it rings three times, and then she must have pressed reject, because it goes straight through to voicemail.

Hey, hey, heeeey! Welcome to April HQ. I can't take your call right now, but if your message is interesting enough, my butler may pass it along . . .

I hang up. I can't believe this. I always thought it would be Dad who got annoyed if I couldn't get better quickly enough. Or maybe Kyle. But *April*? No, no way. Never April.

I see the bus I need trundling down the road, but The Thoughts say: *That bus is unlucky.* So I don't put my arm up to stop it, and I wait twelve minutes for the next one. I let that one go too and then instantly regret it because the next one isn't for twenty minutes. But then that would be the third bus, so I end up waiting for the fourth because it's only another nine minutes away.

I am going to be very late home. Not like Mum will notice anyway.

I finally put my arm out for bus number four. I get on, and every time I try and sit down in a seat The Thoughts scream that sitting in that seat will bring about imminent doom: *April won't forgive you, Dad's never coming back, April hates you like Kyle hates you because you're a total freak, Mum is going to die—*

I'm hopping up and down the almost-empty bus like my bum is on fire, trying to find a seat that feels

257

OK. But none of them do, so I stand, and an old man and a couple of kids near the back of the bus are looking at me like I'm crazy.

Maybe I *am* crazy. I am covered in a sheet of sweat that is turning cold and making me shiver. I check my phone.

Nothing.

When I do get home, Mum is asleep on the sofa. Kyle isn't home yet. Of course.

I take myself upstairs. It takes me ages to get my pyjamas on and stop opening and shutting the door and pulling the blinds open and shut. Nothing I can do makes the room feel right so I count the walls until it starts getting light outside.

The weekend starts to crawl by, and April doesn't reply to any of my messages. I can't think of a single thing that I would like to do – and there seems to be so much time all of a sudden. My routines fill the hours – the compulsions are like a spilled liquid getting everywhere.

Why *do* liquids do that anyway? I wonder. Where do they get off always spreading out and trying to occupy as much of the space as possible?

I bet Mr M would know.

4

4.1

I wake up on Monday, and for one disorientated second, I feel almost OK.

But then I get a sinking sick feeling in my stomach, like when you know you've forgotten something important that you need, only you can't remember what.

And then I remember.

DAYS TO DISCO: FIVE (counting today)

I check my phone.

Messages from April: NONE

I *almost* want to pretend to be ill and skip school so I don't have to face April, but that would mean staying home all day, and I know I'll only drive myself mad wandering round my room checking and moving things.

So I try to tell myself it's just like any other day. I don't even attempt to challenge myself by not using my special bowl. It takes me a while to walk to school, but in the end I'm only actually two minutes late. Mr Montague hasn't even started taking the register yet.

Also: April isn't here yet. Maybe *she's* not going to come in. I don't really get the impression that her parents would be around to stop her.

But April comes through the door at 9.06 a.m. when Mr Montague is halfway through the register.

She doesn't sit next to me.

Instead, she walks to the back of the room and takes an empty desk a couple of seats away from Sophia, casually, with her eyes fixed ahead, like it's the most normal thing in the world for her not to sit next to me. Everyone is turning round to look at April, and then glancing back at me.

And now I feel a twinge of annoyance, because it feels like April is just *trying* to cause drama, and I really didn't think she was like that. My face is getting red and hot, and I stare hard at my pencil case, thinking, *Fine, April, have it your way.*

In physics, Mr Montague is explaining that during solar eclipses, the moon passes in front of the sun, causing temporary darkness during the day. Everyone wants to know when the next solar eclipse will be, so Mr Montague googles it. But it turns out the next one won't be until August 2026.

I will be seventeen by then. I wonder if April

will be talking to me.

At break time and lunch time, Music Room 4 feels like the loneliest place in the world. I keep checking my phone, which I know makes no sense because we've been in the same classroom all morning, and if April wanted to talk, then she would have sat next to me.

I can't write anything down in English (we are supposed to be doing a comprehension on a very boring article about local people campaigning for increased frequency of dustbin collection in their borough). There seems to be something wrong with even four-letter words.

For example, question one says: *What are the residents campaigning about?* I could technically write 'Bins', but that begins with the letter 'B' for bad and ends in the letter 'S' for sad. Worrying about letters making bad things happen as well as numbers is something I used to do when I first learned to write, but I stopped doing it years ago.

How can I be getting worse when I am supposed to be getting *better*?

Later that afternoon we have RS *followed* by history, and it feels as if the day can't get any worse, but then it does, because Mrs Williams tells April off for drawing again, and April tells *her* to 'bog off', and even Bradley is shocked.

April gets sent straight to the head teacher, Mrs Olowe, and blanks me when I try to catch her eye on the way out.

What is *up* with her?

Lauren corners me by the pegs when the lesson ends.

'What are you dressing up as for the Halloween disco, Ben?' she asks.

'Um . . . paper dolls,' I say instantly, before remembering that I wasn't supposed to tell anyone.

'Paper dolls?' says Lauren, sounding a bit confused.

'Um . . . like human size . . . it's a bit complicated. You'll see. It was April's idea.' I'm babbling. 'What, er, about you?'

'Oh . . . bunnies.' She rolls her eyes in the direction of Michelle and Aliya. 'You know the drill – they're cute apparently.' Wow. Maybe Lauren's not as bad as I thought.

I say this to April when I finally find her (by spending twenty-eight minutes hanging around the stop where she gets her bus home), and she scowls. 'Unless she's had a personality transplant overnight, trust me, she is.' Then she scowls even harder – I think she's annoyed with herself for slipping up and saying something to me.

'Maybe she has?' I say excitedly. 'Maybe she went to the Total Cow No More clinic and they did it there?' I giggle, trying to make April join in, but she doesn't. She stares hard at the flashing orange dots displaying the wait-time to her bus on the digital board and acts like I'm not there. I tolerate forty-eight seconds of this before I decide that even I have a threshold for awkwardness, and that it's time to head home.

'I'm not going to art club tomorrow!' she calls out after me, like she somehow couldn't have said that the whole time I was standing there.

Great, just great. Guess I won't go either then.

When I get back, it's just Mum at home. She's made my favourite: tuna on pasta, with sweetcorn and mayo. She says we can watch a film together if we like, but I shake my head angrily.

She tries to coax me into telling her what's wrong which makes me snap, 'Why would I tell you about my problems when you can't even solve your own?!'

She takes a step back, looking hurt. I immediately regret it but still feel too angry to apologise, so I take my food upstairs and slam the door to my room. But then I have to slam it another three times, which kind of lessens the whole 'impulsive kid having a strop' vibe that I was going for.

Another morning waking up feeling like I've given a dragon permission to live in my stomach.

My fingers tingle with all the things I want to touch to try and make stuff between me and April OK. To do stuff Dinesh says Really Just Makes Me Feel Worse.

I sit on my hands and try to concentrate hard on my ceramic planet mobile and absolutely nothing else. My phone bings.

OUTSIDE

I tap my feet on the floor sixteen times for luck and sprint down the stairs, but as soon as I open the front door I know April's not here to make up. She's lurking by the gate, scowling.

'I came for my costume,' she informs me darkly.

'Aren't we getting ready together?'

'No.'

'Do you still want me to dress up?'

She shrugs. 'Do what you like.'

'April . . . I really am sorry.'

She kicks at the weeds sprouting up by the gate.

'Everyone's always sorry. But nothing ever changes.'

I'm not entirely sure what she means by this. I

open my mouth to ask her how I can make it up to her, but she puts her hand out for me to be quiet.

'I really don't want to talk about it. My head's in a funk. Just give me my outfit, *please*.'

I nod and run back inside to get April's paper dress from under my bed. I feel my eyes sting and tell myself to just wait one more minute until I've given April her stupid outfit and got back to my room, so she doesn't see me cry.

I bring her dress down and she takes it and turns and walks off without another word.

I make it inside and shut the door before the tears start. Just. I wish I could talk to Dinesh about it this afternoon, and ask him how to make things right with April, but he isn't around for our session apparently – he's on annual leave. Or maybe he's just fed up with me, like everyone else . . .

*

DAYS TO DISCO: NONE!!

When I get into school today, her head is still 'in a funk'. I can see her sitting at the back of the classroom, scribbling something furiously in her notebook.

I hear Bradley asking Isiah if he's going to ask Aliya to slow-dance. Isiah shrugs like he couldn't care less either way and says, 'Maybe.' Farid, Bradley and Dylan start shouting, 'Yes, my MAN!' and slapping him on the back. Isiah looks annoyed and tries to shake them off. They go *whoop whoop*, until Mr Montague tells them to pipe down, because 'this is a classroom not a zoo, and also it is time for maths'.

Mr Montague starts to hand round some algebra worksheets for everyone, but he gives me a different one to everyone else. The others are just balancing regular equations, but he's given me a worksheet on quadratic equations. I'm about to hand it back to him and tell him he's made a mistake but he meets my eyes and taps his nose like some kind of wise wizard. That's when I realise he's given me a much harder one on purpose, and now we're trapped in some kind of secret nerd alliance. Great. But the much bigger and more pressing question is: what the hell is slow-dancing? I wish I could ask April.

In drama with Miss Valentine that afternoon, everyone's too busy guessing which songs they'll play and who's going to dance with who to join in with the restorative meditation she's set up. Sophia and Ezinne are talking quietly, and I can hear Sophia ask Ezinne if it would be OK for her to dance with Dylan if he asked her, even though Ezinne danced with him at the summer disco. 'But then, you did say you didn't even like him any more, didn't you . . .?'

Ezinne says, 'Fine,' and it sounds very *not* fine. Oh dear, everyone is in a very odd mood at the moment.

*

When I get home, there's a note from Mum on the kitchen counter.

GONE TO STUDIO. BACK BY 8.

I'll be gone by then. The disco starts at 7 p.m. I guess she's forgotten. I really hope she remembers to pick me up – Mr M made it clear that no one is allowed to go home without an adult. What if she forgets and I end up stuck at school all night? That might actually be even worse than slow-dancing (which reminds me, I still don't even know what that actually is). I eat the leftover tuna sweetcorn mayo pasta while googling 'what is slow dancing?'

The first thing that comes up is a YouTube video. The video is full of couples – one with their arms round the other's hips, the other with their arms

268

round their partner's neck, swaying slowly to 'Fix You' by Coldplay.

Eeeesh. No, thank you. I close the tab and tap my feet sixteen times. I take a deep breath and try to think calmly.

April said that you should always be fashionably late to a disco. When I asked how late is fashionably late, April said the thing about fashionably late is that you can't put an exact time on it, otherwise that defeats the point of looking like you don't care enough to be somewhere on time.

In light of this advice, I feel like I should get to the disco just after 7 p.m., but by how many minutes, I'm not sure.

It's another thing I wish I could just ask April.

I'm also not sure if I should wear my costume. Obviously April is still planning on dressing up. But I can't work out if she'll be angrier if I dress up with her, or if I don't.

The Thoughts settle it. Every time I try and put on the paper doll outfit, the grey of the suit sends a little jolt of horror through my fingertips that shoots round my body.

If I wear this, Mum will die. Look what happened last time you tried to wear something different.

I decide I'll just change out of my school uniform

and put on my standard outfit: a black T-shirt and jeans. I tell myself April will be fine. Everyone else will be in costumes, so if anyone's going to look like the odd one out, it's me.

It takes me a while to get to school because I'm stepping in fours in the hope that as soon as it feels right I'll know that Mum will be OK, and April and I will be friends again. Twice I think about just turning round and not going to the stupid disco at all. Somehow, I keep going.

I head through the gate where there's a laminated paper sign that says: YR 8 DISCO IN SPORTS HALL. I walk round to the sports hall entrance. The disco started twenty-six minutes ago. I can hear the *thump thump* of loud music seeping out of the hall.

'Hey, Ben!' Mr Montague is standing outside the entrance with a hand-stamp, waving at me. He's wearing a wizard's hat and a long fake silver beard. I find myself wondering whether Mr Montague was a shy kid who grew into his nerdiness, or whether he couldn't care less what people thought of him from the start.

'How are you doing tonight?' he asks as I give him the two pounds entry for the school charity. 'Hold out your wrists.'

Stamp. Stamp.

'I'm OK,' I mumble.

He pushes the double doors open and when I go in my eyes have to adjust to the new light: the multicoloured darkness of the sports hall lit by disco balls.

All four classes from our year group are here, not just Mr Montague's. If everyone in Year Eight came, there would be a hundred and forty-one students. I find myself instinctively trying to count them to see if there is a good number of people in the hall, but I can't – the lights keep falling on different places in the room and everyone is moving around too fast.

I scan the hall for April but there's no sign of her. I'm wondering exactly *how* fashionably late she intends to be, when I realise:

Other people aren't wearing costumes.

Yes, there are pumpkins and fake spider's cobwebs and some orange paper letters that spell HAPPY HALLOWEEN!

BUT NOT ONE PERSON IS ACTUALLY DRESSED UP.

So maybe everyone just decided they couldn't be bothered? Or worse, the fancy-dress thing was . . . a joke? I try to think if I can remember an actual staff member mentioning costumes. Fizzy horror is creeping into my fingers, because I can't.

I have to text April. I need to let her know that

if she rocks up in costume, she'll be the only one.

I go over to sit on one of the long benches that have been pushed to the side of the hall. I grab my phone out of my pocket and type:

DON'T WEAR DOLL

I hit send, but the send bar only moves about two thirds of the way across the screen and then stops. I realise I don't have 4G, only E, and my message isn't delivering. I feel someone sit next to me and look up to see that it's Sophia.

'Hey . . .' she says a little uncertainly. 'Where's April?'

'How should I know?' I snap. And then, because Sophia and Ezinne were the ones who told me about the fancy dress in the first place, I ask, 'Why is no one dressed up?'

For a moment she looks at me guiltily, like Bumble when he's eaten something he shouldn't, and then she starts to say, 'Well, see, the thing is . . .'

But I never get to hear her explanation, because that's when April comes through the door. In full costume. She's painted her face white like a porcelain doll and drawn red rosy circles high on her cheeks. She looks . . . amazing. Wow.

It feels like the music gets quieter, even though

I don't think it does, and the crowd seem to part so that April is standing in the middle of the hall. She is moving her head slowly back and forth across the crowd, like she can't believe what she is seeing.

Lauren, Michelle and Aliya are moving towards the front of the crowd to get a look, and when the disco-ball lights illuminate their faces, I can see that their faces are twisted in laughter. In fact, pretty much *everyone* is laughing.

'Hey,' shouts Michelle over the music. 'Cute outfit, freak!'

That's when April, whose eyes have been flicking over the crowd, spots me.

Me, on the bench, not dressed up.

Me, on the bench, with Sophia.

Oh my god. Oh my *god*.

Someone starts a chant: *'FREAK! FREAK! FREAK!'* At first it's just a few lone voices, but quickly everyone in the room seems to be chanting at her.

I am trying to get her to see that I am shouting: 'No! I DIDN'T KNOW!' But there's no chance of her hearing me over the chants, and I see her eyes go from kind of glassy and zoned out to very watery, like they might start to spill over. And April doesn't cry. Or if she does, she definitely doesn't let anyone see.

So before I know it, she's whirled round and is running away from Michelle and towards the double doors of the gym.

I turn round too and start to chase after April. I take a few strides – I'm usually embarrassed by my poor coordination and try to avoid running in public, but right now I don't care, and—

I am on the floor.

I genuinely wouldn't be too surprised to have tripped over my own leg, but I see Michelle pull her leg back and I know – she tripped me. I pick myself up and carry on running – it's fine, I am thinking. Mr Montague will have stopped her; asked her if she's OK – but when I get outside the door Mr Montague isn't there any more. And I can't see April. Oh, god.

I have this feeling that she's probably gone to Music Room 4, so I run round the back of the sports hall and to the school's main entrance, where I type in the door code. I thought it might not work this late but it does. *Bzzzz.* The door opens. It's very strange being in the school building when it's all dark and totally silent apart from my feet slapping against the lino floor. I bolt up the four flights of stairs, through the green door and along the nearly pitch-black music corridor.

'APRIL?' I am yelling through the door of Music

Room 4. 'APRIL?'

She isn't there. Just dusty violin cases and music stands in the dark. I start to text her.

WHERE ARE YOU? I DIDN'T KNOW I PROMISE

It's not in four-letter words. I try to rearrange it into four-letter words that work, but that's just taking up time I don't have. This is an emergency. It's more important than any stupid rules. At least it's eight words in total, I try to tell myself. I press send and feel like I am going to vomit.

I remember the time she was upset and hid in the girls' toilets, so I head back down there.

'April?' I call outside. 'April?'

Nothing. Oh, god, I'm going to have to go in. If anyone sees, I'll be forever known as the creep in the girls' bathroom. But I remind myself that no one will see me, because the school is empty.

I always imagined the inside of the girls' bathroom would be super-clean and smell faintly of roses, but really they're just as gross as ours, except for the urinals.

I check every cubicle, and she's not in any of them. Like in the boys' toilets, there's tons of graffiti on the inside of every cubicle door. I don't look at what the graffiti says for long, or count the letters and numbers of words; there isn't time. But still, the same phrases keep jumping out in angry black marker pen:

APRIL IS A LOSER
APRIL NO MATES

I don't stop to investigate further. But as I'm running down to the art room, I am thinking, how could I not know? How could I be her best friend and not know she was reading those words in the toilet, every day. Why wouldn't she tell me?

Then I remember, a few weeks ago, when we were talking about magical thinking:

I'm sure there's loads of stuff I struggle with that you wouldn't get.

April practically invited me to ask. And I didn't. I was too wrapped up in my own head.

Oh, god. I push open the door to the art room. She isn't there.

I text again:

REPLY NOW

I check our classroom. I check the girls' bathroom on the ground floor. April hasn't replied, and she's usually one of those people who replies within seconds.

I really don't know where else to look. I think I might have to tell someone.

I imagine how beyond angry April will be if I tell a teacher on her.

I walk back to the sports hall. I walk as slowly as I can, to give her as much time as possible to reply.

But there's nothing from her. By now she's been missing for twenty-four minutes. Maybe I should have told a teacher earlier. She could be anywhere.

I check my phone once more as I'm about to go through the double swing doors to the sports hall. No messages.

SORRY APRIL. I HAVE TO TELL.

Everyone is jumping up and down and shouting the words to a song I don't know. For a second the room wobbles and I feel like I'm going to be sick. I scan the room for the teachers, and then I see them, clustered in the far-right corner, drinking water in plastic cups.

I make my way towards them.

'Hey, Ben!' yells Mr Montague over the song. 'What's up?'

'I NEED – TO TALK – TO YOU,' I shout back. I can see the other teachers glancing at each other, confused. But Mr Montague stays focused on me.

'Sure! Follow me!'

277

He leads me back outside the sports hall. The doors swing shut behind us and the music fades. The night air is cool and I try to swallow as much of it as possible, to stop the gulpy thing happening.

'What's up?'

'It's April. She's missing.'

'OK. How long has she been missing for?'

I check my phone.

'Twenty-seven minutes.'

'Where did you last see her?'

'On the dance floor.'

'Then what happened?'

'She . . . she ran off.'

'What happened to cause her to run off?'

I stare at the floor. Was Mr Montague in here when everyone started chanting? I don't think so — but even if he wasn't, surely the other teachers saw? How could they not have?

I guess they were probably all too busy talking and I'm going to have to tell him. But I really think April will kill me if I do.

'OK, you don't have to tell me the details. Was she upset?'

I nod.

'And where have you looked for her?'

'Bathrooms, classroom, art room, this music

room we sometimes hang out in . . . I can't think where else.'

Mr Montague's head creases in concern, which worries me. I have never seen Mr Montague concerned. He is generally a very calm and logical man, and I feel like if Mr Montague is concerned, then I should be too.

'Right. OK. I'll be right back.'

I go to sit on the raised kerb round the front of the hall, still feeling like I'm going to be sick. I put my head in my lap and look to my right, and that's when I see something that fills me with horror: April's paper doll costume, torn off and muddy, in the gutter by the school gates.

A few seconds later I hear the music stop, and when I run back round to the gym entrance, the strip lights in the sports hall are flicking on, and suddenly it just looks like our regular gym again. There's collective booing.

Miss Dean, who teaches one of the other forms, calls for everyone to come and sit down at the front of the hall. Mr Thompson and Miss Maleki rush past me, followed by Mr Montague. I hear him tell them, 'April's friend Ben has searched spots he thought she might be, but I need you to do a quick sweep of the site. If you can't find her very soon, and she's not with her parents, then we'll need to get the other kids off site and call the police.'

The police?

Mr Thompson and Miss Maleki nod and keep running. Mr Montague is standing outside, next to me, with a folder full of phone numbers, running his finger down the list. He stops on P for 'Pieris' and reaches for his mobile in his pocket. I can see April's parents have a home number and a work number.

'Call the work one,' I say instinctively.

Mr Montague nods and punches the number in. I hear him explain to someone at the hospital that he needs to speak with April's parents, because their daughter is missing and he urgently needs to know if she has returned home, or is with them. My head repeats that awful word: *Missing, Missing, Missing, Missing.*

'Uh-huh,' he nods. 'OK.' Long pause. 'I understand. Thank you.'

He puts the phone back in his pocket.

'I got through to the receptionist,' he explains to me. 'April's definitely not with her parents, as they're both in surgery. But their flat is only a few blocks away from the hospital. She's sending someone to check.'

I nod. 'OK,' Mr Montague says. 'We'll find her, Ben.'

Back inside, everyone is grumbling about the music being off and the lights being on. Bradley starts a chant of 'PLAY SOME TUNES! PLAY SOME TUNES!' and a lot of people start to join in.

'QUIET!' roars Miss Dean over the noise. Miss Dean is a small woman with a brown bob, who is also the Head of English. I didn't imagine she could roar like that. Then she tells the room:

'A pupil has gone missing.'

Which shuts everyone up.

I turn round and Miss Maleki and Mr Thompson are rushing back in, shaking their heads towards Mr Montague.

'She's not here,' says Mr Thompson breathlessly. Mr Montague's phone starts buzzing. It's the *Star Trek* theme tune. If this was any other moment this would be the most amazing thing that has ever happened, but right now it just feels stupid.

'Sorry,' he mutters, picking it up as quickly as possible.

'Hello?' Pause. 'OK, thank you. I understand. Goodbye.'

He turns to me, Miss Maleki and Mr Thompson.

'She's not at her house. Her parents are due to

finish operating soon and they will be told the moment they're available. Miss Maleki, can you take this folder and go and help Miss Dean to call parents to arrange for pupils to be picked up? We can't have them on the site right now. Mr Thompson, please can you supervise until their parents arrive? I need to call the police. Ben, would you mind going to sit with everyone? I'm sorry, we need to keep everyone in one place.'

'OK,' I say, even though I'd rather be anywhere else in the world than near Lauren, Aliya and Michelle right now. I head over and plonk myself down. I thought they'd be gloating, but actually they're just sitting looking scared and not talking.

Michalle nudges Lauren, and Lauren scoots over to me.

'Text her,' she whispers hotly. 'Make her come back.'

'I have,' I say, gritting my teeth.

'What did she say?'

'Nothing. My messages aren't even delivering any more.'

'Do you think she'll come back?'

'Why do you care? Isn't this what you've wanted for ages? To make her feel miserable. Well, congratulations, you have succeeded.'

Lauren glares at me. 'We didn't mean for . . . *this*. Do you think—'

'Honestly, Lauren, I have no idea. I just want you to leave me alone.'

Lauren nods and bites her lip, rushing back over to Michelle to relay what I have said. Michelle has gone very pale and doesn't look too good.

Now Ezinne and Sophia are shuffling over on my left.

'Ben—' begins Sophia, who looks queasy. 'I'm really sorry – about the fancy dress.'

'Michelle said . . . Well, Michelle said we could sit with her lot at lunch for two weeks if we told you the disco was fancy dress,' adds Ezinne.

'Are you *serious*? You did this just to sit with them at lunch?'

Kids are UNBELIEVABLE, I swear.

'Well, actually, in the end, they didn't let us sit with them after all.'

My *god*.

'I want to be alone right now,' I say. They nod and go back to where they were sitting before.

Parents start to arrive all at once, swarming towards Mr Thompson, and they are *angry*.

'How did you let a child disappear?' 'Which child is it?' 'Did you not have someone supervising the door?'

'Please try and remain calm!' Mr Thompson squeaks at them. 'At present our focus is on finding the pupil, and we will be reviewing the events of this evening at a later date!'

Deeply dissatisfied with this answer, parents are scooping their kids up and ushering them out of the door. I am wondering what happened when Miss Maleki called my mum. Was she at home? Did she even pick up the phone? Was she . . . herself?

I'm one of the last ones left, and then I spot Clarinet Boy, who I didn't realise was in our year, coming towards me. He sits next to me.

'Hey,' he says softly. 'I recognised the missing girl when she came in – I guess she wasn't the missing girl then. Sorry, you know what I mean. Anyway, I, um, know you guys.' He smiles kinda sadly. 'You hide in the music department. Like me.'

It's funny, all this time I thought he just really liked playing the clarinet.

'Yeah,' I mumble.

'What's her name?'

'April.'

'That's a cool name. I'm Pete.'

'I'm Ben.'

There isn't anything else to say, but Pete stays sitting next to me, studying the gym floor intently.

Mum arrives two minutes later. She runs towards me and wraps me in a massive hug, and I don't even care who sees, or what Pete might think. I hug her back, hard.

'Oh, Benny,' she says. 'Benny, I'm so sorry. Let's get you home.'

'But I have to stay!' I protest. 'I have to help find her.'

Mum shakes her head sadly. 'I don't think there's anything else you can really do right now. Mr Montague told me you'd looked everywhere you thought she might be. Come on, they've got the police on the scene. I saw them when I came in. And apparently her parents are arriving any minute. They'll find her, and she'll be OK. She's a clever girl.'

April is clever. She's the cleverest person I know. Maybe so clever no one can find her?

Mum is leading me away from the sports hall.

'I really hope you find her!' I hear Pete calling faintly.

4.2

'I'm so sorry, mate,' Kyle says when we get home. Mum says she's going to make me milk and honey and take me up to bed. I haven't let Mum make me milk and honey for over two years because it is the most babyish drink on the planet, but I just nod. I feel hollow and empty inside, and I want to feel warm.

I drink it all down and Mum strokes my head. I pretend to be asleep, and Mum pads out softly and shuts the door. Mum said she'd keep her phone on loud, and if there was any news from the school, she'd wake me and tell me.

But can I really wait for that? Can I really wait for 'them' to find April?

I look at my texts for what feels like the millionth time.

WHERE ARE YOU? I DIDN'T KNOW I PROMISE REPLY NOW
I'M SORRY. I HAD TO TELL.

APRIL?

THEY'RE CALLING THE POLICE

None of them have delivered. Either April's turned her phone off or it's out of battery. Which means she doesn't know that I would never do this to her. Not in a million years. And I need her to know that.

So where else would she go?

I try and replay every conversation we've ever had about places April likes. There's the Peckhamplex, but April's always going there, so surely her parents would have told the police to search there? We've been to the chicken shop once before and shared a bargain bucket, but no thirteen-year-old is going to sit unnoticed in a chicken shop at – I check the time – 1.08 a.m. And I know April once went to Miss Ruiz's house when she was sad, and Miss Ruiz made her baked beans on toast, but realistically Miss Ruiz would call the school if April came over at night, wouldn't she? I mean, she's clearly a bit of an unusual teacher, but she's not going to harbour a fugitive . . . ?

I wonder if April will be annoyed with me for not running after her fast enough? For not being with her right now. April has only been properly annoyed with me once before. It was the time where—

Oh my god. The place she wanted to show me. The place we had a fight about.

The place I was too scared to see.

Wouldn't that be where she would go? A place she liked to go with Thomas, where she felt safe?

I need to go there. I need to find her.

I pull on the clothes I wore today and creep down the stairs. In the kitchen, I scrawl a note for Mum. There is no way to make it all in four letters and make sense, so, for the sixth time today, and also in my life, I don't write in fours. In fact, I write a proper sentence:

GONE TO FIND APRIL HAVE
NOT RUN AWAY WILL BE BACK

PLEASE DO NOT WORRY.

There is a way of closing the door to the house, where you hold the handle down as you shut it, so that it doesn't slam and make a noise. I step out into the night. I've never been out this late before, and the road is dark and silent and it feels like I am the only person in the world.

I know I have to catch two buses. The first one to Catford and the second one to New Cross. The first

288

bus stop is just a couple of streets away, and when I get there I see that the same bus I took before with April runs all night. The board says it is due in seven minutes, and I sit there with my heart banging in my ears, terrified Kyle heard me leave and is about to come thundering down the road to drag me back home. But he doesn't.

When I see the bus roll towards me, I pull my hoodie up in the hope that the driver won't see how young I look and suspect anything. But the driver just nods at me as I swipe my Oyster card, so I nod back and take a seat. The only other person on the bus is an older man who looks and smells the way Mum does when she has been drinking. I find myself really hoping that he manages to get home OK, or at least to somewhere safe. I almost want to ask him if he's all right, but I feel like I can't really be taking on another mission right now . . .

It takes ten minutes to get to Catford Bridge. This is the first time I have sat totally still by myself since April went missing. For a second I wonder what Dad would think — if he could see me now, on a bus, late at night, by myself. I'm sure he'd be angry with me for sneaking out, but I wonder if he might also be a tiny bit . . . proud?

Stop thinking about Dad, I tell myself. That's not

going to help right now. My eyes flick round the bus instinctively. *One, two, three, four. One, two, three, four.*

And that's when I realise I haven't actually been doing any compulsions since April went missing. I have been too distracted to think about them.

'*Weird,*' I say out loud. The man across from me looks at me.

I stare ahead just feeling queasy and awful for the rest of the journey. I never knew ten minutes could take so long. *Finally* we are at Catford Bridge bus stop, and I have to run over the railway bridge to get the 171 bus from the other side. Down below, the platform is full of people on their way back from a Friday night in town, stumbling in high heels and taking selfies, waiting for their connecting train.

This bus takes seventeen minutes. I count up and down to forty to stop my brain going places I don't want it to. Thankfully there's no traffic at night – and it's strange, sweeping down roads that usually take ten minutes to drive down in the day. *Take me to April.*

I buzz the bell and sprint off the bus at New Cross. 'Slow down, mate, there's nothing worth rushing for quite that much,' someone calls after me, and I'm thinking, *If only you knew.*

I run along the rest of the high street and turn off past the block where April used to live, taking the cut-through path leading to the wrought-iron gates of the small park. I try them but they're locked. What am I going to do? I shake them, calling, 'April, April!' helplessly. Then I see a wheelie bin, which I could use to help me get over. I wheel it over and climb on to it, which means I am just about able to get my leg over and jump down.

I hear the sound of the back of my trousers catching and ripping on one of the spikes, but I keep moving and run down the main tarmac path. I remember I have to go past six street lamps, because that was the number that upset me so much last time. After six lamps, there it is: the smaller mud path. The one with no street lamps. The Thoughts say:

Before you go down the path you must touch your toes forty times to undo the lamps, otherwise something bad will have happened to April.

My fingers itch to do the routine. But I know: it won't just be forty. I'll have to do eighty, then a hundred and sixty, then three hundred and twenty, and on and on. And the thing is: something bad has *already* happened to April.

So, even though it feels like the wrongest thing

in the world, I don't touch my toes.

I get my phone out of my pocket and turn the torch on, holding it out in front of me, and start down the path.

Every step you take down this path without touching your toes makes it more likely that April is hurt.

Enough, I say back to the Thoughts. *Fake magic isn't going to help April now.*

'April?' I call. 'April?'

The trees on either side of the path grow closer together the further I get along, until they are completely entwined in this majorly creepy archway that obscures the moon.

'April? APRIL?'

There's nothing, not a sound, apart from sticks crunching under my feet. And this path is longer than I thought. I turn round and can't see the entrance where I came in. Just blackness. Now that the moonlight has gone, it's hard to see anything at all, even with my torch. I creep forward.

'April?'

That's when I hear it. An awful moaning, like an animal. It's faint, and I have to walk further in to hear it better. That's when I realise the moan has a voice.

'Over . . . *aaahhh* . . . here . . .'

And then silence.

'April! APRIL! Is that you? Call out to me again!'

There's more moaning. I can't make out the words, though. I think it's coming from up ahead, to the left, so I walk that way and shine my torch out along the path and over the bushes. I'm sure it is getting closer—

'April?'

Moan, moan.

Now it seems to be . . . below me?

I shine my torch into the bush next to me and realise that the bush is on a bank, which slopes down the path. I push through the bush and edge my way down, grabbing on to branches with one hand and shining my torch with the other.

That's when I see her.

The bank gets steeper, and then there's a ditch, and there in the ditch is April on her stomach, face down. I gasp. I tell myself to keep it together and shuffle down the bank on my bum to get to her. I hear my jeans rip again.

'April!' I crouch beside her. 'Oh my god, April. Where are you hurt?'

'My . . . leg . . .' I shine the torch on her leg. Her left legging has risen up and I can see that her shin is twisted up to the sky in a way that is very, very not normal.

'My phone . . . dead . . .'

'It's OK. *Shhh, shhh*. I have my phone. I'm going to get help, OK? It's going to be OK.'

I grab my phone and dial 999.

'Police, Ambulance or Fire?' says a voice after two tones.

'Ambulance.'

'Transferring you . . .'

'Ambulance service, what's your emergency?'

'I'm with April, the missing girl from Sydenham, she's hurt, I need an ambulance.'

'The missing girl? Sorry, the line's not great.'

'Yes, she's called—'

'Please hold, I just need to bring up some further details about this case. Did you say she's from Sydenham?'

'Yes!'

The operator is gone for what feels like eternity but I keep telling April she's going to be right back and is going to tell us exactly what to do. April mumbles but I can't tell what she's saying.

The line crackles and I hear the operator's voice come through again.

'Hi there, thanks for holding. Are you school

staff or family to April?'

'No! I'm . . . her friend. Ben.'

'You're a child?'

'Um, yes.'

'OK, Ben, can you tell me where you are?'

'We are in Sanlow Park and April is in a ditch and she's hurt her leg.'

'Is April conscious right now, Ben?'

'Yes, I think so, but she keeps mumbling stuff, she's—'

'Is she breathing OK?'

'I think so.'

'OK, that's good. Please don't move her. The crew are en route. Where exactly are you?'

'Go down the main path from the high street side. Walk for six lamp posts. There is a smaller path that leads off to the left and we are down there.'

'Noted. Thanks for your precision, Ben. Can you stay on the line?'

'Um, yes. That's fine.'

'Estimated time of arrival is six minutes.'

'Thank you.'

'OK, don't hang up.'

I put the phone on speaker and place it on the ground. I lie down next to April and take her hand.

'Six minutes,' I tell her. 'They'll be here and you'll be OK.'

I want to hug her but I'm scared of hurting her more. So we lie like this in the mud and mulchy leaves, until I hear a wail in the distance. Quickly getting closer.

Then I hear shouting:

'April? Ben? April?'

'Down here!' I yell as loudly as possible. 'Down here!'

More running and rustling. The glare of a giant flashlight sweeping down on us.

'They're here, they're down here!' calls a woman's voice.

Five adults in bottle-green uniforms are shuffling down the bank, holding a stretcher. I step back to allow them to get close to April.

'I'm not going anywhere,' I tell her.

But April is. April is going up the bank in a stretcher and into the ambulance, which they've driven right into the park and parked by the entrance to the smaller path.

They lift April in and put her straight on gas and air, like in the movies.

'Can I ride with her?' I ask the paramedic nearest me.

'Yup,' he says. 'Hop in.'

They've secured April's whole body in an orange plastic brace. Another paramedic explains to me it's to stop her moving in a way that might cause any more damage, because they don't know what's broken yet. I ask if I can hold her hand and they say, no, not just yet, just sit tight, but you can talk to her if you want.

I lean down so I can be as close as possible to her ear.

'I didn't know. About the fancy dress. I think you're the most awesome person I've ever met and I would never, *ever* do something like that to you.'

I think April smiles faintly. And then she closes her eyes and is quiet the rest of the way. I look down at her leg and realise I can see something shiny and white poking through torn flesh. It's a bone.

4.3

After that, it's hard to remember what order everything happened in. I know that when we got to the hospital, April's parents were there. It's the hospital where they work, but a different wing. So they'd rushed off to search around their home and the school, and then come *back* to the hospital when they heard she was on her way.

I'd never met them before, but I immediately knew who they were – April looks really similar to her dad. They both started running towards the stretcher as soon as it came through the doors. April's dad was sobbing, 'April! Oh, my April!' and April's mum just buried her face into the side of the stretcher. Then she turned and saw me.

'Ben,' she whispered. 'You must be Ben.' And she folded me into a hug and squeezed me so tight I thought my insides might explode everywhere like toothpaste. Which sounds like I minded, but I didn't. She looked me in the eyes and told me she'd never be able to thank me enough.

I was hoping that I'd just be able to get the bus home and sneak back into bed, and that Mum would never know what happened, but no one would hear of it. The hospital phoned her, and I got told she was on her way. Then *I* was given an examination by another doctor, to check I wasn't hurt at all, even though I kept telling them I was totally fine. The doctor examined me for a few minutes and then said what I already knew: that I was fine, but that maybe some counselling would be helpful, given what had happened. I grinned and told her that I was already *in* counselling, so that wouldn't be necessary. I don't know why I told her this since it's not information I usually feel good about telling anyone.

But the rules feel kind of different now, so maybe I'm more like THE Doctor than I thought? Like, I got a bit older and I changed my list of rules to live by, the way different incarnations of the Doctor do. Anyway, she didn't think it was weird or anything. She just smiled and said, 'Well, that's great.' And then she shook my hand and told me it was a privilege to meet me, that I was a very brave boy and my parents should be very proud of me.

Which made me think about Mum, and how much trouble I would be in, because I was sure she'd be cross with me for sneaking out, and not very proud at all. And also whether she'd tell Dad, and what he would say if she did.

In the end, she was sort of both. I mean, she hugged me and said, 'Benjamin Hardie, I have never been more proud and cross with you than I am now.' She said I was grounded, and that she would take me to the official *Doctor Who* shop in Upton Park at the same time – which will be logistically challenging.

Then she wanted to take me home. I wanted to stay with April, but the nurse said what April needed now was to sleep, and that she would make sure April's phone was plugged in and charging so that I could text her and she would see it first thing when she woke up. Before Mum could take me home, I had to have an interview with a police officer about what had happened. The police officer took me into a small hospital cubicle behind a plastic curtain and asked me lots of questions and made notes on everything I said. I thought I might be in trouble; that there might be some law against children leaving their houses in the night. This policeman looked very stern and it was hard to tell what he was thinking. But then, at the end of the interview, *he* also asked to shake my hand

and told me he had never met such a brave young man.

It was all very odd, and then me and Mum got a taxi home. By this point it was getting light outside, and even though the streets were very empty, I saw a few people who were opening their metal shop fronts for the day, and some girls in high heels and short dresses who *still* hadn't made it back from the night before. I had never been out this late, or seen this in-between time of the day. I thought I'd be up for hours when I got home, thinking about everything that happened and how strange it had all been, but after Mum stroked my head and turned out the light, I don't think I can have been awake for more than half a minute . . .

*

This morning when I wake up in my bed with the sunlight in my eyes, I am sort of wondering if it all *was* just a weird dream.

But then I check my phone and I have nine texts, which is more than I have ever had all at once before. Four are from people in my class. Sophia, Ezinne and Jia want to know if I have any news about April. And one from Dylan (???!!), who I didn't realise knew I existed, let alone had my number. He must somehow know I found April, because his text just says:

HEARD THE NEWS. U LEGEND X

One is from a foreign number I don't recognise, and when I open it, it says:

Hey Ben, I'm Thomas, April's big brother. I'm working abroad at the moment with very sporadic reception, and I only found out what had happened to April this morning. I just wanted to tell you how grateful I am. I heard that you found April and I can't thank you enough. We never told anyone about our spot in the park at the time, but thank god April told you. I will be flying home for a break in the next few weeks and I very much hope to meet you. You're a true hero and April is lucky to have you. T xxx

One is from Kyle, it reads:

BRO UR FAMOUS! WHAT A HERO. HAD TO GO TO WORK. CAN'T WAIT 2 TELL EVERY1!!

At the bottom of the text there's a link to a BBC article, which I click on. It was posted at 8.09 a.m. this morning, and the headline reads:

BOY, 12, RESCUES MISSING GIRL

A twelve-year-old boy was an unlikely hero in a missing person's case that police and rescue services had been unable to solve. A thirteen-year-old girl, whose name cannot be revealed for legal reasons, went missing from a school event and was unable to be located for five hours.

The boy, name also withheld, located the girl in a ditch in a park, before telephoning in her whereabouts to rescue services. The girl is currently recovering in hospital. Her injuries are said to be serious but not life threatening . . .

Oh my *god*. This is too weird.

The other three messages are from April, sent between 6.08 a.m. and 7.16 a.m. The first one just says:

BEN!!!!

The second says:

LEG BROKEN IN 3 SPOTS. GOIN 4 OP NOW 2 FIX. CRACKD RIBS ASWEL.

The final one reads:

IM RLLY SRRY

So I guess it really did happen after all.

Dad texts me while I'm downstairs eating my breakfast.

Your mum has told me what's happened. I'm proud of you, of course, but want to check you're OK. Shall we go out for some chicken this week, big man?

I haven't heard from Dad in a while. I think I should feel relieved, but instead the hot wavy feeling fills me again until even my fingertips are tingling with it. I lock my phone and carry on eating my Coco Pops. In the blue bowl.

Dad can wait. I need to go and see April.

*

I visit April that afternoon, and again on Sunday. I get the bus both times, there and back. Her parents have taken emergency leave and are with her pretty much round the clock, which is a first – I mean, don't get me wrong, when April's spoken about them I always got the feeling they adore her. It's just weird to finally see them with her in person, fussing and bringing her whatever she wants to eat and drink. There is a heap of Crunchie wrappers and Coke cans on her bedside table. April seems to not really know what to do with their full-time attention.

I bring her comics both times so she has something to read at night when we are all gone. All the doctors and nurses keep high-fiving me and calling me 'the man of the hour' which is, um, nice but also weird. There were even a few journalists waiting outside the hospital to talk to me, but Mum had told me that I probably shouldn't speak to them and I should just say, 'No comment.' Which I did. And again, I felt like I was in a movie.

April has had surgery to get her leg back into place, and she needed two metal plates to secure it there, which will stay round her knee for the rest of her life. I tell her that means that every time she gets on an aeroplane, even if she lives to a hundred, she'll always set the security metal detector off. She tries to scowl at me, but it turns into a smirk.

On Sunday evening, April's mum and dad go home to get April some more clothes, because she's going to have to stay in for a few more days. That means that for the first time since I found April, it's just the two of us.

I feel like April might want to discuss, er, you know, the matter of her disappearance, but remind me never to assume that April would handle MAJOR TRAUMA like a normal person.

'It's not that rubbish, by the way,' she says. 'Mine and Thomas's den.'

'What?'

'Well, our den isn't just a ditch. I was trying to *find* the den, which means finding the right bush. There was this sort of hollow bush thing we used to make a camp in. But my phone died so I had no torch, and I think I turned off the path too early, and it wasn't the hollow bush, it was a ditch . . . Anyway, I want you to know we didn't just hang out in a ditch, Thomas and me. We had a proper camp.'

It seems important to April that I understand she wouldn't hang out in ditches, but a hollow bush would be totally adequate. 'OK,' I say.

We're quiet for a while.

'I promise I didn't know. About the fancy dress,' I say.

'Well, why weren't you dressed up too then?' says April, trying to sit up. 'I don't get it.'

'*Shh, shh,*' I say, trying to get her settled back on the pillows. 'Don't get all worked up. You need to rest.'

'OK, nurse,' she scowls.

'I didn't dress up because when I tried to put the outfit on, The Thoughts told me something awful would happen.'

'Well, something awful did happen,' says April sulkily. '*Because* you didn't wear the outfit.'

'Yeah, but, April, be fair – I thought everyone else was going to be dressed up, just like you. So I thought *I* would be the odd one out. Anyway, you were so annoyed with me I thought it might annoy you more if I showed up wearing the same thing as you. I thought you didn't want anything to do with me.'

'Of course I still wanted you to dress up with me. I was annoyed with you. I was trying to make a point by picking up my outfit from yours, but you didn't even text me.'

'Well . . . I didn't realise you were making a point. I thought you just wanted to go solo.'

Honestly, people are too confusing.

April nods. 'Thank you. I think I'm tired. I think I'm going to go to sleep now.'

I say that's good, she should rest as much as possible. I tell her I'm going to go now, because Mum said I have to be home by 8 p.m., but that I'll try and visit her in the evenings, after school. I'm not sure if she hears; she's pretty much asleep already. The nurse did tell me she'd be that way, after the operation.

I make my way out of the ward and through the double glass doors on to the street. This time there's only one reporter on the way out, who yells,

'What was it like to rescue your girlfriend?'

'She's my best friend, not my girlfriend. And no comment.'

*

It's weird being at school without April on Monday. But what's weirder still is what *school* is like post-April disco saga.

I thought I'd have no one to talk to. But I have never had *more* people talk to me than today. Everyone knows I found April. They've all read the article online. Everyone is calling me a hero.

Well, pretty much everyone. Lauren, Aliya, Michelle, Ezinne and Sophia are too upset to get sentences out properly. They've been crying and shaking all morning, saying they never meant for this to happen. Saying they feel so bad. I can't get my head round this 'we never meant for this to happen' thing. What *did* they mean to happen? For April to just be miserable enough for them to get their kicks? But somehow, because she's in hospital, that's worse than just *feeling* miserable?

Lauren, Aliya, Michelle, Ezinne and Sophia spend the first hour in a meeting with our head teacher Mrs Olowe, Mr Montague and their parents.

When they get back, Mr Montague says we all

need to have a talk about what happened. Everyone is very still.

'There are certain people here who are in more trouble than others,' begins Mr Montague. 'And, yes, from everything that's been relayed from multiple sources, it seems we know who started this. But it wasn't just those people. Most of you went along with the costume prank, and the chant. And all of you who did bear partial responsibility for what happened. Every single one.'

The room is silent apart from the tick of the clock and Jules's heaving sobs coming from the back row.

'I know you're all upset. I've spoken with your parents over the weekend and I believe that you are all genuinely sorry about what happened. And honestly, at your age, mistakes are made. You may see difference in someone and want to mock it, and it may be only in years to come, when you're a grown-up, that you know that that was wrong. But we need to address this now. April is in hospital. You have some hard evidence for just how bad these things can get. But not all cases like this end in hospital, and that doesn't make them less bad.

'I *never* want to see this behaviour in my classroom again. Do I make myself clear? Never.'

Everyone is nodding.

'I know, in my heart, that you are all better than this.'

And with that, pretty much *everyone* starts crying. Even Bradley, Farid, Isiah and Dylan are looking pretty emotional.

'I'll be leaving a scrapbook at the front of the classroom for anyone who wants to write April a message, and I'll make sure it gets sent to the hospital when everyone who wants to has signed it.'

The rest of the day is a blur. At first break, the queue to sign April's scrapbook goes round the classroom, and kids from the other forms come too. I see Clarinet Boy, I mean Pete, in line, and he gives me a shy grin. Even Lauren, Michelle and Aliya queue up. I know it's not nice to comment on other people's appearances, but they look . . . Well, they looked rough. Like something truly awful has happened to them all.

I guess it has.

*

This afternoon Isiah comes and sits next to me! At April's desk! For a second I honestly think he's confused and has gone to the wrong side of the classroom.

I turn to him, surprised, and he goes, 'Don't worry, I'll move as soon as April's back. Just thought you could maybe use the company.'

He gives me this kinda goofy awkward grin, which is weird because I've never seen Isiah as a goofy sort of person. Isiah is *cool*. I mean, come on, he's probably the most popular guy in the class.

I don't know what to say, so I just nod and say, 'OK,' because it's true that I could use the company. All of our lessons today are with Mr Montague – back-to-back maths, physics, English and chemistry. I'm so nervous about Isiah sitting next to me that I revert to default Benny and pretend he isn't there and get on with my work. I would like to talk to him, I just have no idea what to say . . . What do popular people talk about?

But then in English Mr Montague says we need to write a short story with the person next to us. Which means I *have* to talk to Isiah. I sort of wonder if Mr Montague saw Isiah move next to me and crafted this activity on the spot so that I *have* to talk to him. I can't work out if I'm grateful to him or not.

'What shall we write about?' Isiah says.

'I dunno, you choose,' I say, because I'm worried he'll laugh at anything I suggest. BUT even though I thought he'd choose something flashy and cool, Isiah says, 'Let's do something sci-fi – you're into that, right? I don't watch *Doctor Who*, but I've watched some *Star Trek*. Do you watch *Star Trek*?'

Do I watch Star Trek*??!!!*

We decide our story should be set in Ancient Egypt, because people are always wondering how the pyramids were built without any machinery and saying it shouldn't be possible. So in *our* story the sphinxes (lions with human heads) that you often see in books about Egypt are actually aliens from the planet Rena who landed in Ancient Egypt and *they* built the pyramids.

Isiah gets pretty excited and says, 'This is AWESOME! When April comes back she can illustrate it!'

Which makes this sort of sad guilt swell in my heart because I realise for the past few minutes while we were writing our story that I hadn't thought about April, and I hope that it's OK if someone is in hospital and you don't think about them *all* of the time.

By the end of English, I'm wondering why I ever thought Isiah was so scary in the first place. We're still whispering about how we should end our story even after Mr Montague says it's time to stop writing so he can set us some homework. He has to ask us to be quiet! Honestly, if I told Kyle this happened, I don't think he'd ever believe it.

When the clock hits 3.30 p.m. and Mr Montague says it's home time, Isiah calls, 'Hey, don't forget to ask April if she'd be up for illustrating this for us!'

'Sure,' I smile, wondering if April will believe me.

*

Kids have actually been waving goodbye to me as I disappear through the gates after school this week. I give small waves back. It is very strange not being invisible, and I can't work out if I like it or not. It's also weird spending less of my day doing routines: The Thoughts are still there, whispering in the background, but I guess the difference is that somehow I'm not listening to them so hard.

On the bus to see Dinesh on Thursday, I am looking out of the window at Lewisham shopping centre and flashing back to the time when Mum practically emergency-stopped the bus to go and buy the T-shirts with me, when she says quietly, 'I thought about what you said, Benny. About my . . . thing. About how if I really cared, I would do something about it.'

I don't say anything, just turn and look at her, totally speechless, because I can't believe she's actually bringing this up of her own free will. She takes a deep breath.

'I'm going to try and get a . . . referral. Like you did. And I'm going to try my very best to sort it out.'

Wow. *Wow*. I squeeze her hand, hard. Just the once – not four times.

'I can come with you – if you like,' I say. 'On the bus and in the waiting room. Like you do for me.'

Mum smiles. 'Thanks, Benny. But I think this is an adult thing I need to do by myself. Although . . . Dad said he will come with me to the assessment.'

'You . . . spoke to *Dad*?'

She nods. 'Yes – on the phone. I think I've tried to hide it for long enough. Don't you?'

'Yeah, I just can't believe you spoke to him. I'm really happy you did,' I add quickly.

'I've got rid of it all,' she adds flatly, staring hard out of the window at a chicken shop, like she's angry with it.

I don't have to ask what. I know she means the bottles.

'And there are . . . these groups I've heard you can attend. With other people like me. Who try to help each other stop . . . drinking. There's one in

314

the community centre a few streets away from where we live. I'm going to try going to the Monday one, starting next week.'

I think about all the things April said that helped me, and I say to her, 'I think you can do it. It won't be easy, but I believe in you.'

She squeezes my hand back, and we don't say anything for the rest of the journey.

Dinesh collects me from the waiting room at 4.28 p.m. It feels like years since I saw him, even though of course it's only been a week longer than usual because of his annual leave. Still, I have so much to tell him.

Dinesh starts by saying that he knows about what happened with April – he was informed by social services. He says that while he can't professionally recommend twelve-year-olds going on rescue missions in the middle of the night, I have his sincere respect. And then he asks me how I am doing now.

'I'm . . .' I look round the yellow room I have come to know every centimetre of so well over the last few weeks, wondering how to say this. 'I'm finding it all pretty weird.'

'I'm sure. You've been through a massively traumatic event.'

'It's not that, though. Well, yes, of course it is a bit. But it's more . . . what happened after. When I went to find April, it didn't feel that brave. It just felt like the right thing to do. Like what anyone would do, if they thought they knew where their missing friend was. And now everyone keeps telling me I'm so brave, and that I'm a hero. And . . . I don't really feel like that.'

'Were you scared?'

Was I? I guess a bit. Scared I wouldn't find her at all. Scared I'd be in trouble. But I've been more scared . . . 'I mean, I know it sounds stupid,' I say slowly, 'but I feel like I was more scared when I wore the red T-shirt to school for non-school uniform day. And it's not like anyone's going, "Oh, Ben, wow, you wore a red T-shirt, my god, what a hero." So getting called all this stuff for a thing that wasn't actually as difficult . . . it's just weird.'

'I think you're a hero. For wearing that T-shirt.'

'Really?' I can feel my heartbeat in my fingertips and my ears – I want Dinesh to understand. I *need* him to understand.

'Of course. *And* I think you're a hero for finding April too. But I get that wearing the red T-shirt might have been a braver thing to do than finding April. It can be frustrating that people usually

316

notice big, dramatic acts of bravery much more than our own more private triumphs. But between you and me, I think challenging the fear in your head is the bravest thing you can do, and, well, once you've done that, everything else feels pretty easy in comparison.'

He gets it. Dinesh gets it. I smile at him. Now I don't feel quite so strange, even if no one else ever sees it like that.

'Also, I was able to put finding April before stupid stuff in my head.'

'Oh, yes?'

'I was able to text her, and write a note to my mum, in words that didn't have four letters. I thought I was going to have to touch my toes forty times because on the way there were six lamp posts. But finding April felt more urgent than that stuff, so I didn't. It's sort of made me think . . . I don't know . . . If that stuff doesn't really need to be done when everything's as wrong as it can be, well, then, when does it need to be done? So now doing routines seems kind of stupid and pointless. Does . . . that make sense?'

'A lot.'

We're quiet for a bit, and then Dinesh says it's the end of the session, and that since I am, quote 'bossing life', he doesn't think he needs to set me any challenges this week.

I almost tell him about Mum and Dad, but decide not to. Some things are best kept to yourself.

4.4

April is back at school after a week. I nearly wear black boxers under my school uniform on the morning of her return – I want so badly for it all to go OK. But at the last minute I go back to my room and change into the new blue ones Mum bought me to help me 'challenge my routines'.

I'm sweating slightly on Monday morning when April hops through the classroom door with her leg in a blue plaster cast. I'm worrying I should have stuck with the black ones, and also about whether everyone somehow knows I'm thinking about my pants, but that's when an amazing thing happens: everyone starts cheering.

Knowing April, I think she might tell everyone to get lost. But she doesn't. She actually smiles and looks kind of shy. Then she says, 'Thanks for the scrapbook, it was cool.'

In maths, Michalle passes a note forward. April opens it at our desk. It says:

Glad you are back. I am really sorry.

April draws a thumbs-up and passes it back.

Honestly, I think my brain is going to explode. In a good way. I really hope this weird Lauren-Aliya-Michelle-April truce lasts.

At break time we aren't able to take the back stairs to Music Room 4 as there's no lift that goes to that floor, so we have to take the lift down the main stairs to the playground. We sit on a bench so April doesn't have to stretch her leg out on the ground.

And people keep running over with permanent markers, because *everyone* wants to sign her cast.

Even me. Even though it is blue.

The rest of the day is a blur, but in a good way. So many people want to talk to April – which is OK; anything to distract me from wondering whether Mum really will go to that group she mentioned this afternoon, or whether she didn't really mean anything she said, and when I get home I'll find her on the sofa heckling *Gardener's World* . . .

At home time I pack my stuff up as slooooowly as possible and try to get April to stay and chat with me at her bus stop, but she's like, 'Ben, I'm actually really exhausted and need to get home, but I'll talk to you tomorrow, OK? It's art club, don't forget!'

When her bus comes I watch it drive down the road until it turns the corner, and then I dawdle all the way home.

I tell myself that even if Mum is at home, even if she hasn't gone to the group, it's not such a big deal . . . The fact is she considered it, that's the important thing, right?

I don't really manage to convince myself.

The weird thing is that as I turn on to our street, I see that our car is parked outside the house, even though Dad took the car when he left. I unlock the door and push it open slowly. What if something really awful happened to Mum and that's why Dad's back?

But when I get upstairs, Dad is in the kitchen by himself, flicking through some post at the table. The shock of seeing him in the kitchen is so big that it's hard to find my words.

'Hey, local hero!' Dad replies, concerningly cheerful. 'Mum's gone to her . . . group . . . so she asked if I could be around for you to make supper and stuff. What do you fancy? I could do us . . . some soup . . . tomato pasta and cheese?' He rifles through the cupboard, chucking tins and packets out at random on to the surface. 'Or we could even just order in a pizza! Here –' he turns round to face me – 'come and give your old man a hug?'

I still haven't said a single word. My throat starts doing the gulpy thing and I back away from him. The hot wavy feeling is seeping everywhere, surging all the way down to my feet and my toes, and all I know with one hundred per cent certainty is that I don't want a *hug*.

I let the wave take over, and it tells me to run. So that's what I do – I keep backing out of the kitchen and run upstairs to my room, and when I slam the door the whole door frame thuds so hard the wall shakes.

I sit on the corner of my bed, trying to sort my thoughts and get my breathing steady. I hear Dad's footsteps on the staircase. He opens the door and peeks round, and I wish I'd put something in front of it so he couldn't open it. I turn and face the window.

'Can I come in?' he asks.

I say nothing and clench my fists.

'Hey,' he says softly, moving towards me. 'What's up?'

'What's *up*?' I roar, twisting back to face him. 'What's up is that you don't get to just walk back in here and pretend like nothing happened!' I realise I am standing, shouting. Dad steps back and turns away from me.

'I . . . I'm sorry,' he says. 'Maybe I should come back when you've calmed down.'

'Yeah! Maybe you should! Or maybe you should just go away again and not tell me where or even try and get in touch, and then it won't be a problem for you, will it?' I've never felt quite like this before. I don't just feel the wavy anger going around me – it's like I *am* the wave. I shove him towards the door but I'm not strong enough to move him. He wraps his arms around me and I start shouting, 'I hate you, I hate you, I hate you, I hate you!' into his tummy.

'I'm sorry,' he repeats. His voice sounds strange, and when I look up I see his eyes are wet. 'I should have told you. I suppose I . . . thought it would be better if I didn't make a big deal about it – didn't bother you and Kyle too much. No fuss, you know.'

'Right, so you thought you could just leave and we wouldn't *notice*?' I say, genuinely shocked that this made sense in Dad's head. 'You're . . . you're my *dad*. I needed you. Mum hasn't been good at *all*, and I started counselling to get better from all my . . . "Benny stuff". But you wouldn't know because you haven't even called me *once*. There's stuff I have to do to challenge it, and it's *hard*.' I trail off and clench my fists so I don't shove him again. 'I *needed* you,' I repeat angrily.

'Well, yeah, when you put it like that, I, I . . .' He sighs. 'Can we sit?' he asks.

'S'pose,' I nod, staring at the floor. He comes and perches on the corner of my bed and pats the duvet for me to sit down opposite him.

'I'm sorry, Ben,' he begins. 'I'm afraid I've . . . well . . . I've handled this really badly, haven't I?'

I nod, kicking at the floor, and try not to start looking around the corners of the room in fours. Even though I'm angry with him, I still want him to see how much better I am.

'I really thought I was doing the right thing by you and your brother,' Dad carries on. 'I . . . I wasn't thinking. Of course you needed me. I need you too, you know.'

'Yeah,' I say bitterly. 'You can be really stupid sometimes.'

I think he might tell me not to speak to him like that, but instead he stretches a hand out and squeezes mine, and this time I don't pull away.

'Yeah,' he says quietly. 'Yeah, I can.'

I realise I have no idea how long Dad plans to be here for – is he just going to stay while Mum's out and then disappear again into the middle of nowhere? I guess I'm glad he's apologised, but how am I supposed to feel OK when I have no idea what's going on?

'Are you . . . Are you coming back here then? For good?' I ask, annoyed at how hopeful my voice sounds.

Dad sighs, and now it's his turn to shuffle his feet awkwardly. 'We're not . . . Your mum and I . . . I don't think we're . . . going to be getting back together. Of course it's great that she wants to go to her group and . . . sort herself out. And I want to support her, and you and Kyle, as much as I can in that. But your mum and I, we're . . . Well, in many ways we're just not very compatible.'

I want to tell him that loads of people aren't compatible, like, in fact, April and I aren't very compatible, because she's a rebel and I hate doing anything out of the ordinary (except recently, apparently), and the Doctor loves Rose even though he is a nine-hundred-year-old alien who has seen whole galaxies and Rose works in a shop on Earth and hasn't seen much of anything at all.

But I think maybe some of this is just weird adult stuff that I'm never going to understand . . . So I just nod and stare hard at the floor.

'I might try and rent a flat – not in Plaistow, but nearer here, to you and Kyle, and see you at weekends and things. Would you like that, eh?'

I shrug, Kyle-style.

Then Dad asks if I want to watch *Doctor Who* with him, since he's here all evening. I smile, even though I still feel hot and wavy, and say that, yes, I would like that. The two of us make our way down to the sitting room. I choose 'Gridlock', one of my favourite ever, *ever* episodes. The Doctor and his companion Martha get stuck on another planet's motorway: it's an underground highway so full of traffic that it takes six years to travel ten miles. Finally the Doctor realises that no one ever gets off the motorway – in fact, the cars are just going round and round in a loop – and they'll never get off unless they *force* their way out. I realise I'm laughing to myself, because the looping motorway kind of feels like my brain before Dinesh came into my life.

I want to tell Dad, but I'm not sure he'd get it, and I'm not sure he *deserves* to know any important stuff about my life. At least . . . not yet.

When 'Gridlock' ends, Netflix automatically starts playing the next episode, 'Daleks in Manhattan', and Dad raises an eyebrow at me which I know means *One more episode?* and I nod back at him, like, *Yeah, duh.*

We're all still watching when Mum gets home. She walks into the sitting room, and I realise I was so focused that I didn't hear her come in.

'How did it go?' asks Dad shyly, pausing 'Daleks in Manhattan'.

'It was . . . Well, it was quite good actually. There were a few other mums there, which was helpful.'

She shakes her hair out of her high bun, kisses me on the head (not Dad) and plonks herself down on the sofa.

'Yeah, I think I'll try and go every week. As long as Mondays work for you?' She looks at Dad.

'No problem,' says Dad, giving me a wink. 'We've got a lot of *Doctor Who* to catch up on anyway.'

My stomach gives a happy flip, like someone nuked the slugs, but I don't smile too much because I want Dad to know I'm not ready for us to start acting like everything's fixed and back to normal.

'Sock it to him!' I imagine April saying.

Dad slaps his thighs and says, 'Right then!' getting up to leave. He wraps me in a hug, even though my hands stay at my sides, and says, 'I really am proud of you, Benny boy.'

I lean into his chest and breathe in the smell of

him – woody peppermint and laundry detergent – somehow still the same. I hope he does come back next Monday.

'Bye, Dad,' I say.

5!!

For the last few weeks of term, things are good at school. We even *sometimes* hang out with Michelle and Isiah's crews at break, and Sophia, Ezinne and Pete have had lunch with us in Music Room 4 a few times. Mr Montague made everyone shuffle seats and sit with someone they don't usually talk to. That means I'm not with April, which sucks, but I ended up next to Rachel, and it turns out she's also great at maths and is actually pretty cool. So now Mr Montague gives us *both* the harder maths sheets, and we call ourselves the Uber-Nerds.

On Mondays, when Mum goes to her group, Dad and I have been working our way through the fourth Doctor, Tom Baker's classic episodes of *Doctor Who* from the 1970s. Dad used to watch them as a kid, and he always says Tom Baker is his favourite Doctor. I say I don't mind as long as Dad watches all of Peter

Capaldi's episodes with me after. Kyle makes sure he's never home because he says he never wants to talk to Dad ever again. Dad says they are 'working on it'.

I've still been seeing Dinesh on Thursdays, even though we'll be ending quite soon. I was put down to have twenty sessions with him, which seemed like loads when we started, but they're going by super-quickly. I'm a bit nervous about what life will be like when I'm not seeing him – especially because if I need counselling again I'll have to go back on a mega waiting list. Still, Dinesh says that in our last session we will make a list of all the things we've worked on together – in case I forget and need to look at it again. That makes me feel a bit better.

I'm fighting the brain bully every day, and sometimes I get frustrated, because after I was able to stop doing routines to find April, I thought I had smashed them for good. But I still forget what I'm supposed to be doing and find myself going back to my old ways. Especially right before bed, and first thing when I wake up when my brain is in that weird kind of half-sleep.

But it is true that I am feeling much better, and happier too. And Dinesh says not to get frustrated

— that these things take time, and I'm fighting like a champion and should be proud.

The REALLY EXCITING thing is that I'm going away with April the day after Christmas to stay with her grandparents in Manchester for a few days! Apparently they go to visit them most holidays. April says it's super-boring, that we'll spend the whole time in their living room playing board games. But to me that sounds like an adventure because I love board games, and I'm looking forward to being able to play them without spending half the time worrying so much about whether the counters are the 'right' colours or that the dice lands on the 'right' number. And Thomas is coming back from Syria for a few weeks. So I'll get to meet him, *and* April says he's going to bring a load of his classic *Doctor Who* DVDs for us to all watch together on his laptop.

It's basically heaven.

Except I won't be with Mum. And I worry about her.

I do a sweep of the house to see if it really is true — that she's thrown all the bottles out. And I don't find a single one. What I do find, tucked under her bed, is a book called *The Alcoholic's Recovery Guide*, which makes me pretty happy. The book has a bookmark in it on page 157, which means she's actually reading it. That makes me even happier. And I don't even care that 157 is not divisible by four.

On the day that I'm due to leave with April, I use my new writing skills to write Mum a note, so she'll know that I'm still thinking about her even when I'm not around. I hide it in the book by the bookmark, and I hope she won't be annoyed that I was snooping.

It says:

YOU CAN DO IT, MUM.

LOVE YOU.

Even though I'm not totally sure she can do it. Or that she's going to do it straight away, no steps back. And now I've seen her try to get better, the idea of her going back again . . . Well, it terrifies me. I check her phone, which I know I probably shouldn't have been doing, and I see she's joined a WhatsApp group chat where people from her support group seem to be keeping in touch during the week. She also tells me she's going to meet up with some of the mums from her group for coffee while I'm away, and that makes me feel a bit better. But still.

My phone bings. It's from April:

OUTSIDE

I grab my duffle bag and take the stairs two at a time. Kyle has already left for work, but Mum's in the kitchen and she comes to the front door with me. April's in the front seat with her blue leg elevated on the dashboard. Her mum's driving and her dad is in the back, next to a guy with shoulder-length hair who I recognise from April's phone background: Thomas.

April has found the *Doctor Who* theme tune on Spotify and is blaring it out so loudly on the car speakers as I get in that her mum says, 'April, you are going to burst our eardrums,' even though she is laughing. April's dad rolls down the window and calls hello to Mum, who gives a little wave back.

'Have fun!' she calls to me as I cram myself in the back next to April's dad and Thomas.

April is already talking at a hundred miles an hour about how I'd better prepare myself for a journey that takes all of time and please can we stop at the service station on the motorway with the McDonald's and also she already is bursting for the loo.

'Hey, Ben!' Thomas yells over the music. 'So, the most important question of all: who's your favourite Doctor?'

He is wearing a Dalek T-shirt, and if I can't get the Doctor to take me on a trip in his TARDIS, I think this might just be the next best thing.

'Um . . . I'm not sure,' I say. 'I mean, it changes. Usually the Doctor in the last episode I watched is my favourite!'

'Ha ha,' laughs Thomas. 'Same.'

'ACTUALLY,' shouts April, 'there's a MORE important question than that . . .' Thomas and I look at each other, confused. April continues, putting on a booming quiz-show-host voice, 'Are Ben and I the best friends in a) the world, b) the galaxy or c) the UNIVERSE?'

'The UNIVERSE,' I shout without hesitation, because I really do think that in all of space and time, there's never been another Ben and April.

'*Waheeeey!*' yells April, turning the music up even louder.

'Apriiiil! Not so loud,' warns her mum. 'And take your leg off the dashboard.' But I can see in the wing mirror that she is smiling slightly. April turns the volume back down the *tiniest* amount and sits up, while her mum starts the engine and pulls the car out into the road.

I am turning around to wave to Mum one last time, and she's waving back at me. I watch her get smaller and smaller as we drive down our street, until we round the corner, and I can't see her any more.

Acknowledgements

Firstly, thank you to every child and young person who has ever shared their experiences of OCD with me, either online or in person. You are the brave and wonderful people who inspired me to write this book, and I hope you find a friend in Ben. Thank you also to the parents and other adults who read my writing about OCD and suggested I write something for younger readers – the children, grandchildren and other young people in your life. You gave me the drive to take a leap and embark on Ben's story.

This book would not have come into being without my agent Dan Lazaar – he encouraged me to write for children and has been with *When I See Blue* since before there were any words on the page. Thank you for believing in me and sharing your expert guidance and knowledge with me every step of the way. Thank you also to Victoria Doherty Munro – for tirelessly rereading literally every version of the first draft and your invaluable thoughts and input as Ben's world took shape. You both were mine and Ben's first supporters and breathed this book into existence with me!

Thank you to my UK agent Martin Hickman, for being my sounding board, trusted advisor and friend, not just on this book, but always. You were the first person to believe I could write any books at all and I couldn't have done any of it without you. To Naomi Greenwood – you are a dream to have as an editor. Working with you has been a delight and *When I See Blue* is the best book it could be because I was lucky enough that you wanted to take it on. You even spotted things about Ben's thoughts and rituals to be tweaked that I hadn't, and he thanks you for that because it would have stressed him out if they'd been missed. Back and forth editing can become a slog and your jokes in the margins make it 1000 times better! Thank you to Michelle Brackenborough for creating such a dazzling front cover, and to Jenny Glencross for your wonderfully thorough copy edit. Thank you to Ruth Girmatsion for being such a brilliant desk editor, and getting this book to the finish line!

Thank you to Professor Paul Salkovskis for giving me permission to use your children's OCI in Ben's assessment, as well as all the work and research you do for people with OCD. A big shout-out also to OCD Action, OCD UK and the International OCD Foundation (IOCDF) for being brilliant charities that tirelessly advocate for those of us with OCD.

I want to thank Josh and Divya for helping me to craft the character of April through sharing your experiences with me. Thank you to Hannah for all your advice about teaching and UK schools (I did attend one but it's been a while!) – I know the students you teach are very lucky to have you. Thank you to Amelia for all the medical advice that helped me shape April's parents' professional life (and also for all the medical/personal advice you've given me over the years!). Thank you to my mum, dad, and all the friends and family who supported me while I wrote this. Thank you to my dog Rocky for sensing when I needed a break from writing (as well as when I didn't, you sneaky pup) and persuading me to go to the park with you.

Finally, thank you to my wonderful partner Josh, for reading this at the beginning and having so much constructive and helpful advice for me. I always thought living with another writer would be a nightmare, but it turns out that it sometimes . . . isn't?! Much of *When I See Blue* was written and edited during Covid times. It's been a little cramped but we've kept it together, so cheers to us – I wouldn't have done it with anyone else.

Resources

When I See Blue is a work of fiction, but the issues experienced by Ben and his mum Leila are very real. If you have OCD, or are worried you might, or if you are concerned about a parent, carer or family member's drinking, you may find the organisations listed below helpful.

OCD-UK *works for children and adults affected by OCD. They provide advice, information, support services, and campaign to end the trivialisation and stigma of OCD.*

ocduk.org

OCD Action *provide support and information to anybody affected by OCD, work to raise awareness of the disorder amongst the public and front-line healthcare workers, and strive to secure a better deal for people with OCD.*

ocdaction.org.uk

OCD Youth *aims to increase awareness and access to support for anyone under 25 affected by OCD. It is run by young people with OCD, for young people with OCD. They organise trips and outings, run a youth forum and e-helpline, take part in campaigning activities, create resources and much more!*

ocdyouth.org

IOCDF (International OCD Foundation) *is an international foundation who help those affected by OCD and related disorders. They aim to increase access to effective treatment through research and training, and foster a supportive community for those affected by OCD and the professionals who treat them.*

iocdf.org

Nacoa (The National Association for Children of Alcoholics) *is a charity for everyone affected by a parent's drinking. They offer information, advice and support, including message boards, events, and a free helpline.* **0800 358 3456**

nacoa.org.uk

We Are With You *provide support and can help source ongoing support for anyone affected by drug and alcohol use and mental health issues. Both adults and children can speak to trained advisors on their instant chat service, via their website.*

wearewithyou.org.uk

Adfam *is a national charity tackling the effects of alcohol, drug use or gambling on family members and friends. They run events, local projects, and their site has an interactive map so you can search for support in your area, as well as a helpful resources section.*

adfam.org.uk

ORIGAMI BOX

1. DIAGONAL FOLD

2. DIAGONAL FOLD

3. TURN OVER & FOLD

4. FOLD & TURN BACK

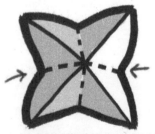

5. PINCH MIDDLE FOLD

6. TO FORM PYRAMID

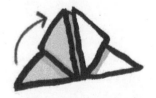

7. FOLD POINTS TO TOP

8. TURN & REPEAT

9. FOLD TO CENTRE

10. REPEAT X3

11. FLIP

12. FOLD UP

13. FOLD IN HALF

14. TUCK IN

15. REPEAT X3

16. PULL OPEN

17. BLOW INTO TOP TO INFLATE

18. PULL INTO BOX SHAPE

LILY BAILEY

Lily became a journalist in London in 2012, editing a news site and writing features and fashion articles for local publications including the *Richmond Magazine* and the *Kingston Magazine*.

As a child and teenager, Lily suffered from severe obsessive-compulsive disorder (OCD). She kept her illness private, until the widespread misunderstanding of the disorder spurred her into action. In 2014, she began campaigning for better awareness and understanding of OCD.

Her first book, *Because We Are Bad* (2016) was published internationally. In 2019, Lily won the Illumination Award for media personalities and influencers who accurately and respectfully represent OCD and related disorders. She continues to write and speak publicly about mental illness, and blogs for *Psychology Today*.